Here's what crit
Gemma Halliday's Wine & Dine Mysteries:

"I rank *A Sip Before Dying* as one of my favorite fun reads. I say to Gemma Halliday, well done. She wrote a mystery that encompassed suspense flavored with romantic notions, while giving us a heroine to make us smile."
—*The Book Breeze Magazine*

"Gemma Halliday's signature well-written story filled with wonderful characters is just what I expected. All in all, this is the beginning of a great cozy series no one should miss!"
—*Kings River Life Magazine*

"I've always enjoyed the writing style and comfortable tone of Gemma novels and this one fits in perfectly. From the first page, the author pulled me in...when all was said and done, I enjoyed this delightfully engaging tale and I can't wait to spend more time with Emmy, Ava and their friends."
—*Dru's Book Musings*

"This is a great cozy mystery, and I highly recommend it!"
—*Book Review Crew*

"I could not put *A Sip Before Dying* by Gemma Halliday down. Once I started reading it, I was hooked!!"
—*Cozy Mystery Book Reviews*

BOOKS BY GEMMA HALLIDAY

High Heels Mysteries
Spying in High Heels
Killer in High Heels
Undercover in High Heels
Christmas in High Heels
(short story)
Alibi in High Heels
Mayhem in High Heels
Honeymoon in High Heels
(short story)
Sweetheart in High Heels
(short story)
Fearless in High Heels
Danger in High Heels
Homicide in High Heels
Deadly in High Heels
Suspect in High Heels
Peril in High Heels
Jeopardy in High Heels

Wine & Dine Mysteries
A Sip Before Dying
Chocolate Covered Death
Victim in the Vineyard
Marriage, Merlot & Murder
Death in Wine Country
Fashion, Rosé & Foul Play
Witness at the Winery

Hollywood Headlines Mysteries
Hollywood Scandals
Hollywood Secrets
Hollywood Confessions
Hollywood Holiday
(short story)
Hollywood Deception

Marty Hudson Mysteries
Sherlock Holmes and the Case
of the Brash Blonde
Sherlock Holmes and the Case
of the Disappearing Diva
Sherlock Holmes and the Case
of the Wealthy Widow

Tahoe Tessie Mysteries
Luck Be A Lady
Hey Big Spender
Baby It's Cold Outside
(holiday short story)

Jamie Bond Mysteries
Unbreakable Bond
Secret Bond
Bond Bombshell
(short story)
Lethal Bond
Dangerous Bond
Bond Ambition
(short story)
Fatal Bond
Deadly Bond

Hartley Grace Featherstone Mysteries
Deadly Cool
Social Suicide
Wicked Games

Other Works
Play Dead
Viva Las Vegas
A High Heels Haunting
Watching You (short story)
Confessions of a Bombshell
Bandit (short story)

CHOCOLATE COVERED DEATH

---

a Wine & Dine mystery

GEMMA HALLIDAY

Dedicated to Charlotte Rose, my littlest chocolate lover.

CHAPTER ONE

———

I stood back and admired the display in front of me. The tower of individual Chocolate Molten Lava Cakes sat alongside Oak Valley Vineyard's own Zinfandel and Pinot Noir, looking both tempting and delicious. Crispy outsides, gooey centers, and a delicate dusting of powdered sugar along the top. The desire to smuggle one out on a plate and enjoy with a glass of Pinot was almost overwhelming. I adjusted a bottle so that Oak Valley's label was more prominent and then slid one of the dozen glasses just a bit to the right so that the spacing between them was perfect. We had a guest list of at least fifty people who had RSVP'd to our Wine and Chocolate Tasting event at the Chocolate Bar, a small local bakery, and I couldn't afford for it to be anything but a success.

"Are you ready?" a familiar voice asked from behind me.

I spun on my stiletto heel and faced my best friend, Ava Barnett.

"Ready as I'll ever be," I replied, only halfway feeling it. In truth? Nervous energy practically knotted my stomach into macramé beneath my little black dress.

Ava moved in close to give me a hug, the camera slung around her neck digging into my chest as she squeezed. She was my dedicated photographer for the night, and she was taking the role seriously.

"Don't worry, Emmy. You've got this," she whispered in my ear.

Ava Barnett and I had been practically joined at the hip since childhood, and I considered her more of a sister than acquaintance. We even looked alike—sorta. We both sported blonde hair—though mine ran more toward unruly-with-a-mind-of-its-own than Ava's shampoo-commercial shimmer. We were both about a size eight—though Ava's was a slim, lithe eight, while mine was a loves-her-chocolate eight-bordering-on-ten. And we both enjoyed fashion—even if my style ran a bit more toward jeans and classic cuts while hers was an eclectic bohemian mixture that perfectly matched her upbeat artist's personality. That evening, for example, she was dressed in a long, flowy skirt and peasant style blouse in a creamy linen edged in bright embroidery. She'd brought the hippie-esque vibe into the present with modern silver jewelry of her own making and a pair of killer heels that rivaled my own in height.

I gave her a smile as she released me. "Thanks," I replied. I shook off the nerves and pointed toward the cake display. "You get photos of all of this already?"

"Several," Ava assured me. "They'll be great promotional pieces."

I nodded in agreement. Promotion was one thing we sorely needed.

I was about to double-check, for the third time in as many hours, that her camera battery was fully charged, when our hostess for the evening, Leah Holcomb, owner of the Chocolate Bar, bustled into the room carrying a tray of chocolate éclairs.

"I have two more of these in the back," she informed us, gently setting them down on an empty table near the windows. She stood, wiping a stray strand of brown curly hair from her forehead. "This should be the last display. Gosh, I hope this goes well."

I knew Leah had as much invested in tonight's success as I did. While I'd recently taken the reins at my family's struggling winery, trying to save it from being gobbled up by the corporate giants hovering just on the other side of our sinking bottom line, Leah had mortgaged everything she owned to open the Chocolate Bar after her divorce last year. I'd met her when, after a particularly depressing meeting with my accountant, Gene Schultz, I'd wandered into her newly opened shop and spent the next two hours chatting and indulging in about a million calories worth of her heavenly creations. Both of us, as it turned out, were playing the daily scramble for customers, and we figured that pooling our list of VIPs for this joint event could help put us both on the radar of the right kind of clients—wine lovers with a sweet tooth.

"Well, I think everything looks great," Ava said, ever the cheerleader. "And it smells even more amazing," she reassured Leah.

Leah's tense smile relaxed a little, but I could still see a small sheen of moisture on her forehead, betraying the fact that her nerves probably matched mine. "Thanks. I'm going to go freshen up a bit before the guests start arriving."

"Oh, hang on just a minute!" Ava instructed, moving toward a large canvas bag she'd stowed behind a display counter. "I have something for you both first." She rummaged around, digging into its depths. "I know it's somewhere..." she mumbled, more to herself than us.

"Ava, you really don't need to—" I started.

"Ah! Here they are!" Ava straightened up with such gusto that she came within millimeters of hitting Leah's pièce de résistance—a seven tiered raspberry chocolate layer cake.

Leah closed her eyes—if I had to guess, praying to some gods of sugar and cocoa.

Ava sheepishly stepped away. "Sorry."

Relief flooded through me that the arrangement was unharmed.

Leah's shoulders relaxed away from her ears as she smiled and accepted the small blue box bearing the logo of Ava's shop, Silver Girl.

"You didn't have to get me anything," I told her, accepting an identical one.

But Ava waved us both off. "I know, but I know how much this night means to both of you, so it's just a little something. Open it," she instructed.

We did, Leah being the first to get the ribbon off and lift the lip. I saw a glittering silver chain holding a yellow stone set in the center of a flower shaped pendant.

"It's for good luck," Ava told us as I opened my own box.

While my flower was slightly different—each made, I knew, by hand—it also held a small yellow stone.

"That's citrine. It brings the holder luck," Ava informed us.

"Thank you," I said, meaning it.

"This is so generous," Leah added, clasping hers around her neck.

Ava beamed, clearly enjoying her gifting. But as I saw her gaze flit toward the large glass front windows, the smiled faltered a little. "Uh-oh. Don't look now, but I think I see a couple early birds arriving."

Leah sucked in a breath, her hands immediately going to her hair as she looked down at the dusting of flour on her tasteful gray A-line dress.

"Go," I told her. "I'll hold them off while you freshen up."

Leah nodded at me. "Five minutes," she promised.

"Don't worry. We got this," Ava reassured her again.

Sounding much more confident than I felt as the first guest of the evening walked through the front doors.

* * *

I had to admit that Leah had done an exceptional job organizing the night. The room was buzzing, and I swore we had our fifty invited guests, and then some, all sipping, nibbling, and generally enjoying themselves. My stomach clenched every time I saw someone roll their glass and sniff the contents, but I knew our wines were good. Better than good, I reminded myself, watching an older man in a tight suit swish Zinfandel around in his mouth and swallow with a nod of appreciation.

"Do you have anything white?" a woman in a long-sleeved emerald dress asked me, the diamonds at her ears sparkling as she punctuated the question with a toss of platinum hair over one shoulder. Caroline Danvers. She'd been on Leah's VIP list, though I recognized her from an event I'd catered at the local golf club recently.

"It's so good to see you, Caroline," I said, turning to the table behind me. "Yes, we have a Pinot Blanc that goes very well with the tart bite of the raspberries in the chocolate layer cake."

Caroline glanced at the gorgeous towering dessert as if it were something alien instead of a delicious creation. Clearly size-two Caroline didn't do carbs. But, she accepted the glass I offered her and sipped daintily.

"Not bad," she conceded. "Where did you say your winery is again?"

"Just east of town." I handed her a brochure with our address on it.

Caroline squinted at it, flipping over the glossy photos. "Jenny," she called to a woman over her shoulder.

A slim brunette with a short bob, wearing a tailored pencil skirt and blazer that screamed *power suit*, appeared at her side. "Yes?"

"Uh, this is…" Caroline looked my way, at a loss for a name.

"Emmy Oak," I said, offering the newcomer my hand.

"Jennifer Foxton," she replied as she shook lightly.

"Emmy owns a winery," Caroline told her friend. "It's kinda cute." She showed Jennifer the brochure.

"Uh-huh." Jennifer's interest level looked about as low as my current bank account balance.

"Did you book a place for the fall fundraiser yet?" Caroline asked.

I felt my hopes rise. Bookings were few and far between for us lately and sorely needed. "We have a large tasting room and plenty of outdoor space for events of all sizes," I chimed in.

Jennifer gave me a cool smile. "Sorry. It's not that kind of party. My husband is Jonathan Foxton." She paused, letting the name sink in, as if it should mean something to me.

I tried to keep a neutral expression, not wanting to insult her with the fact I hadn't the slightest clue who he was.

"*Senator* Jonathan Foxton," she supplied.

"Of course," I lied, the name still meaningless to me.

"Uh, *state* senator," Caroline amended, sending a smirk toward her friend. "Let's be truthful, darling. He's in Sacramento, not Washington."

Jennifer laughed the comment off, though her eyes were cold as she shot back, "Well, at least *my* husband is in the country. Where did you say Trevor was tripping off to again, *love*?"

"Tokyo," Caroline responded. "For work."

"Sure. Work." Jennifer smiled, but it was all predatory teeth. "Anyway, Washington is not far off for Jonathan." She paused, turning to me again. "He's already campaigning for November."

"Good for him," I managed to get in between the two barbing each other.

"But I think we'll look elsewhere for the event venue, Caro," she told her friend. "We're not really into rustic." With that, Jennifer turned and glided back in the direction she'd come from.

Caroline shrugged, returning the brochure to me. "Thanks anyway."

"Uh, keep it," I encouraged. "You never know when you might need a venue." I shot her a big smile.

She shrugged and slipped the brochure into her bag before turning to join Jennifer, who was now busy greeting another similarly dressed Glamazon woman who'd just walked in the door. Though, I had a bad feeling Caroline would be tossing the brochure right into the trash that evening. At least she had liked the wine. Or at least deemed it "not bad." Not exactly glowing praise, but I'd take what I could get.

"Ohmigod!" Leah was suddenly at my side, her voice a mock whisper of urgency. "Is that Heather?"

I followed her line of sight to Caroline's group, homing in on the newcomer of the Glam Squad—a tall brunette in a short white dress that showed off her dedication to the gym. Or at least to her plastic surgeon's office. While I didn't know her personally, I did recall a Heather as one of the VIPs Schultz had recommended to me. "I'm not sure, but I did invite a Heather Atherton. She's supposed to be a wine broker."

Leah shook her head, her color going a shade paler. "Sure. But she's also married to James."

"James?" I asked, still not sure why Leah was so upset.

Leah turned to look at me, her eyes bordering on tears. "James Atherton. My ex-husband. *That's* his new wife."

Oops. "Leah, I'm so sorry. I had no idea." I didn't think I'd ever caught the name of her ex-husband before. Clearly Leah had reverted to her maiden name after the split.

Leah shook her head. "God, please don't tell me he's here too…" She trailed off, her eyes scanning the crowd.

"I'm so, so, *so* sorry!" I told her. While the most serious relationship I'd had lately was with a carton of Mint Chip, I could only imagine how awful it would be to have your ex-husband crash your party. Especially with someone who looked like Heather Atherton.

I glanced back to the group. Clearly Heather was a friend of Caroline and Jennifer's, as they were sharing air kisses all around at her arrival, though I put Heather at least a few years younger than the other ladies. Her white dress clung to her slim hips as she flipped her shimmering chestnut colored hair over her shoulder. Her perfect manicure accentuated the diamond engagement ring on her left hand, which had to be at least five carats, and her eyelashes and boobs were as fake as her smile.

"She looks like a freaking model," Leah said beside me, mirroring my own thoughts. "I think I'm going to be ill."

"She's not *that* pretty."

Leah shot me a *yeah right* look.

"I am so sorry," I said again. "Look, I'll tell her you're not comfortable with her here and ask her politely to leave—"

But Leah quickly shut that thought down. "You will do no such thing. That would only make us both look bad." Leah swallowed, her throat bobbing up and down while her gaze stayed on the tall woman's exposed back in her low-cut dress. "It's okay. I mean, how could you have known? It's my fault. I should have mentioned something. I mean, I know James runs in these circles."

Honestly, this was the first I was hearing of it. Leah had never really mentioned much about her ex-husband except that they had a seven-year-old son together and the marriage had ended badly. Now didn't feel like the time to pry though.

"I should have checked your list more carefully," Leah went on, shaking her head.

"I promise I'll run interference," I said, still feeling like a heel for my gaffe. "You won't even have to talk to her." Though even as I said it, I wondered if it was a promise I could keep. While Leah might not have known Heather was on the guest list, Heather certainly must have known she was coming to her husband's ex's bakery. And from the look of her flat tummy and tiny tushy, I doubted it was to scarf down the éclairs.

"I, uh, need to go to the kitchen and find a knife to cut the layer cake," Leah said, waving a distracted hand toward the kitchen.

If I had to guess, Leah needed to be anywhere that the new wife wasn't.

Feeling guilty as I watched Leah retreat, I decided to make good on my promise and grabbed a glass of Pinot Noir, heading in the Glam Squad's direction with it.

"Traffic was ghastly," Heather was saying to her companions as I approached. "Tourists. Too many in this town."

"Totally," Caroline agreed. "And you look amazing tonight, by the way."

"And don't you look lovely, too," Heather replied. Though her smile took on an air of smugness as she scanned Caroline head to toe.

"See," Jennifer said, swatting Caroline on the arm. "I told you that dress would look better on you than me. I mean, you fill it out much better with those hips of yours."

More smirks all around.

But Caroline didn't bat a false eyelash before retorting, "It does require someone who has the right bust for it. I mean, it's not as forgiving as, say, a blazer."

Jennifer's eyes flashed, though her expression remained neutral. Either she was a practiced politician's wife or had done a round of Botox that afternoon.

I cleared my throat, inserting myself in the middle of the cattiness. "Can I offer you a glass of our 2016 Pinot Noir?" I asked, handing it to Heather.

"Thank you," she said politely, taking the wineglass but not sipping, I noticed.

"Emmy Oak," I said, introducing myself. "My family owns Oak Valley Vineyards."

She sent me a bored smile.

"I, uh, hear you're a wine enthusiast."

"Broker," Heather corrected. "Only rare, collectible bottles." She glanced down into her glass as if already ascertaining that it was not up to collectible standards.

"We have some older bottles in our cellar you might be interested in. Vintage Napa history," I said, trying to tempt her.

"The only *vintage* she's interested in tonight is the old wife," Jennifer joked.

"Jenny!" Heather chided. "That's not nice."

But I could see the first genuine smile on her lips as she said it.

Oh boy. While Leah had a few years on my own twenty-nine, I wouldn't put her any older than thirty-five at the most. Hardly "vintage." I glanced over my shoulder, glad to see Leah was still hiding in the kitchen and not within earshot.

"Uh, yes, Leah mentioned you're married to her ex-husband, James," I said, stating the obvious.

"Oh? Leah mentioned me?" Heather asked. The smile grew.

"In passing," I added quickly, trying to somehow save face for my friend. "Is James, uh, here?"

But Heather shook her head. "He had a conflict."

I did a mental sigh of relief on Leah's behalf.

"Besides, this is more of a cute little girls' night event," Caroline chimed in.

I glossed over my efforts being called a "cute little" event and addressed Jennifer instead. "Can I get *you* a glass of anything?"

Instead of answering, Jennifer turned to Heather, who was still holding her untouched Pinot Noir. "What do you think, Heathy? Should I let her get me a glass of anything?"

Heather looked from Jennifer to me. Then she gave her glass a slow, deliberate sip. She drew out the answer, dabbing her mouth with a cocktail napkin before replying, "It's alright."

Gee, so far I'd had a "not bad" and an "alright" from these ladies. Tough crowd.

Jennifer shrugged. "I suppose I'll have a taste."

"I'll be right back with a glass." I clacked my stilettos back to the table, only too happy to put some distance between me and the Glam Squad. This was going to be one long night.

* * *

The next couple of hours passed in a blur of handshaking, glass filling, and brochure dispersing. The crowd was a good one—ranging from lively couples in cocktails dresses here for the free booze to serious enthusiasts in suits discussing tannin and oakiness, and I even spotted a guy in a cowboy hat, giving the scene some local flavor. While not everyone was as Ice Queen as Caroline and company, they were a discerning crowd, and praise was subdued enough to keep me on my toes. Leah spent most of the evening in the kitchen, only popping out to refill the dessert tables and cut the impressive layer cake. And Ava did a fantastic job of photographing the VIPs while highlighting the food and wine in the shots as well. By the time the guests started taking their leave, most of the bottles I'd brought were emptied, and only a scant few treats were left on the silver trays.

"Looks like a successful evening to me," Ava said, eyeing the quickly emptying room.

"We'll know if bookings start coming in."

"*When* they start coming in." Ava gave me a wink.

I grinned. "I like the way you think."

"Did Leah avoid the Model Thing okay?" Ava asked.

I nodded. I'd briefly filled her in earlier on the accidental invite situation during a lull in the crowd. "I think so. At least, I didn't see anyone clawing anyone's eyes out, so that's a good sign."

"What restraint," Ava joked.

I laughed along with her, though I realized I hadn't actually seen Leah in awhile. With the guests dispersing, it felt like a good time to check in on her and at least relay some of the praise I'd overheard for her chocolaty creations. "I'm going to go see if she needs any help cleaning up in the kitchen."

Ava nodded. "I'll keep an eye out here in case anyone wants one for the road."

"Thanks," I called, heading toward the kitchen.

As the door swung closed behind me, I took a moment to enjoy the stillness. The sounds of murmured goodbyes, tinkling glasses, and retreating footsteps filtered through the closed door, but the kitchen was blissfully silent. I took a beat to inhale the scents of sugar, cocoa, and crispy burnt edges.

"Leah?" I called. The quiet said I was alone, but she could have been hiding out in the pantry. "Leah!"

I walked past the ovens, rounding the corner to a small office, and noticed that the back door to the alleyway behind the bakery was ajar. I wondered if Leah'd popped out for a moment of fresh air. I knew I could use some.

I made my way to the door, allowing the night air to cool my warm skin as I stepped outside. Even though we were well into summer, after the sun went down, the evenings were still crisp. The dim streetlight at the end of the alleyway created shadows, and I squinted, willing my eyes to adjust to the darkness.

"Leah, are you out here?" I asked, a chill creeping across my skin.

The alleyway wasn't huge, but it was big enough for a delivery truck and for Leah to park her car. Across from the doorway was a large dumpster, next to which sat cardboard boxes holding our winery logo, now filled with empty glass bottles. But instead of them being stacked tidily like I had left them, several were now tilted on their sides, bottles scattered on the ground. I sighed, crossing the alley to pick them up. Broken glass was the last thing Leah needed back here. I picked the first one up and pushed it against the fence.

And that's when I noticed a long, slender leg sticking out from behind the dumpster.

I sucked in a breath. "Leah?" I called, my voice sounding far away as my heart hammered in my ears. I took a step forward, peeking around the side of the dumpster. "Leah?"

Only, the dress covering the top part of the woman's leg was not a tasteful gray linen, but a clinging white silk.

Heather Atherton.

And she wasn't just getting some air. If the cake knife sticking out of her back was any indication, she'd never be getting any air again.

CHAPTER TWO

———

"Name?"

"Emmeline Oak."

"Address?"

"Oak Valley Vineyard," I said automatically, spouting off the street address. "I, uh, live there."

The uniformed officer gave me a quizzical look before entering the information into his electronic notepad. "You work there too?"

I nodded. "I own it. I mean, well, my family owns it. But my dad passed away, and my mom…well, she's not up to it anymore. She's in a home. Her choice—not mine. I mean, I'd much rather have her at *our* home, but she doesn't want to be a burden. *I'd* never consider her a burden, but we come from a long line of stubborn women. Anyway, yeah, I guess technically I'm sort of the caretaker of the winery, not the owner." I paused. I was talking too much, wasn't I? I looked up to find the officer still eyeing me. Yep, definitely too much.

"And you were the one who found the deceased?"

The deceased. I licked my lips, trying not to replay the image of Heather's body crumpled behind the dumpster.

"Ma'am?" the officer prompted.

I nodded. "Yes, I, uh, found Heather Atherton. She was the new wife. Though, I guess now she's the second old wife, and he's the widow. Or, what do they call man widows? Widower?"

The officer was still staring. "I'm not really sure, ma'am. But I think you might be in shock."

I closed my mouth with a click. I thought I might be too.

I glanced up to see Ava and Leah both making similar statements to similar uniformed officers—Ava by the windows and Leah through the open kitchen door. After finding Heather, I'd done a good amount of screaming, then had run back into the bakery to find both Leah and Ava in the kitchen, having ushered out the last of the guests. I vaguely remember telling them what I'd seen, all in a sort of rush, and there'd been more screaming (from me), some panicked tears (from Leah), and the good sense to call the police (that would be Ava). I think we'd each downed a glass of Zin while waiting the few minutes for the police to arrive, but it had done little to dull the horror of the scene I couldn't seem to stop playing in my mind. While I hadn't been Heather's biggest fan, the sight of her body—encased in a designer dress, three-hundred-dollar heels, and diamonds—just discarded alongside the trash, was all I could think about.

"Officer White?" a voice called to the uniformed officer from across the room.

I looked up to the source. Standing in the doorway was six feet of broad shoulders, worn jeans, and dark hair above dark, assessing eyes.

Detective Christopher Grant.

I swallowed, not sure if I was relieved or worried to see him. Grant was with the sheriff's office's VCI, Violent Crimes Investigations Unit, as I'd learned a couple of months ago when a dead body had turned up in my wine cellar. At first I'd thought Grant was all Bad Cop attitude and hard edges. He'd been transferred to Sonoma after a shooting gone wrong, which he still hadn't shared all the details of with me. I had a feeling there were some gray areas of the law involved. However, the last time I'd seen Grant, he'd been flirting with me in my tasting room. While it had been surprising, it hadn't been altogether terrible, and I might even have flirted back a little.

But right now, none of that promising mischief twinkled in his eyes. Right now, Grant was all business, his hard assessing gaze squarely on me.

I swallowed again, really wishing for a second glass of that Zin.

Grant crossed the room in three easy strides, pausing only to get a quick update from Officer Quizzical before approaching me.

"Emmy," he said, nodding toward me.

I waved back, not sure I trusted my voice. Something about Grant always put me on edge, and after the night I'd had, I was already precariously close to going over it.

"I hear you found the body?"

I nodded again. "Heather," I managed to get out.

"Did you know her?" he asked, taking me by the elbow and leading me to an empty table along the far wall.

"I knew of her," I answered, trying to ignore the heat tingling along my skin at his touch. Finding a chair for me to sit in, he released his hold, yet the tingles remained where his fingers had been.

"Tell me," he prompted.

"She was one of my VIPs for the tasting," I said. "But I'd only just met her in person tonight."

"She came to the tasting alone?"

I nodded, looking up at Grant. His arms were crossed over his chest, the muscles in his arms flexing with the effort beneath his blue cotton shirt. It was tucked into a pair of jeans that sat low on his hips, and his stance was both protective and commanding.

"You said you knew of the victim. What can you tell me about her?" He grabbed a second chair and sat across from me, the hazel flecks in his eyes intent as they held mine.

"Not much," I said truthfully. "Schultz recommended I invite her. She's a wine broker and has some influence in the community."

"Go on."

"That's about it. Except that she was married to Leah's ex-husband."

Something changed in his eyes, but he quickly covered it by dropping his gaze to his notebook. His slightly too long hair fell over his forehead, and his hand distractedly brushed the dark strands back into place as he phrased his next question.

"That would be the owner of this place, Leah Holcomb?"

"That's right. She and James divorced last year. That's when she opened the bakery."

"The split was amicable?"

I shrugged. "I don't know the details. But when is a divorce ever pretty?"

"What about the deceased?" he countered. "Was Leah on good terms with her?"

"Well, I don't know that I'd call it *good*."

Grant's gaze flickered up to meet mine. "Oh?"

I paused. "I mean, not that it was bad either. It was...well, awkward maybe?"

"Maybe? Or it was?"

Why did I suddenly feel like I was being interrogated? "She was Leah's ex-husband's trophy wife. How do *you* think that story goes?"

The corner of Grant's mouth ticked upward ever so slightly, but he quickly covered it by consulting his notes again. "How was their interaction this evening?"

I shrugged. "I don't think they even spoke to each other during the event."

"And after?"

I frowned. "What do you mean after?"

"Where was Leah after the event ended?"

I blinked. "I-I don't exactly know. I was actually looking for her when I found Heather."

Something flickered in his eyes again. "So Leah was missing?"

"Well, I don't know about missing. I mean, she was here in the kitchen when I ran back inside."

"But not before." It was statement, not a question.

I cocked my head to the side, getting a pretty good idea of where he was going. "Leah did not have anything to do with this," I told him.

"I didn't say she did," he responded. But the flecks in his eyes told a different story, buzzing with activity. "What time did Heather leave the party?" he asked, switching gears.

"I-I'm not really sure." I tried to think back, but I couldn't recall specifically seeing her leave. I remembered Caroline ducking out early—something about a golf lesson first thing the next morning. Jennifer had stayed on a bit, meeting up with a couple of other ladies I knew were the country club set as well. I didn't recall when she'd left, but I thought I'd seen a group of them leave in a car together. Had Heather been with them? "I don't remember seeing her go," I finally said. "She might have left with Jennifer Foxton."

Grant nodded. "I'll check in with her." Clearly he'd already gotten the deets on her as well, as he didn't even ask who she was. Or maybe Grant paid more attention to state politics than I did.

"Was chocolate cake served tonight?" he asked.

"Uh…yeah. I think we have some left if you want…" I trailed off, realizing he wasn't asking for a late night treat.

"Did Leah serve it?"

I licked my lips. "Yes. It's her bakery. Why?"

He paused, his eyes searching my face. I could feel an internal war over how much to give away and how much to play close to the vest. Finally, he must have conceded some ground to the giveaway, as he said, "The murder weapon had a dark residue on it."

"Chocolate?" I asked, my stomach clenching at the implications.

Grant nodded slowly.

I closed my eyes and thought a dirty word. The knife Leah had used to cut the layer cake. Her prints would be all over it. And she had been missing.

"Leah could never hurt anyone," I protested again.

"How well do you know her?"

"Well enough to know she didn't do this."

Grant let out a sigh and leaned back in his chair. "Convince me."

I licked my lips. "Okay, yes, Leah wasn't a huge fan of Heather. But could you blame her? The woman was ten years younger and looked like a supermodel."

Amusement flickered across Grant's features, but just as quickly it was gone. "Go on."

"Look, if Leah was going to murder her, why do it in her own bakery?"

Grant raised one eyebrow my way.

"I mean, not that she *was* going to murder her," I added hastily. "But you know, if ever she…" I needed to take my foot out of my mouth and close it tightly before I had Leah hung. "Look, Leah is just not capable of this. She's a single mom. Moms don't kill people. They bake pie."

"And chocolate cake?"

I threw my hands up in the air "Anyone could have picked up that knife!"

"Where did you last see it?" Grant asked, his notebook out again as his pen hovered over it.

I'll admit, I thought about lying for a second. But I knew from experience I was a terrible liar.

"In Leah's hands as she cut the cake," I admitted.

Grant moved to write that tidbit down, but on instinct, I reached my hand out to stop him by covering his.

"Look, you have to believe me," I pleaded with him. "Leah did not do this."

Grant looked up from his notebook, his eyes connecting with mine. I was usually good at reading people, but try as I might to decipher the intense look in them, I came up empty. I had no idea what he was thinking.

Grant moved his free hand over mine and gently removed it from his. But as he placed it into my lap, his thumb ever so lightly grazed mine in a small, deliberate caress. It was the slightest of touches, but my entire body flushed from it.

"I'll be in touch," he said softly. Then he quickly let go of my hand and rose, returning to join the rest of the officers swarming all over the Chocolate Bar.

* * *

The clock was ticking close to one in the morning by the time we were finally cleared to go home. I was eternally grateful I'd ridden to the event with Ava, because as cool as I'd tried to play it with Grant, the entire evening had shaken me more than I wanted to admit. Enough that I wasn't sure I would have trusted myself behind the wheel of a car. We rode in silence in Ava's car—a vintage 1970s olive green convertible Pontiac GTO that she loved like it was her baby—and I'd never been so happy to see the tall oak trees lining our gravel drive as we pulled up to the familiar comfort of Oak Valley Vineyards.

Our ten acres were small by commercial standards, but the land had been worked by generations of my family, dating back as far as the early developments of the region. My grandfather had built many of the Spanish style buildings that made up the winery—including the tasting room, kitchen, and offices built beside the cellar where our wares sat in cool darkness, ripening to a perfectly smooth age. My grandmother and namesake, Emmeline, had affectionately dubbed the cellar as "the cave," and it had been a favorite childhood place of mine to hide from the world. Especially after my father had passed.

I'd only been a teenager then, and with a rebellious streak, I'd left home for a stint at the CIA—just not *that* CIA. Culinary Institute of America, though the training had been almost as hard, and I was pretty sure chef instructors yelled even louder and more often than drill sergeants. After graduation I'd moved to Los Angeles, where I'd been on my way to making a name for myself among the Hollywood foodie crowd. A career that was cut short when my mother began to lose herself, her beautiful mind falling into the early stages of dementia. The sale of the winery had seemed imminent. As much as I had loved being a personal chef to the who's who of tinsel town, I loved my family's legacy even more. So, I'd come home to save Oak Valley. Or, at least put up a decent fight.

"Well, that was some night," Ava said as I unlocked the door to my little cottage at the back of the winery.

Like the rest of the buildings on the property, it had been built by my grandfather, but with upgraded plumbing and AC, the two bedroom place was cozy, comfortable, and homey.

On autopilot, I walked into the tiny kitchen that I hardly ever cooked in, thanks to the fancy commercial kitchen my parents had put in the main building years before. I pulled two wineglasses down from my cupboard, filling them with the remains of an uncorked bottle of Chardonnay in my fridge. "Grant interview you?" I asked.

Ava nodded. "Like a freight train. Man, that guy is unnerving. I suddenly wanted to confess anything I'd ever done. I was *this* close to telling him I cheated on my second-grade spelling test." She held up two fingers an inch apart to illustrate her point.

"I know the feeling," I agreed, handing her a full glass.

She paused. "If I drink this, I'm sleeping here."

I gave her a sheepish grin. "I was kind of hoping you would." I had a bad feeling the image of Heather's body was about all I'd be seeing behind my closed eyes that night, and the comforting thought of Ava in the guest room was a welcome one.

"Then, bottoms up," she agreed, sipping. Once she put her glass down, she added, "You know, I have a bad feeling Grant thinks Leah did it."

"I got that feeling too," I admitted. "He wanted to know where Leah was after the party started to break up. Did you see her?"

Ava shook her head. "I was in the front, saying goodbye to the last few guests. I thought she was in the kitchen."

"So did I." I sipped from my glass, feeling the cool liquid hit my empty stomach.

"Well, I'm sure she was around," Ava reasoned.

I nodded, though I wasn't positive "around" was the type of alibi Grant was looking for.

"Did you know Leah's ex-husband?" I asked. While I'd been MIA from the Sonoma scene for a few years, Ava had stayed in our childhood stomping grounds after high school, building a reputation in the local artists' community with her silver works.

Ava scrunched up her nose as she thought. "Not really. I mean, I know he works at Bay Cellars."

I raised an eyebrow her way. Bay Cellars was one of the larger wineries, mass producing inexpensive wines that sat on every grocery and drug store shelf in the country. While their bottling plant was just outside town, they had small vineyards all over California. In fact, their MO was to buy up struggling family farms, then chuck their grapes into the large corporate vat that spat out generic tasting varietals at alarming speeds. Not that I had any strong feelings on the subject, but I'd felt their vulture's eye on Oak Valley more than once.

"What does he do there?" I asked.

"Sales or something, I think. I'm not sure. I never actually met him—just word of mouth. I know he and Leah divorced last year, and he married Heather a couple months after."

"A couple months?" I asked. "That seems quick."

Ava shrugged. "Maybe it was a whirlwind romance."

"Maybe," I agreed, sipping my drink. Then again, maybe Leah's ex-husband had been seeing Heather before the divorce.

Giving my friend that much more motive for her murder.

*   *   *

The sun arrived way too early the next morning, smacking me in the face a scant few hours after my head had finally hit my pillow. I groaned against the onslaught, reluctantly pulling myself out of bed and into a hot shower. By the time I'd done a quick blow dry and makeup routine and dressed in a pair of jeans, suede ankle boots, and a soft periwinkle top, Ava had already gone to open her shop, Silver Girl, to capitalize on the Saturday tourist trade.

I made my way into the main kitchen, where the thought of coffee beckoned me.

Conchita Villarreal, our house manager, was just pulling a tray of Mexican Chocolate Scones from the oven as I arrived, and my mouth practically watered at the competing scents of cocoa, sugar, and cinnamon. Conchita's dark hair was shot through with a generous helping of white, and it was thrown up today in a floral clip that I knew her husband, Hector, our vineyard manager, had bought for her birthday last month. Conchita and Hector had been with us nearly forever, Hector having grown up on the land like I had, in my father's time. He and Conchita had married young, though they'd never had kids of their own. Some days the couple were almost like surrogate parents to me, and I had a feeling it was mutual on their part.

"So how was the tasting last night?" she asked.

I bit my lip. Apparently she didn't know yet. I quickly filled her in on the details, or at least as much as I knew. Which, honestly, was not a lot. But she clucked and gasped at all the appropriate parts as I relayed the events of the previous evening.

"Who do you think could have done it?" she asked when I was done.

I shrugged. "Not Leah," I decided. Though I had to admit that her lack of alibi was a small doubt in the back of my mind.

"Did Heather know anyone else at the tasting?" Conchita asked.

I nodded. "She had a couple of friends with her. Ladies she knew from the golf club."

"Maybe not so good friends?" Conchita asked, wiggling her eyebrow suggestively.

I thought back to Caroline and Jennifer, and the catty banter between the three ladies. "They didn't seem terribly close, but I don't know what motive they could have for killing her."

"What about the husband?" Conchita asked. "It's always the husband who did it in crime shows."

"I suppose that's possible," I said. "But, again, I don't see why. Kill the ex-wife maybe, but why the hot young trophy wife?"

"You never know. Maybe things weren't so hot between him and Hot Wife."

I nodded. I liked that idea. I liked it a lot better than the finger being pointed at Leah, anyway.

Conchita shrugged. "Well, I'm sure that detective of yours will figure it out."

I felt myself blush. "He's not *my* detective."

"Yet." Conchita winked at me.

I shook my head. "You are a hopeless romantic."

She nodded. "Someone has to be, or you would never date."

Truth be told? I didn't date now.

"Anyway," she said, waving the subject off. Thankfully. "Eat up. You have three interviews this morning."

I closed my eyes and thought a bad word. I'd forgotten all about the interviews. Recently our winery manager had quit, citing something about a larger place in Napa offering him dental and a 401K. I had a hard time blaming him—I'd kill for dental. But it had left us with an opening to fill and not much to provide in the way of perks. I was dreading the interview process. And with everything that had happened the previous night, I'd forgotten all about the fact that I'd scheduled three for that morning.

After another cup of fortifying coffee, I met with candidate number one: a twenty-three-year-old guy with no experience in the wine industry except that he "really dug" drinking wine. When I asked him why he had applied for a manager position without any experience, he'd said the salary had led him to believe it was an entry level "managing" job.

Which was at least better than what candidate number two had explained when asked why he'd applied. He'd already been fired from all the big wineries. He claimed it was a misunderstanding in each instance and he was totally innocent. Which would have been more believable if he hadn't then asked about our policies on random drug testing.

I'd like to say things went better with candidate number three, but the moment he entered my office, I knew it was a no-go. He was so drunk he could barely stand, and asked how many free bottles of wine the managers got. Per day. Luckily, he told me he'd Ubered in, so I politely asked him to Uber right on out.

I was wallowing in pity and browsing the rest of our online applications, wondering if I could take a second job to pay for a real manager, when Jean Luc ducked his head into my office. Jean Luc was our bar manager—or sommelier, as he preferred to be called. He was a slim, tidy man with a mustache that rivaled Hercule Poirot and had a flair about him that was such stereotypically French pomposity that it bordered on comical. It also played to the casual wine lovers' sense of sophistication when entering our tasting rooms, which was a definite plus.

"We have a lady in zee tasting room," he whispered, his French accent heavy with glee. He knew as well as anyone that our tasting room had been sparsely populated lately. "And she eez asking for you, Emmy."

I felt an eyebrow rise. "For me?"

He nodded. "She says she met you at the Wine and Chocolate Tasting party last night?"

The other eyebrow went north. Maybe something good would come out of the evening at the Chocolate Bar after all. "I'll be right up," I promised him.

He gave a nod. "I will keep her beezy until you arrive." And he disappeared to work his charming magic on our guest.

Thankful for the respite from picking among the interviewees, I pulled my hair up into a tidy ponytail and made my way into the tasting room, where, true to form, Jean Luc was putting on a very elegant and intricate show of decanting a bottle of Chardonnay and pouring a dainty serving into a glass for our lone guest.

A guest, I realized, I knew. Caroline Danvers.

"Caroline," I greeted her, trying to cover my surprise. "How nice to see you again."

If she was grieving the loss of her friend, it certainly didn't manifest in the physical. She was dressed in a sporty white skirt and athletic top, though the amount of gold jewelry adorning her neck and wrists said she didn't expect to be working out at athlete levels. Her hair and makeup looked more appropriate for a gala than the gym, and none of the dark circles I'd found under my eyes that morning were in evidence. Or maybe she just used more expensive concealer than I did.

"Nice to see you too, uh...Amy?" Caroline asked.

"Emmy," I corrected automatically. "I see you're sampling the Chardonnay. May I get you a lunch menu as well?"

"No thanks. Just here for the wine." She grinned at me, downing the entire contents of the glass in one gulp.

Jean Luc curled a lip at her behind her back, but he was professional enough to cover it when Caroline turned and pointed at her empty glass for more. I gave him a nod, and he poured a more generous amount.

"I, uh, I'm surprised to see you here," I admitted.

She paused, glass halfway to her lips. "I know. It's a bit more—oh, what did Jenny call it last night?—*rustic* than I'm used to. But one must push one's boundaries, right?"

I cleared my throat, trying to ignore the insult. "I meant because of what happened last night. To Heather."

Her smiled faltered a minute, but she covered it with a large sip from her glass.

"I'm so sorry for your loss," I offered.

"Thank you," replied Caroline. She picked up a cocktail napkin and dabbed at her dry eyes. "I think we're all still in shock."

"I'm sure this must be difficult on everyone who knew her well," I said. I paused, almost feeling bad for asking, but... "How well *did* you know her?"

"What?" Caroline asked.

"Heather. Had you known her long?"

Caroline shrugged and took another deep draw from her glass. "Not really. Jennifer introduced us to her. 'Us' being the Links Ladies, you know."

I didn't exactly know, but I could guess. The Links was an exclusive golf club in town, and everyone who was anyone was a member. Needless to say, I hadn't made that sort of status yet. Nor could I afford the membership fees. "Jennifer and Heather were close, then?" I prodded.

Caroline frowned. "Oh, I don't think so. I think her husband knew James. Or something like that. Anyway, when Heather married into the group, Jennifer sort of took her under her wing. You know, made the right introductions and all."

"Of course," I agreed, having no clue whom the "right" introductions would be to.

"Anyway, I suppose that's all for nothing now." Caroline's face hinted at the first bit of sadness I'd seen from her, before she emptied her second glass.

Jean Luc gave me a questioning look, and I nodded again, watching him refill it a second time.

"Caroline, how were things between Heather and her husband, James?"

Caroline looked up from her glass, eyes narrowing at me. "What do you mean?"

"I just wondered if their marriage was on good terms."

She held my gaze for a moment, and I suddenly wondered if I'd pushed too far. But just as I was about to apologize, she gave another bark of laughter. "So, I guess even *you've* heard the rumors, huh?"

I hadn't, but I hoped I was about to. "What do *you* know about the rumors?"

"I know that's all they are! Vicious rumors. I mean, sure, Heather spent a lot of time lately at the club, but it was her love of the game, nothing more." She paused, pointing one sharp red fingernail my way. "And anyone who tells you otherwise is a liar."

Methinks she doth protest too much. Clearly something was going on at the club, and I had a feeling it wasn't just putting. But, I filed that tidbit away, not wanting to push Caroline off the edge. Instead, I switched gears and asked, "Do you know if Heather knew anyone else at the tasting? Anyone else in attendance that she was close with?"

Caroline sipped her drink, eyes sizing me up over the rim. Then finally she set it down, slightly unsteadily, on the bar and said, "That's actually why I'm here."

Finally. I'd had a feeling it wasn't for the *rustic* atmosphere. "Oh?" I said.

"Look, I need to know the name of one of your guests."

"*My* guests?" I asked.

Caroline nodded. Also slightly unsteadily. Three glasses of Chardonnay on an empty stomach would do that. "Yes. He was at your party. I saw him talking to Heather just before I left."

"Did they know each other?"

"They seemed to. Though, I haven't a clue who he was. Not our type, I'll tell you that."

"Not your type? What do you mean?"

"Well, for starters, he was in a cowboy hat." She scoffed.

I thought back to the event, remembering seeing someone in a hat. At the time I'd found him a bit out of place and had to agree with Caroline's assessment that he hadn't seemed the country club set. "Go on," I prompted.

"Anyway, I saw Heather talking to him outside behind the bakery."

"Wait—did you say *behind* the bakery? As in, in the alleyway?"

Caroline blinked at me. "Did I? I mean, yes. They were just around the corner of the building as I drove away."

I felt my heart rate pick up. Was it possible Caroline had seen Heather's murderer moments before he'd shoved her behind a dumpster?

"What did he look like?" I asked.

More blinking as her false eyelashes fluttered. "Well, he was tall. Dressed all in black like some Johnny Cash wannabe. Dark hair. Kind of crude looking really. And Heather was waving her hands around at him. Like she was mad."

Now we were getting somewhere. "What else?"

"Well, that's all I saw. I drove away then. I mean, I didn't know she was about to be killed."

"Did you tell this to the police?" I asked, thinking of Grant.

Caroline scoffed again. "Well, of course not. I mean, what if he was just a friend of Heather's. Or maybe..." She trailed off, and I thought of those *rumors* that were only rumors. "Well, anyway, I wanted to find out from you who he is first."

I shook my head. "Honestly, I don't know," I told her. Not everyone on my guest list had been a personal acquaintance. Schulz had provided some names, and a few had been local influencers who I'd known of but never personally met. The truth was, this guy could have been anyone.

I just hoped I hadn't invited a murderer to the party.

CHAPTER THREE

———

After calling Caroline a car and carefully depositing her inside, I went back to my office. I thought about calling Grant about Caroline's Man in Black, but her uncertainty over his identity gave me pause. It was entirely possible he was just one of my VIPs who'd had a disagreement with Heather about the merits of red wine versus white with chocolate mousse. In which case, the last thing I wanted to do was be the one instigating an interrogation.

I pulled up my guest list from the event, going over it for anyone who fit the description of the Man in Black. The few male guests I hadn't met in person prior to the event, I googled and was able to come up with faces for them from social media and news mentions. Three were too old—sporting either white hair or none at all instead of the dark hair Caroline had mentioned. One more was barely my height of 5'5", which didn't quite strike me as "tall," and the other was a British transplant. While I couldn't promise he hadn't donned a cowboy hat and black clothes for the party, it felt like an unlikely fit. Whoever the Man in Black was, I was fairly confident he wasn't on my guest list.

Which left Leah's.

I glanced at the clock. It was just after one.

I dialed Leah's number, but it went straight to voicemail. Though, I could well understand if she wasn't taking calls today. I bit my lip, vacillating between not wanting to intrude and honestly wanting to check on her well-being. In the end, curiosity over the mystery guest pushed things into the check-on territory, and I grabbed my purse and headed to my Jeep, stopping only to grab a few of Conchita's scones on my way out the door.

Twenty minutes later I was outside Leah's condo off Riverside Drive, baked offerings in hand as I rang the doorbell. A beat later I heard footsteps shuffling toward me, and Leah opened the door.

Bags hung under her eyes, as if she'd had a sleepless night, though I noticed said eyes were dry and free of the telltale redness that would indicate she'd been crying. She was dressed in an oversized sweater that seemed to swallow her up.

"Emmy!" She enveloped me in a hug, and I only barely avoided crushing the scones.

"How are you?" I asked.

She shrugged. "I've had better days. Come in."

I did, offering her the plate of pastries. "I thought some comfort food might be in order."

She grinned. "Thanks. I actually don't think I've eaten anything today." Though, as she took the plate from me, she set it on the small kitchen table, not touching it.

"The police were just here," she said, sinking into the sofa in the adjacent living room.

I sat opposite her. "Detective Grant?"

She nodded. "You know him?"

"A little," I hedged. "What did he say?"

She shrugged, her shoulders bobbing up and down. "He just asked a bunch of questions about last night. Honestly, Emmy, I think he was treating me like a suspect."

I thought that too, but I didn't say so. Instead I said, "What kind of questions did he ask?"

"Mostly about where I was."

I bit my lip. "What did you say?"

More shrugging. "I told him I was at the event all night. I mean, I don't remember exactly where I was when Heather left. I was in the kitchen, then the main room. I may have ducked into the restroom for a few minutes."

Which all sounded plausible, except that I had been in the kitchen and Ava in the main room, and neither of us had seen her.

"Anyway, he said the Chocolate Bar has to stay closed until they're done processing it." She frowned. "Sucks."

I knew that weekends were usually a busy time for Leah. Coffee and her delicious chocolate delicacies were a treat that the locals devoured. Even those who didn't like to admit they indulged were often spotted inside the store, their dark glasses disguising their identities from their personal trainers.

"Did he tell you how long that will take?"

She shook her head. "Not really."

"I talked to someone today who said they saw Heather outside the shop last night," I said, watching her reaction carefully. "Heather was talking to someone. A man in a cowboy hat. Do you know him?"

Leah pursed her lips together. "I don't recall seeing anyone in a hat. But, then again, I spent most of the night hiding out in the kitchen."

"He was tall, had dark hair?" I prompted.

But she just shook her head. "Sorry, I don't know. I mean, I invited a lot of people. I suppose anyone could have worn a hat."

She had a good point.

"And it wasn't as if we had a bouncer at the door. Anyone could have come in off the street."

Which narrowed our Man in Black down to anyone in Sonoma. Who, honestly, could have been talking to Heather about anything under the sun. The timing was unlucky, but it didn't necessarily mean he'd had anything to do with her death. And, if I was being honest with myself, it wasn't as if Caroline made the most reliable witness.

"Why do you ask?" Leah said, pulling me out of my thoughts.

I shook my head. "No reason," I decided. While Caroline's story had been compelling, the more I thought about it, the more I realized what a wild goose chase it could be. "How are you holding up?" I asked Leah, dropping the subject.

She hugged her oversized sweater tighter around herself. "Okay, I guess. Trying to hold it together for Spencer, you know." Her eyes suddenly teared up with real emotion at the mention of her son. "He's at my mom's right now. I didn't want him here when the police were."

I felt an immediate pang of sympathy. Spencer was Leah's seven-year-old son. I'd only met him a couple of times, but he was a four-foot-tall walking encyclopedia of all things Transformers and loved anything with fur that breathed. Death was hard enough on adults, but I couldn't imagine how Spencer must be taking the death of his stepmother—never mind the fact that his mother might be the police's number one suspect.

"Is he okay?"

She nodded. "He's actually handling it pretty well. Maybe better than I am." She hugged herself again. "I mean, not that he and Heather were close or anything."

"How well did *you* know Heather?" I asked, hoping I wasn't prying too much.

She frowned. "I'm not mourning her death, if that's what you mean."

Which I hardly expected. "I guess I was just wondering if you knew who might have wanted to harm her."

Leah gave a wry smile. "Anyone who had met her?"

I had to admit Heather hadn't seemed overly warm and friendly to me, but the barbs I'd seen her give her friends seemed a far cry from a cake knife in the back. Yet I could tell by the edge creeping into Leah's voice that it was a sore subject. I decided to switch gears. "You never told me much about your divorce from James."

Leah sighed. "There's not much to tell. I mean, classic story. We married young when he was just entry level at Bay Cellars. Had Spence, bought a place in the suburbs. James worked his way up the corporate ladder, and as soon as we were making decent money, he decided he needed a trophy wife to go with his new big shot image."

"Ouch," I said.

She shrugged again. "We're better off without him."

I hesitated to share the rumor Caroline had told me, but I carefully phrased my next question. "Did you know if Heather and James were having any problems?"

She raised an eyebrow my way. "Why? Who told you that?"

"No one, really. It's just a rumor," I said truthfully.

Leah let out a bark of laughter. "Well, wouldn't that be ironic."

"How so?"

Leah crossed her arms over her chest. "I caught James cheating on *me* while we were married."

"With Heather?" I asked.

She paused. "Not specifically," she admitted. "Look, I saw all the signs and chose to ignore them for Spencer's sake. James came home smelling like perfume, he had lipstick on his clothes, late nights at work. All the clichés, and I know I was an idiot not to pay attention to it, but I wanted to believe we could make it work."

I put a sympathetic hand on her arm but remained silent as she continued.

"Finally, I couldn't ignore it anymore when I saw charges for a motel room on his credit card statements. He'd used his card! It's like he wasn't even trying to hide it anymore."

"I'm sorry," I offered.

She shrugged. "I confronted him, and he finally broke down and said he'd been seeing someone and wanted a divorce. But he never told me who. Of course, I suspected later when he and Heather married practically before the ink was dry on our divorce papers."

So Heather had not only been the hot new wife, she'd also been the other woman who'd broken up Leah's marriage. Or at least had a contributing hand in it, from Leah's point of view.

"You never confronted Heather about it?" I asked.

Leah shook her head. "Look, I just wanted to move on and put all of that behind me. Start a new life for Spencer and me, you know?" She sniffed. "Easier said than done now, right?"

I phrased my next question carefully. "Leah, how badly do you think James would want to avoid another messy divorce?"

Leah narrowed her eyes. She was a smart cookie, and I could see her mind following my train of thought. "You think maybe James had something to do with Heather's death?"

I bit my lip. "Do you?"

Leah inhaled deeply, digesting that question. "No." She shook her head. "No, I can't believe James would be capable of that kind of violence."

"He never displayed any while you were married?"

She was still shaking her head, though whether it was to convince me or herself, I wasn't sure. "Violence? No. Pompous, egotistical, liar? Absolutely. But there's no way he would kill someone."

I wondered how much of that assessment was based on reality and how much was based on the fact we were talking about her son's father. Did Leah really think her ex-husband incapable of killing, or was this too just for Spencer's sake?

* * *

I left Leah with a hug and a promise to check in on her tomorrow and headed back to my Jeep. But before I pulled out of the condo complex, I googled James Atherton on my phone. The profile of the Bay Cellars acquisitions manager immediately popped up, showing a man in a brown suit, with a megawatt smile and a generous dusting of salt and pepper at his temples. He wasn't exactly classically handsome, but he wasn't repulsive either. The type of average, forgettable face that blended into a crowd. I could tell he was a good decade older than Heather had been. Had Heather been seeing someone younger at the golf club? Maybe James had found out about it and stabbed her in a fit of jealousy. Or maybe it had been more calculating—setting up an alibi with his scheduling "conflict" that night when in reality he was getting rid of a problem before it could start demanding alimony.

On a whim, I called the phone number under James Atherton's name. I nervously picked at the skin around my finger nail as I listened to the call connect and then divert to his voicemail.

"You've reached James Atherton," said a voice that was deep and laced with a hint of self-importance. "I can't take your call right now, but please leave a message at the tone, and I'll respond ASAP."

I almost hung up, but as the beep sounded, I found myself saying, "Hi, this is Emmy Oak. My family owns Oak Valley Vineyards and...we're thinking of selling," I said, frankly surprised how easily the little white lie came to me. "I wondered if you might be free to chat. Please call me back." I ended the call with my cell number and hung up, hoping my ten little acres were enticing enough to arrange a face-to-face meeting with the recent widower.

Then I dialed Ava's number.

She picked up on the third ring. "Silver Girl fine jewelry, how may I help you?"

"Hey, it's me," I said. "You busy?"

"Unfortunately, not really. It's slow for a weekend here. I think the wine walk downtown is sucking my business."

"Sorry."

"No worries. It's only once a year. So what's up?"

I quickly filled her in on my visit from Caroline and chat with Leah. "She seemed so defeated," I told her when I finished.

"I wonder..." Ava trailed off.

"What?"

"Well, I kind of remember the guy in the cowboy hat from the party. Caroline's Man in Black."

"Did you know him?" I asked, hope lifting.

"No."

I heard hair rustling on the other end as she shook her head.

"But it's possible I caught him on camera at some point. I mean, I took a crapton of photos."

"Could you send them to me?" I asked.

"Sure."

I heard more rustling as she moved around her shop.

"Gimme a sec, and I'll email them over."

I waited, listening to her connect her camera to her computer and send the files through cyberspace to me.

"Okay, check your inbox."

I did, putting her on speaker and pulling the phone away from my ear to see a large attachment come in. I opened the preview, scrolling through what looked like hundreds of pictures. "Wow, this is going to take forever."

"Sorry. I said there were a crapton."

I sighed. "I should probably just tell Grant all about everything and leave it all to the authorities, right? I mean they have the resources for this kind of thing."

"Maybe," Ava hedged. "But what would you really tell him? That Caroline saw someone in a hat talk to Heather, and Heather may or may not have liked to golf a lot?"

I blew out a breath. "Well, when you put it like that."

"Let's face it. All we have are rumors."

"So we should just leave it alone?"

"Oh contraire, my friend," Ava countered, a hint of mischief in her voice. "Look, who's in a better position to find out if the rumors are true—us or Grant?"

I thought of Grant interviewing Caroline. I had a feeling she'd consider a detective to be as beneath her as a man in a cowboy hat. Not that Ava and I were really "her kind," but lips were likely to be slightly looser around a couple of nonthreatening blondes than a VCI detective.

"I don't know…" I said.

"Maybe we could at least find out if there's any merit to Caroline's story about Heather and someone at the club. Just ask around a bit."

I guessed that sounded safe enough. "Any chance your dad might be able to get us an invite to the Links?" I asked.

The only other time I'd been there as a guest, it had been at the invitation of Ava's father, Ken Barnett, a longtime member who had been golfing on their course since before it was trendy to do so.

"That would be a no-go," she responded. "Mom and Dad are on an Alaskan cruise. Fiftieth wedding anniversary."

"Wow. Good for them."

"I do know someone else who is a member." She paused. "But I'm not sure you're going to like it."

Oh boy. "Who?" I was afraid to ask.

"David Allen."

I cringed. David Allen was a tall, dark, and brooding artist from a seriously dysfunctional wealthy family, whom I didn't trust as far as I could spit. I'd met David Allen a few months ago when his stepfather had been found poisoned in my wine cellar. While David had been cleared of the murder, I wouldn't exactly say he'd been 100% innocent. But something about his bad-boy artist vibe had intrigued Ava, and they'd recently struck up a friendship that I warned her not to let veer into much more. Whether she was heeding that warning or not, I wasn't sure.

"You're right," I told her. "I don't like it.

"But you'll go along with it?"

I thought of the way Leah had teared up at the mention of her son. What would happen to Spencer if Grant actually did more than suspect Leah—like arrest her?

"I'll go along with it," I agreed. "Call David Allen."

CHAPTER FOUR

———

The Sonoma Links was lavish, boasting a world class eighteen-hole golf course that often played host to local tours or charity events. It was the place to see and be seen, whether you were actually playing golf or just gossiping about it in the lounge over an oaky Chardonnay. We valeted the car and walked up to the cream-colored building, with a terra-cotta roof, that practically frowned upon us as we stepped under the portico, almost challenging us to prove we were good enough to enter. I held my head high and looked down my nose, hoping I blended with the three other women entering the foyer alongside us.

The glass doors effortlessly glided open to reveal a vaulted ceiling that was at least two stories high, surrounded by gables of glass allowing the brilliant blue sky to reflect upon the white marble floor. The muted sounds of flutes competed for air space with the soft scent of the lilies, and the walnut reception counter was so highly polished I could see my reflection as we walked up to it.

The man standing behind it gave us a toothy smile. "Good afternoon, ladies. May I help you?"

"Good afternoon"—Ava glanced at the nameplate on his breast pocket—"Byron," she finished, pulling a smile to match his. "We're guests of David Allen."

Even hearing the words out loud made me cringe. I tried to put on a toothy smile to match the other two, but it might have come out more of a grimace.

"Welcome. If you could just sign the visitors' book first," he said, "I believe Mr. Allen is on the terrace."

"Thanks." Ava tucked an imaginary strand of hair behind her ear and moved toward the visitors' book. Her signature was large and swirly, and she even added a little heart above the *i* when she wrote my full name in beside hers.

"Thanks so much, Byron," she trilled, fluttering her eyelashes demurely.

His grin flashed bright as she gave him a one-finger wave and led me through the foyer.

"What was that?" I asked, following her through a large set of white oak and glass doors that led to a terrace.

"What?"

"All the eyelash fluttering and flirty smiles?"

"I wasn't flirting," she said, punching me playfully on the arm. "But it never hurts to have a friend at the club, right?"

She had a good point. I'd be happy to have any friend other than the one we were about to meet.

We made our way down a short corridor toward the sounds of clinking glasses and lively chatter that led us to the outdoor bar. The view that greeted me off the terrace was nothing short of breathtaking. The light terrazzo tiles accentuated the green of the fairways that sprawled for miles in front of the wide steps leading down toward it. To my left was a large area where expensively dressed ladies sipped wine and champagne under umbrellas, with servers dressed only in white attending to their every whim. On the fairway, the air filled with the distant thump of metal clubs hitting golf balls.

I spied David sitting at a small table near the back, under a banner touting that the Wine Country Invitational would be hosted there the following day. His too long hair hung rebelliously in his eyes, and his tall length was encased in dark jeans and a black T-shirt that hung loosely on his frame. His expression was exactly the way I'd remembered it—boredom bordering on contempt.

"David!" Ava hailed him as we approached.

He looked up, and the boredom turned into an almost wicked smile as he caught sight of us. "Hello there, doll," he said, rising to greet Ava with a hug.

Then he turned to me. "And Doll's friend," he said, tipping his head my way.

"Emmy," I corrected.

The corner of his mouth turned up. "Trust me, I remember you." He gestured to the table. "Please, sit."

We did, Ava taking the spot closest to him, while I sat across the table.

"Can I buy you ladies a drink?" he asked, not waiting for an answer before he hailed a server and ordered three glasses of a sparkling rosé. I made no attempt to stop him. Hey, it was after noon, and who was I to turn down free rosé?

"So what have you been up to lately?" Ava asked our host.

He shrugged. "Business as usual."

"Still card sharking?" I asked. While David's above board profession was struggling artist, I knew from my previous encounters with him that he enjoyed a card game now and again. And, miraculously, he almost always won. I still wasn't sure if he was brilliant or a cheater, but I guessed it was probably a combination of both.

David shook his head at me. "Shark is such a dirty word," he said, chiding me.

"It's a dirty practice."

David's wicked grin grew. "Then guess I'm just a dirty boy."

I shifted in my seat. I told myself it was the heat of the sunlight on my back, but it probably had more to do with the predatory gleam in David's eyes.

"So, what brings you ladies to the links?" David asked, turning to Ava as he splayed his arms across the back of her chair in a casual pose. I thought I detected a whiff of marijuana along with his expensive aftershave.

"Well," Ava said, "other than enjoying your company, we were hoping to get the lowdown on a little club gossip."

David shook his head. "I'm afraid you've come to the wrong place, babe. You know me. I couldn't care less about whose Tesla is parked in whose garage." He winked my way, as if making sure I got his innuendo.

I was never quite sure if David was flirting with me, or just playing at the flirt to make me uncomfortable. Either way, it had the aforementioned effect, my cheeks heating slightly.

"Did you know Heather Atherton?" I asked him, challenging his flirt head-on with eye contact.

"The dead girl?" he asked.

I nodded, pausing as the wine arrived and I took a cooling sip.

"I'd seen her around," he answered, sipping at his own glass. "She was hard to miss. Didn't she used to be a model?"

Honestly, I had no idea who she was prior to being Mrs. Atherton. But I could well imagine the willowy brunette I'd met at the tasting on the cover of *Vogue*.

"I think she was a wine collector," Ava offered. "Right, Emmy?"

I set my glass down. "Right. A broker, actually. She was also an avid golfer."

David raised one dark eyebrow at me. "If you say so."

"Or," Ava said, shooting a look my way, "she was just spending a lot of time on the links for another reason."

The wicked grin quirked the corners of David's lips again. "Well that sounds like a more interesting story. So you think Mrs. Atherton was playing hole in one with someone at the club?"

I rolled my eyes. "Enough with the sixth-grade euphemisms."

David threw his head back and let out a full laugh. "I forgot. You like to be direct, don't you, Miss Wine and Dine?"

"So, be direct with me," I prompted. "Any idea who Heather might have been seeing here?"

"*If* she was seeing someone?" Ava added.

But David just shrugged his shoulders again. "I'm not exactly in the loop with the ladies who lunch," he told us. "But, if I had to make a wild guess..." He arched one dark eyebrow again, drawing out the suspense on purpose.

"Yes?" I asked, hating that he had me on the hook.

"*That* might have had something to do with her sudden interest in golf." He nodded toward the driving range to our right.

Ava and I both turned our eyes in the direction he'd indicated. Several men and women in polo shirts and golf shorts whacked buckets of balls out onto the expansive green. But it was the man closest to us who immediately held my attention. He was tall and bronzed, and his blond hair gleamed in the sunlight like a golden halo. He wore a polo shirt in the same club blue as Byron. Only this man's uniform hugged his body like a second skin, showing off biceps that rippled with muscles. The tanned thighs beneath his white Bermuda shorts looked strong enough to crack walnuts. He currently had his arms wrapped around the back of a middle-aged woman, hands covering hers on a golf club as he guided her through the finer points of her swing. The look on the woman's face was pure ecstasy.

"Who is he?" Ava asked.

I swore I detected a gleam in her eyes as she watched the golden god.

"Cole Jackson. New golf pro. Came on about six months ago, and I hear demand for lessons has almost doubled."

"He's that good, huh?" I asked.

David grinned again. "I wouldn't know. I don't *swing* that way."

I couldn't help the small chuckle that escaped me.

"So not all my innuendos are childish?" he asked, still grinning.

I shook my head at him, though I had to admit he had a certain rough-around-the-edges charm. "So the ladies love the new golf pro. You think Heather was seeing him for more than just lessons?"

David picked up his glass, sipping slowly. "I don't know. You'd have to ask *him*."

* * *

Twenty minutes and an empty glass of rosé later, Ava and I were standing in the pro shop, watching Cole Jackson bid his female client goodbye. As the woman walked away, her shoulders drooped, and I swore I detected a note of sadness in her eyes. Parting was such sweet sorrow. She went in the direction of the locker rooms, and Cole sauntered toward the back offices.

I stepped forward, hoping to catch his attention.

"Uh, excuse me?"

He turned a pair of perfectly blue eyes our way. Or, I should say, Ava's way, as they quickly dismissed me and honed in on my best friend. I watched his gaze subtly yet seductively roam her soft, flowy skirt and low-cut blouse, his lips curving into a smile of approval that showed off a row of white teeth that would make any dentist proud.

"Yes?" he asked Ava.

"We, uh, were hoping to speak to someone about golf lessons." I was on a roll with the little white lies today.

His gaze flickered briefly toward me before he answered Ava. Or more accurately, answered Ava's cleavage. "Lucky you, you've come to the right place." He took one of her hands in his, shaking it in a way that looked part greeting and part caress. "Cole Jackson."

To her credit, Ava didn't react other than to smile breezily his way. "Ava Barnett. And this is my friend Emmy."

"Nice to meet you." I waved. Which earned me the slightest flicker of attention my way again before his eyes want back to Ava. It was enough to give a girl a complex.

"And you say you're looking for golf lessons?"

Ava nodded. "My dad is a member here. I'd love to be able to keep up with him."

Apparently my best friend was something of a small fibber too.

But it had the desired effect, as Cole's smile widened, his eyes crinkling enticingly at the corners. "Well, why don't we step into my office," he suggested, motioning toward the back.

I could well imagine many a female club patron being ecstatic to hear those words.

I trailed along behind as Cole led Ava and "the girls" to a small room with a desk and a pair of leather chairs. I couldn't help my gaze going to his hips, swaying sexily with every step, almost hypnotizing. I wondered if it was intentional or natural swagger.

"Can I offer you anything to drink?" he asked as he sat behind the desk.

"No, thank you," I replied as Ava and I sat opposite him. For a high-end golf club, the chairs were surprisingly uncomfortable.

"So, you said you're interested in lessons," he said, flashing Ava that bright smile again.

I cleared my throat to get his attention. "Yes. A, uh, mutual friend told us how amazing you are," I said.

Cole nodded. "Who's your friend?"

"Heather Atherton," I offered, watching his expression.

Cole didn't so much as blink, and I wondered if maybe he hadn't heard of her demise yet. "Oh?" was his only reaction.

"Yes, she spoke very highly of you. You know before her..." I trailed off.

Cole's smile finally dropped, his eyes going to the table. "Yes. A very tragic end to a beautiful life."

Which held zero sincerity and sounded a lot like a rehearsed line.

"You knew her well?" Ava asked.

"She was a client," came the noncommittal reply.

"How long had you been working with her?" I jumped in.

His eyes shot up to meet mine for the first time, a questioning note in them. "Why do you ask?"

"Uh...I just wondered how long it took for her swing to improve so much." I shot him a big toothy smile of my own, doing my best to project innocent curiosity.

I wasn't sure it totally came across, but his expression softened.

"We worked together for a few weeks. But, she did have daily lessons."

"Daily?" I felt my eyebrows rise. "That sounds like a lot."

"She was very dedicated," he said.

I tried to read between the lines, but he wasn't giving me much.

"I'm so sorry for your loss," Ava said, her big brown eyes warm with sympathy.

But Cole remained a cool customer, just flashing that white smile again. "I appreciate the sentiment, but, really, I barely knew her."

"You had *daily* lessons with her and barely knew her?" I asked, unable to keep the note of disbelief out of my voice.

While the smile seemed reserved for Ava, the flashes of distrust kept being sent my way. This time it was accompanied by a pair of narrowed blue eyes. "What exactly are you trying to insinuate?" he asked.

"Nothing," I backpedaled. "I just—Heather made it seem like you were close. Very close."

"Heather was a married woman. And I was her golf instructor." While the words were a simple statement, the tone held a hint of menace to it that suddenly made me wonder where Cole Jackson had been the night of Heather's demise.

"Did Heather's husband ever play with her?" Ava asked.

"What?" His sandy brows drew together, his gaze bouncing back to Ava. Only this time he looked her in the eyes instead of the D cups.

"James," I supplied. "I assumed he was a member here as well. Did they ever play golf together?"

Cole snorted. "As if he would have taken time out of his busy day to spend time with her."

I felt a surge of hope. That was an interesting statement. "So they didn't spend much time together?"

Cole shook his head. "I promise you, Heather spent as little time as possible with that man. All he did was put her down. She hadn't said the right thing to this person, hadn't acted the right way at that party. The man cared more about his reputation than he did his own wife."

Clearly we'd hit a sore spot. "Did Heather tell you this?" Ava asked.

He paused before nodding. "You're her friend. I'm sure you've heard it too."

Right. Like any real friend would have. "Yes," I said, vigorously agreeing. Maybe too vigorously, as his suspicious glare came my way again.

"Poor James," Ava said, her perfectly pale brows drawing together. "He must feel awful about it all now that she's gone."

Cole snorted again. "Relieved is more like it."

"Oh?" I asked. "How so?"

His gazed bounced from me to Ava before he leaned in confidentially. "Look, you didn't hear this from me, but the last time I saw the two together, they were arguing."

"Really?" I said. "Did you happen to hear what it was about?"

"I don't know. They were at the valet picking up a car, and there was lots of hushed tension. The only word I really caught was *alimony*."

"Wait—was Heather leaving her husband?" Ava asked.

Cole turned a blank face her way. "I wouldn't know. I'm just the golf instructor."

Which I didn't believe for a second. My smart money was on Ava and me not being the only liars in the room.

"So, shall we discuss *your* lesson?" he asked, turning the charm back on for Ava.

She shot me an unsure look.

I shrugged.

"Uh, yes, let's discuss," she said, sending him a smile that was almost as wide and fake as his.

I let the new info marinate in my mind as I sat quietly, listening to Cole give her the sales spiel and a handful of brochures. I could tell he was very good at his job. The plaque on the wall above his head told me that much, in glowing commendations, even if his smooth smile hadn't already hinted at charming the ladies of the Links into his pro shop. Charm seemed to be his stock in trade, and if Heather had fallen for it, and asked James for a divorce and alimony, maybe James hadn't taken the idea of cheating spouse quite as calmly as Leah had. Maybe he'd decided to end things on *his* terms. I surreptitiously checked my phone as I listened to Cole's pitch. Nada. Nothing back from James Atherton.

Of course, there was also Cole himself. I'd bet a bottle of Screaming Eagle Cabernet that he was closer with Heather than he was letting on. What if she'd asked James for alimony, he'd refused, and Heather had ended it with Cole—sticking with her sugar daddy instead of her hot golfer on the side. Could Cole have been angry enough to kill Heather? I wondered just what he might be capable of if he took a blow to his goliath sized ego, like being dumped by Heather Atherton?

When Cole finally let us go with a promise to call Ava later to schedule their first lesson, my booty was numb from the uncomfortable chair and my mind was still spinning with possibilities.

Warm air hit me in the face as we stepped outside of the air conditioned pro shop.

"Ohmigod, I thought we'd never get out of there. What a salesman," Ava said, fanning herself with a brochure as we walked under the flowering overhang toward the main club entrance.

"He seems to be selling quite a lot to the ladies here," I said, gesturing to another woman in white heading, with a little spring in her step, toward the pro shop we'd just left.

"I guess he is pretty hot," Ava admitted.

"Yeah, but he knew it, and that's a major turnoff."

"What's a turnoff is these prices," she replied, whistling. "How do these women afford him?"

Walking past the bar as we left, I noted the $400 bottle of wine being consumed. For me that bottle would only be opened on special occasions, yet the two men in golf pants and loafers were drinking it like water.

"Maybe they can well afford it," I replied.

"Do you think their lives are as charmed as they look?" Ava asked, her heels clacking across the tiles as she pushed the brochure into her handbag.

My thoughts immediately jumped to Heather. "Not all of them."

Ava must have read my mind, as she said, "Poor Heather. She marries into the country club set only to be ridiculed by both her husband and her so-called friends. No wonder she turned to the arms of the hot golf pro."

"Wonder what her husband thought of that," I mused out loud.

"*If* he knew," Ava added.

"If," I agreed, checking my phone again for a nonexistent call back from him.

CHAPTER FIVE

After saying my goodbyes to Ava, I headed home to get some much needed work done. With my winery manager gone, unfortunately my workload had suddenly doubled. Which was compounded by the fact that our bottle washing machine had died just before our manager had quit, and we now had to wash all the recycled bottles by hand before they went into the sterilizer. Or, more accurately, *I* had to do it. I could have begged Conchita to help, but considering it was my lack of funding that was forcing us to use recycled wine bottles in the first place, I felt it only right that I picked up the slack.

"Hi, Hector," I called to our vineyard manager as I entered the shed where the wine production was done and pushed my sleeves up, ready to get to work. Our production shed was large, was as old as my great-grandmother, was timber clad, and had a cement floor that was washed religiously. The far corner held a sterilizer and the dead washing machine, and the filtration system and bottling line was along the other wall.

"How's my Emmy?" Hector asked, his voice holding a calm, deep comforting tone that instantly put me at ease. Years of too much sun as he tended the grapes had left Hector with more wrinkles than he knew what to do with. But when his craggy face grinned, sunshine and mischief radiated from within, and the years melted away from his appearance. "Life treating you well today, my girl?"

"Could be better, but it could be a lot worse," I replied honestly.

"Yeah, we could have had the latest delivery of bottles." He grinned.

I groaned. "That'll be tomorrow's job. What are you up to?"

"One of the day workers alerted me to a mess in the western plot. Looks like a wild pig got into the vines last night."

Feral pigs were the worst. They dug for the roots, destroying the grapevine. "Much damage?" I asked, mentally crossing my fingers that we hadn't lost a lot.

"I think it looks worse than it is, but I'll know more when I get started on the cleanup."

I hoped Hector was right and that the vines weren't destroyed. We could handle a broken fence, but to lose the plants would mean there would be no grapes, and no grapes meant no wine. And that was something we couldn't afford.

Hector waved as he exited the shed, and I turned my attention to the pile of bottles.

I zoned out, feeling the hot, soapy water heat my skin, the lemon scent of the liquid drifting up and calming me. After the dead body in our cellar a couple of months ago, Ava had recommended an app to help me relax and sleep. It recommended clearing your mind and focusing on just being. I tried the practice now, hoping to calm the swirling thoughts of murderers and cake knives out of my mind, but it turned out it was a lot harder to think of nothing than I realized. The longest I could go before my mind wandered into a different direction was three seconds. I didn't think that was very good, but we all had to start somewhere, right?

Once the last bottle was loaded into the sterilizer, I hung up my gloves and headed into the main building for a much needed coffee. And maybe a leftover chocolate scone. That was going to relax me far more than an app.

I grabbed a plate and sat at a stool at the kitchen counter with my laptop, opening up the attachments Ava had sent me earlier.

Waiting for the photos to appear, I enjoyed a bite of the reheated scone and sipped my coffee. The bitter, sweet, and silky flavors of the coffee, cinnamon, and chocolate played nicely together on my tongue, and I was a step closer to achieving Zen.

The photos finally downloaded, and I pulled up the first one in my previewer—an artful shot of the molten lava cake tower next to our signature label Pinot Noir before the guests had arrived. Ava was right—it would be perfect for our next event promotions. I scrolled through more pictures of the food and wine before guests started appearing in the backgrounds. I slowly flipped through every photo, pausing when Caroline Danvers' face filled the screen. Jennifer was a step behind her, and Heather was just walking in the door. I felt a pang of sadness that these were the last pictures of Heather anywhere. I made a mental note to send copies to her husband. You know—in the event he ever got back to me. And wasn't her killer.

I went through several pictures of the three frenemies—slowly sipping wine, sending each other wan smiles, heads together as they chatted, probably about whose fillers were overdone and whose shoes were last season. Then Ava moved on to other groupings, getting shots of people sipping, laughing, and generally enjoying themselves with my wine. All lovely for promotional purposes. Not much help for ferreting out a murderer.

Until I spotted something in the corner of one of the photos. A cowboy hat.

I paused, hitting the magnifying glass icon on my computer to zoom in. Sure enough, it was a tall dark haired man all in black. His facial features were a little grainy zooming in so far, but I scrolled to the next couple of shots, finding one where he was more in the foreground. He looked in his late forties to early fifties—though his face was lined and weathered, so it was hard to gauge. His eyes were dark and hooded, and he had a small scar cutting through his right eyebrow that instantly made me think *bar fight*. I could tell right away he was definitely not any of the men on my guest list that I'd googled earlier. Either he was one of Leah's guests, or he'd crashed the party. Possibly to kill Heather? I wasn't sure, but Caroline's story about him and Heather arguing suddenly had legs as I noted the way he was scowling as he shot a glare across the room—right at Heather Atherton.

"Am I interrupting?"

I jumped about mile in my seat at the sound of a deep male voice at the doorway to the kitchen. My heart only mildly calmed down as I looked up to find Detective Grant filling said doorway, his broad frame awaiting entry.

"You scared the crap out of me," I admitted. I immediately shut my laptop, as if I'd been caught with a hand in the suspect jar.

"Sorry," he said, coming into the room. "Jean Luc said you were in here." He gestured to the stool beside mine. "Mind if I sit?"

"No, please," I told him, my manners recovering. "Hungry? We've got more chocolate scones."

His eyes flickered to the half-eaten dessert on my plate. "Tempting, but unfortunately, I can't stay."

The disappointment at those words was stronger than I would have liked to admit. "So this is a fly-by jump scare?" I teased, trying to cover the emotion.

Grant's eyes crinkled at the corners, the soft hazel flecks twinkling at me, and I tried to ignore how good even the hint of a smile looked on him.

"Actually, I just wanted to stop by and check in on you."

"Check on me?"

"After last night. I meant to come by earlier, but the day's been crazy."

Truer words were never said. I could scarcely believe it had only been twenty-four hours ago that Ava had been taking those pictures at a party.

"You holding up okay?" he asked, sincere concern lacing his voice.

I nodded. "A lot better than Leah is," I blurted out. And immediately regretted it, as some of the hard angles came back to his jawline at the mention of his prime suspect.

"I know she's your friend, Emmy, but this is a murder investigation."

"A murder she did not commit!" I protested. "A lot of people had much better reasons to want Heather dead."

He raised one eyebrow and leaned an elbow on the counter toward me. "Such as?"

I swallowed hard. I hadn't intended to share the rumors with him until I had something to back them up. But with his questioning gaze pinning me, I felt the sudden and profound urge to confess. "Okay," I finally said, "how about her husband, for starters?"

"James Atherton?" he clarified.

I nodded. "He and Heather were having marital issues. She was asking for a divorce and alimony."

The other eyebrow went north. "He told you this?"

"Well, no, I haven't exactly talked to James."

"Then Heather did?"

I bit my lip. And shook my head. "No."

"Where did you hear it?"

"From the guy I think she was having an affair with."

"You *think* she was having an affair?"

I nodded again. "Unconfirmed but highly suspected."

Grant ran a hand through his hair. "Okay, so this highly suspected individual told you that Heather was asking for a divorce and alimony?"

I paused as I thought back to my conversation with Cole. "Well, not exactly like that. He said he overheard Heather say the word *alimony*. To James. And they were arguing," I added.

He sighed deeply, shaking his head at me. "Any chance they could have been arguing about the alimony James pays his ex-wife, Leah?"

I felt a sheepish blush creeping into my cheeks. "I didn't know he paid Leah alimony."

Grant nodded. "He does. Enough that I could well see his current wife being interested in it."

"But Heather was having an affair," I defended. At least, I thought she was. Though, all Caroline had said was that Heather spent a lot of time at the club, and Cole had denied everything. As I sat in the crossfire of Grant's Cop Face stare, I realized all I had were a lot of theories and a lot of people *not* saying anything.

"Emmy, where did you hear all of this?" Grant asked.

"At the Links club."

His eyes narrowed. "Develop a sudden interest in golf?"

"No, I was just—"

"Prying?" he supplied for me.

My turn to narrow my eyes. "Following up on a lead," I corrected.

Grant let out another deep sigh. Gee, you'd think I was exasperating him or something.

"Look, Emmy, *I* am a police detective. I follow leads. You are a winemaker. And, I might add, a witness the prosecution may want to call to the stand in a trial."

I bit my lip. "Trial? You mean, Leah?"

"I mean, leave this alone," he said. While it was clearly an order, the tone in his voice was softer. Less Bad Cop than Concerned Hot Guy.

I hated how my insides responded to Concerned Hot Guy. And despite my better judgment, I found myself nodding.

"Promise me you won't get into trouble?"

"What am I, twelve?" I gave him a wry smile.

He grinned. "Point taken." He stood, stepping into my personal space. "But please stay safe."

I licked my lips and nodded again. Mostly because with him standing so close, I wasn't sure my brain could formulate a word. I could feel the heat from his broad chest radiating just inches from me, and the subtle woodsy smell of his aftershave felt like it was suddenly all around me.

Then he reached a hand out and tucked a bit of flyaway hair behind my ear, his fingers gently brushing my cheek. It was the softest of touches, but my skin sang with heat where his hand had been.

"I'll call you later?" he said, phrasing it as if asking for permission.

I nodded dumbly again.

Then he sent me another small smile and walked away.

Leaving me overheating faster than a chocolate scone in a microwave.

CHAPTER SIX

———

Through the crack in the curtains, sun streamed in, assaulting me awake Sunday morning. I glanced at my bedside clock. 9:15. I almost never slept that late, but the tossing and turning I'd done the night before could hardly be called sleeping. The green glowing numbers stared back at me, taunting me to try for another hour. My body wanted to stay right where it was for another *few* hours, but my mind was already alert. And once that happened, I knew there was zero chance of getting back to sleep.

It had been after midnight by the time that I'd made it to bed, and even then sleep had been slow coming, visions of Heather's body mingling with Cole Jackson's smug smile and Leah's defeated posture. Not to mention Grant's scorching eyes and soft touch inspiring a whole host of other emotions. None of which were restful.

I checked my reflection in the bathroom mirror. As a testament to the amount of tossing and turning I'd done in lieu of sleep, my hair sat in a blonde bird's nest at the back of my head. My eyes were carrying baggage, and I had a pillow crease embedded on my cheek. No wonder I didn't have a boyfriend.

I ignored the banshee in the mirror and threw on a pair of Ugg boots and a sweater over my pajamas then trudged toward the main kitchen. Being Sunday, Hector and Conchita had the day off, so I was on my own to brew a pot of coffee.

"Well, good morning, sunshine!"

The cheery and unexpected voice jolted me awake, and I might have even let out a scream at the sight of the man standing in my kitchen, cup of coffee in hand. He was short—close to my height—and had enough padding in the middle that someone might have referred to him as jolly. Especially with the large grin on his face, coupled with slightly larger than normal ears on either side of it. He was dressed in pressed slacks and a navy sweater, and I had absolutely no idea who he was or what he was doing in my kitchen.

"What are you doing in here?" I asked, taking a step backward. Though, he looked almost too friendly to be a burglar.

"Just making some coffee." He held up the cup as evidence.

"I mean, exactly who are you?"

"Eddie!" He grinned at me again.

"Why are you here, Eddie?"

He blinked at me, as if not understanding the question. "Here?"

"Here in my kitchen, yes."

More blinking. "Oh, well, the main door was locked, but the kitchen one was unlocked, so I let myself in here instead."

I took a deep breath. "Why. Are. You. At. My. Winery?"

"I-I'm Eddie."

I felt a headache starting to brew and dearly coveted the coffee in the annoying man's hands. "Yes, we've established that."

"Eddie Bliss. I'm here for the winery manager's position?"

I closed my eyes and thought a dirty word. "We had an interview scheduled for this morning?" I vaguely remembered setting something up last week, though that felt like a lifetime ago now.

His smile was back as I opened my eyes. "Yes. You said eight o'clock sharp, but no one was here, so I took the liberty of making some coffee. Would you like a cup?"

More than life itself. "I'll get it myself, thanks," I told him, crossing the room to the machine. I grabbed a mug from the cupboard that said *I wine without my morning coffee* and poured a generous amount of the dark liquid into it. Steam rose, slightly lifting my mood.

"I, uh, hope I didn't overdress," Eddie said.

I turned around to catch him eyeing my pajamas.

I pulled my sweater tighter around my middle. "No. You're fine."

"Curtis is always telling me I'm too finicky about the way I dress. He says I should go for business casual, emphasis on the casual, but I prefer business to be business, you know?"

"Hmm," I answered, sipping from my cup. The warmth seeping into my hands through the ceramic slowly cut through the fog in my brain.

"Curtis is my partner, by the way." He paused. "Oh shoot. Curtis said I shouldn't tell you I had a partner either. I mean, the word *partner* implies things. I guess the name Curtis does too. Whoops, cat's outta the bag. I'm gay." He did jazz hands in the air, accompanied by a wide smile again.

I swore this guy had, like, a hundred teeth.

"Anyhoo, I hope I didn't get the time wrong. I thought the email said to come at eight, but no one showed up until nine. Ish," he added, glancing at the clock above the sink that clearly displayed the time as 9:29.

"No. You had the right time," I assured him. "My fault. I had a long"—week? year? life?—"day, and I'm sorry the interview slipped my mind."

Eddie's face fell. "Oh. So you don't want to interview me then?"

Truth? That was the last thing I wanted to do at current. But considering he was already there—dressed for business, no less—and I sorely needed someone to fill the position, I figured I might as well get it over with. "Why don't we step into my office?" I suggested.

Eddie's grin came back full force, and I think he might have even skipped once down the short hallway to my office. I sat behind my desk, mustering as much dignity as I could in pajamas with little unicorns on them.

"So, Eddie, what previous work experience do you have in the wine industry?"

"Oh, in the wine industry? None!" He practically beamed at me, his expression reminding me of an older version of Dopey from the seven dwarves.

"None?"

"Nope. Not a lick."

Internal sigh. "May I ask why you're applying for a winery *manager* position?"

"Oh, don't get me wrong—I don't have any experience in the wine industry. But I have experience with wine. I drink a *lot* of it."

I was starting to wonder if he was drunk now.

"And," he added, "I can manage the heck out of people."

I picked up my pen. "Okay, so you have management experience then?"

"Nope!"

I put the pen down. "Eddie, why don't you just tell me your qualifications for the job."

Eddie's smile faltered. "Look, I'll level with you, Ms. Oak. I really don't have any."

I grabbed my coffee and took a long drag, hoping the magic warmth would do its thing against the headache that was blossoming into a full-fledged hammering at my temples. "Then why are you applying for this job?"

"I've been a house husband for the last twenty years. Curtis was always the breadwinner, but his health has forced him into early retirement."

"I'm sorry," I said, immediately thinking of my mother. She, too, had been forced from the life she loved much too early.

"Thank you, but he's okay now. He had a heart attack just before the holidays, but as long as he doesn't overdo it, he's okay. So you see, I feel like it's my turn to take care of him now. Get out there in the workforce and make a splash!"

Which was a lovely sentiment, but sentiment wasn't going to run my winery. I opened my mouth to say just that, but he continued on, clearly not yet done with his plea.

"And before you worry, I know your wines."

I raised an eyebrow at him. "You do?"

He nodded. "I drank a whole case in preparation for this interview."

I felt my other eyebrow rise.

"Oh, not all at once. I mean, not today." He ended with a feeble laugh.

"Eddie, you seem like a nice guy, but I'm not—" I started.

"Hear me out!" he protested before I could get any further. "I also know how to run a household, which I admit is not the same as a winery, but I am superduper with organization, I am a stickler for cleanliness, and I am totally a people person."

I sighed. A superduper stickler people person. Why couldn't he just be a qualified experienced person?

Because, said my common sense, I wasn't paying enough for experience and qualifications. Superduper was about all that was in my budget.

I looked up at Eddie's huge Dopey grin again, the hope in his eyes tugging at my chest even as the businesswoman in my head screamed *No, no, no!*

"Fine," I said, much to that screaming businesswoman's dismay. "We can give you a two-week trial."

Eddie clapped his hands and yipped with glee. Actually yipped. Like a terrier in a field of squirrels.

"But," I warned, holding up one finger, "it's just a trial. No promises."

Eddie nodded vigorously. "When do I start?"

"Monday," I told him on a sigh.

"I'll be right on time. Early even!" Eddie promised. "Wow, and to think Curtis said not to get my hopes up. That no one would hire someone without qualifications. Won't he be surprised?"

Curtis sounded like a wise man. Too bad I couldn't afford to be a wise woman.

* * *

After working out the details with Eddie, I shuffled back into the kitchen, had another cup of coffee, and contemplated my breakfast options. Usually Conchita kept a stocked refrigerator, but this week we'd both been too busy with the Wine and Chocolate event to go shopping. Besides, it wasn't as if we had a high demand for gourmet meals at the winery lately. I contemplated a mushy apple and week-old indistinguishable leftovers, deciding maybe a trip into town for supplies was in order.

I tossed the apple and leftovers (which turned out to be lasagna from two weeks ago—yuck!) into the trash and walked back to my cottage to shower. Then I dressed in a linen shirtdress with a brown leather belt and nude low-heeled sandals. I did a blow dry thing with my hair, hopefully applying enough product to turn it into something resembling a normal person versus a home for pigeons. While the bags were still present under my eyes, I added a swipe of red lipstick to detract.

I grabbed my car keys, jumped into my Jeep, and made my way into town.

The Sonoma Valley wasn't a huge area, though a large portion of our population at any given time was tourists flocking to the bed and breakfasts to enjoy the wine tours or Silicon Valley millionaires with vacation homes. The mountain backdrop, soft rolling hills, and warm environment were perfect for growing grapes, and as I negotiated the fifteen-minute drive into town, I was once again stunned by the beauty of the vineyards. I didn't think I would ever become immune to it. It was in my blood, and even though I had enjoyed every second that I had lived in LA, coming home had been the right thing to do for our winery, Mom, and most importantly for myself.

My stomach had growled more than once on the trip, and as I drove past the Chocolate Bar and saw the *Open* sign, I made a fast U-turn and pulled to a stop out front. Groceries could wait. A slice of Leah's Chocolate Chip Coffee Cake and a latte were too enticing to pass up.

The glass storefront glistened in the morning light, and the large chocolate colored logo written in swirling script on the door was my first friendly greeting as I pushed into the shop. The bell above the door jingling its hello was my second.

The aroma of coffee and chocolate blasted me, and for a moment I stood in the doorway inhaling deeply, feeling my mood lift in earnest.

At the sound of the bell, Leah emerged from the back, wiping her hands on her pink apron with the Chocolate Bar's name emblazoned on it. Relief was apparent in her face as she saw me. "Hey, it's you."

"Expecting worse?" I joked.

She shrugged. "You never know lately. This whole thing has got me on edge."

"I'm sorry," I said, meaning it.

"Well, I'm just hoping it blows over soon."

I thought of Grant's visit the night before. I didn't imagine he'd let things just blow over.

"So, what brings you by?" Leah asked.

"I was hoping for a slice of chocolate chip coffee cake? Maybe a latte to go with it?" I glanced at the bakery display. "And maybe one of those for the road?" I added, gesturing to a box that resembled a pink egg carton. I knew from experience that it held six cupcakes, and did an excellent job of keeping them safe for the journey home. Not that mine always made it that far.

"No problem. Take a seat. I'll bring the coffee out in a moment," she told me, disappearing into the back.

I sidestepped the timber tables and metal chairs, and headed toward my favorite spot—the well-worn leather couch with the view of the road and the distant mountains beyond. A moment later, Leah approached and placed a large hunk of cake and a steaming mug on the coffee table before taking a seat in the club chair opposite me.

"Got any calls for events from the party yet?" she asked.

I shook my head. "Sadly, no."

"Me neither. And business here has slowed to a trickle." She paused. "You're the first customer I've had in an hour. Turns out, no one wants to eat at the scene of a crime."

I took a bite of cake, thinking that was a crying shame considering how tasty it was. The moist confection was studded throughout with creamy chocolate chunks that practically melted on my tongue.

"Has Grant been back?" I asked, trying at nonchalant.

Leah shook her head. "No. Thank God. Hopefully, he's moved on."

That, I doubted. I set my fork down. "Leah, did Heather resent the alimony James was paying you?"

She blinked at me, clearly taken aback by the question.

"I'm sorry," I said, holding up my hands in a surrender motion. "I don't mean to pry, but Heather was overheard arguing with James about alimony."

"As if it's any of her business! I was married to the man for ten years," Leah said, the color rising in her cheeks.

"I know," I agreed.

"I earned that money. It wasn't charity. Do you know how I put my own life on hold for his?"

Clearly this was a sore subject. "I agree. No one is disputing that you deserve alimony."

"Darn right they aren't!"

"I was just wondering if maybe it was a source of contention in Heather and James's marriage."

Leah crossed her arms over her chest. "I wouldn't know. Honestly, I don't know if James even shared his financial information with Heather. From what Spencer told me, she was just on an allowance."

"Would it be too personal to ask what kind of alimony he was paying you?"

"Yes," she shot back.

I bit my lip. I'd definitely overstepped.

Leah must have seen the regret on my face, as she let out a big breath. "Sorry," she said. "I'm not mad at you. It's just all of this—all of my dirty laundry suddenly being everyone's business. Spencer and I were doing fine in our new life until Heather showed up and made a mess of everything."

I didn't point out that the situation hadn't turned out all peaches and cream for Heather either.

"No, I'm the one who should be sorry," I apologized. "I didn't mean to pry. I just was hoping to find some other direction to push Grant toward."

Leah reached across the table and took one of my hands in hers. "I know. And you have no idea how much I appreciate that."

I squeezed back, glad we were back on good terms. "Can I show you a picture?" I asked her.

"Of?" she said, leaning back to her chair again.

I scrolled through my phone. "I found a photo that Ava took of the Man in Black."

Leah gave me a blank look.

"The man who was seen arguing with Heather just before her death." I turned the screen so Leah could see him. "Do you recall if he was one of your VIP guests?"

She took the phone from me, a frown forming between her eyebrows as she inspected it. "Sorry, no. Most of the people I invited were from my former life. You know—people James's job afforded me access to before the split. I didn't invite anyone I didn't know." She handed the phone back to me. "And this guy is a stranger to me."

I watched her, seeing no sign she was being untruthful. Which meant the Man in Black had crashed our party. Specifically to see Heather? I looked at the photo again myself. He definitely only had eyes for her, and the look in them was not one of adoration.

The bell above the door jingled, and Leah stood to greet the customer.

I turned my attention back to my latte and cake, savoring each bite as I idly scrolled through news stories on my phone. The local paper had, of course, run a story on Heather's death, but, at least according to them, the sheriff's office did not have any official suspects. While I knew they had at least one unofficial suspect, it was good news that they hadn't released a statement yet. Unofficial meant there still was not enough evidence to point to Leah. I hoped it stayed that way.

A blog by a local foodie reporter, Bradley Wu, did a piece on Heather's life, which was interesting but unenlightening. She'd briefly worked as a cocktail server at a country club in San Jose, where she'd met James when he'd been there for a golf tournament. According to Wu, the two had hit it off immediately with "true love at first sight" and married quickly in a "fairy-tale whirlwind." Bradley had a bit of a flair for the dramatic. No mention of the first wife or whether or not Heather had been the "other woman." They did note that she'd "dabbled" in the wine trading business prior to her marriage, but since tying the knot, she'd been able to focus full-time on it, making quite a name for herself in the last year as the go-to woman for rare and vintage varietals.

I was just scrolling through some photos of Heather at a recent event in Petaluma, when my phone buzzed with an incoming call from a number I didn't recognize.

"Emmy Oak?" I answered.

"Ms. Oak, it's a pleasure. This is James Atherton."

I immediately glanced guiltily over my shoulder at Leah, as if I were somehow betraying my friendship to her by taking this call in her bakery.

"Uh, yes. Hi," I stammered.

"I got your message about wanting to chat about the sale of your winery," he said.

I cringed even though I'd been the one to leave the message and knew it was purely a fictional desire. It just hit a little too close to home. Or too close to what my future looked like in my nightmares.

"Right. Yes. I, uh, got your name from your wife, Heather," I told him. Which was really only half a lie. It was because of Heather that I'd gotten it, even if it hadn't come directly from her.

He was silent for a beat on the other end, but the salesman in him quickly took over. "Yes. Well, I apologize that I wasn't in when you called, but I'm free to meet with you any time today, if you'd like."

"How about now?" I asked, shooting another glance at Leah, who was helping a customer at the bakery counter.

"Now?"

"Yes, I can be there in half an hour."

"Well, you are eager, aren't you? Alright, half an hour it is."

"Perfect. I'll be at your offices then."

He quickly rattled off the address before we hung up. I downed the rest of my coffee, left some money on the table, grabbed my pink to-go container, and gave Leah a little wave goodbye as I headed out the door. All the while still feeling slightly guilty that I was ducking out on seconds of her cake in order to interrogate her ex-husband.

CHAPTER SEVEN

———

Bay Cellars was one of the largest wineries in the region, sprawling just outside of town and employing a dizzying number of employees who did everything from menial labor to high volume sales. They distributed to every grocery chain in America and could arguably call themselves a household name. When it came to wineries, they were the polar opposite of Oak Valley Vineyards—their wines were inexpensive and mass produced to turn over the profits as fast as possible. And judging by the size of their operation as I pulled up to the factory, they were doing a mighty fine job of it.

My stomach tensed as I walked through the main entrance. I would have liked to think it was pride, but as I looked around the room, noting the displays of fine glassware, row after row of beautifully labeled bottles, and the dozen or so people in the massive tasting room, I shamefully admitted it was envy growling like a monster.

A dark haired woman dressed in designer jeans and a cropped leather jacket covering a high necked shirt stepped out from behind a massive stone reception counter and approached me.

"Welcome to Bay Cellars," she said, her voice high pitched and tinny. "Are you here for a tour or a tasting?"

"I'm actually here to see one of your sales managers. James Atherton?"

She nodded. "Of course. Let me ring upstairs for him." She stepped back behind the counter, picking up a receiver and dialing. After a short murmured conversation, she turned back to me. "He'll be down in just a moment. You can wait for him in our tasting bar if you like."

I thanked her and made my way into the crowded room where a sommelier was just placing clean glasses along the bar. The crowd of weekenders eagerly stepped up. He held a glass out to me and raised his eyebrows questioningly.

"Would you care to join us?" he asked.

"Sure. Why not?" I decided. May as well see what the competition had to offer. I mean, I didn't want to be rude.

"You won't be disappointed," he said, pushing the glass across the marble bar top toward me.

"We're starting with our reds," he announced to the crowd. "It's a Tempranillo. Originally these grapes are from Spain, but the climate here in Sonoma is perfect for them as well. You'll detect the aroma of the savory cherry and floral notes," he explained as ten people, including me, picked up their glasses and swished the beautifully colored liquid around, before inhaling the delicious aroma.

"Oh boy, that's a big glass," one of the women in the group announced, with a small giggle.

"We're trialing different styles of glasses today, as the size and shape of it can change the taste of the wine," the sommelier explained.

"How so?" the lady asked.

"It changes where the wine hits the palate, awakening different taste buds."

I nodded my approval. He knew his stuff—I'd give him that. And the idea of different glass sizes was interesting. I wondered if maybe we could arrange a tasting around that. Give the customers samples of the same wine using different glasses and see what different notes they could detect. I made a mental note to run the idea by Jean Luc later.

"Enjoying yourself, Ms. Oak?"

The voice made me jump as I spun to find James Atherton's sparkling white smile. I'd been so engrossed in the wine that I hadn't even heard him walk in.

"Yes, thanks," I replied, setting my glass down on the bar.

"That's our latest Tempranillo. We only serve it seasonally here, but we're finding the limited run raises demand."

He winked at me, as if sharing a seller's secret. "Shall we go up to my office?"

I nodded, noticing that he was much taller than I'd anticipated from his photos. Over six feet, I guessed as I followed him down a corridor and up a spiraling staircase to the business offices. He was also a bit heavier than his photo had shown, and the salt was winning over the pepper in his hair, indicating that the publicity photos I'd seen of him were at least a few years old. Though, if he was feeling any grief at his recent loss, he was hiding it well. None of the bags I'd seen in the mirror that morning were present under his eyes, and the salesman's smile on his face seemed etched there permanently.

"Please, have a seat," he said, leading me into an office with a breathtaking view of vineyards and rolling hills. A large desk sat in the center, several glass cupboards holding bottles stood opposite the windows, and a wall of commendations and photos sat behind us. Clearly business was good for James.

I did as he suggested, sitting in a soft leather chair opposite his desk. It was cool against the bare skin on the back of my thighs below my shirtdress.

"So, you're thinking of putting Oak Valley Vineyards on the market," he started, clasping his hands in front of him on the polished surface of his mahogany desk.

I nodded, hating even pretending at this game. "Uh, yes. We're...just having a hard time making ends meet."

He nodded. "Understandable. In this market small family operations can hardly compete with us."

I inwardly cringed at how matter-of-factly he said it.

"Exactly how many acres do you have?"

I licked my lips. "Around ten."

He nodded again, this time turning to his computer and typing some notes. "And the varietals of grapes you're currently growing?"

"Pinot Noir, Chardonnay, Pinot Blanc, Zinfandel, and some Petite Sirah," I rattled off.

He paused. "You're spread pretty thin for ten acres."

"We do small run batches," I explained. "You know, it ups demand."

His eyes shot to me for a minute, but I just gave my best innocent grin back, pretending he hadn't just said that a moment ago.

Finally he turned back to his computer. "Anything else of value on the property?"

"We also have a tasting facility and commercial kitchen for catering and events."

He waved those off. "That will all be torn down. We're only interested in the grapes."

Even though I knew this was hypothetical, the idea of tearing down the buildings my grandfather had built by hand caused my stomach to churn. And did little to endear me to the man sitting across from me, who would dismiss such history.

"I'm sorry. I haven't offered my condolences on your loss yet," I said, hoping to get to my point in being here.

"What?" James's head snapped up. "Oh, uh, yes. Heather." He paused, the first sign of emotion I'd seen poke through the salesman façade clouding his eyes. Though, whether it was sadness or guilt, I couldn't say. "You said you knew her?" he asked.

"Briefly," I told him honestly. "I was co-hosting the event where she…passed," I finished, trying to think of the kindest terms to describe her murder.

"Ah." James said, steepling his hands on his desk again. "Yes, I should have recognized the name."

"I'm so sorry for your loss," I told him.

He nodded somberly. "Thank you."

"They, uh, they're saying she was killed?" I asked, hoping to open up conversation.

"Yes. I hear the police are looking at my ex-wife."

I'd heard that too. I tried to read from his expression if he believed Leah capable of it or not, but his face was neutral, giving nothing away.

"Was there bad blood between the two?"

James shook his head. "Honestly? I wouldn't have thought so. Not like that. But, as you probably know, my ex-wife owned the bakery where the event took place."

"And you weren't there?" I said. Which I knew already, but exactly where he *was* was of interest.

"No, unfortunately I had a meeting scheduled elsewhere. Which, actually was canceled at the last minute. I was on my way into town when I got the call about Heather."

I perked up. If his meeting had been canceled, then there was no one who could actually vouch for his whereabouts when Heather was killed.

"I got there as soon as I could," he continued. "But of course it was too late to do anything."

"I'm sorry," I said for a third time. He was doing a bang-up job of saying all the things a grieving husband should, but none of it seemed to reach his eyes. Which, I noted, had been dry the entire time.

"I, uh, wondered..." I trailed off, shifting forward in my seat.

"Yes?" He looked at me expectantly.

"I saw Heather at the event." True. "And she was talking with someone." Also true. "Arguing." Hearsay, but possibly true. I pulled up the photo of the Man in Black on my phone. "This man. Do you know him?"

James leaned forward, squinting at the picture. I had the feeling he probably needed glasses, but it if was true, he was too vain to reach for them. "No, I'm sorry. I don't know him."

"Could he have been a friend of Heather's?"

James's expression darkened. "I couldn't say. Heather had lots of friends."

His voice had an edge to it that told me I was in danger of pushing too far.

I tucked my phone away, switching gears. "Heather was an avid golfer, wasn't she?"

He nodded. "That's right."

"I heard she was even taking lessons with the new golf pro." I watched his reaction carefully. "*Daily* lessons."

While he'd had a lifetime of boardrooms to cultivate a poker face, he couldn't hide the way his eyes narrowed slightly and his back teeth clenched. "I wouldn't know anything about that."

I'd have bet money that was a lie.

I tried to come up with a delicate way to ask if his beautiful young wife might have been cheating on him and looking for a divorce and alimony. I must have tried too long, as James turned back to his computer.

"How long did you say Oak Valley has been operating?"

"Four generations," I told him. "Since the early 1900s."

His salesman smile was back. "Impressive."

"Thank you."

"Most older facilities have long ago shut down."

There was that cringe in my belly again.

"I don't suppose you have any bottles from earlier eras in your stockrooms?"

I nodded. "Actually, we do. Not from the original harvests, of course, but we have a few that date back to my grandparents' time, and several from the later twentieth century."

James nodded, the smile growing. He seemed to show more emotion at the idea of rare wine than at his wife's passing.

"Heather was a wine broker, correct?" I asked, trying to steer the conversation back to my reason for being here.

James snorted. "That ridiculous hobby." He shook his head.

I perked up. This felt like a sore spot. "Oh? I thought she had a burgeoning business."

He let out a sardonic laugh, shaking his head. "You did, huh? Well, Heather was a master at making things look pretty and shiny."

"What do you mean by that?"

"What I mean was that 'business' of hers was costing me a pretty penny. I don't know how she talked me into putting up the capital to fund her inventory, but instead of seeing any return, I've been bailing her out of some bad purchases ever since."

I frowned. Heather had been on my VIP list courtesy of my accountant, Gene Schultz. And Schultz rarely made a mistake where money was concerned. "Are you sure?" I asked. "I got the impression that she was doing a brisk business."

"Briskly into bankruptcy," he countered. "Look, Heather knew wine, but she had no head for business, and really, she just wasn't used to dealing with this type of clientele."

"What type would that be?"

"High end. Take last week, for instance—I heard her on the phone arguing with a client."

"You did?" I asked, mentally edging forward on my seat. "Arguing about what?"

"I don't know, really. Something about a wine bottle. But I heard her tell him just where he could stick that bottle." He shook his head. "I told her you can't talk to this type of client like that. It's not how high end business is done."

"Did she tell you who the client was?" I asked, suddenly seeing a whole new theory open up. If Heather had an angry client, it was possible he didn't stop at a phone call, maybe even cornered her at the party and confronted her.

James shook his head. "No. She didn't say."

"But it was a heated argument," I clarified.

James's eyes narrowed as his posture stiffened defensively. "Wait—you're not trying to say one of her clients might have hurt her?"

"Do you think that's possible?" I countered.

But he shook his head vehemently. "Absolutely not. These aren't riffraff off the street we're talking about. She dealt with a select wealthy clientele only."

And, of course, no one with money had ever killed anyone. "How did she meet these clients?" I asked.

He frowned. "I-I don't know," he stammered. "I mean, I guess she met most of them at the club."

"The Links?" I clarified.

He nodded. "Yes. Jennifer introduced her around." He paused. "That would be Jennifer Foxton. *Senator* Foxton's wife," he added, clearly enjoying the namedrop. "The senator and I go way back."

I nodded, trying to feign the appropriate amount of awe even as I was mentally making a note to chat with Senator Foxton's wife about the client Heather had been arguing with.

Before I could come up with a delicate way to pry more, James turned back to his computer screen again. "Now, about the Chardonnay grapes. About how much yield do you expect this year?"

Sadly, far less than I feared Bay Cellar's offer would be to buy the vineyard.

* * *

Twenty minutes later I left James's office with an extremely high offer to buy and a bad taste in my mouth about what would happen if we were ever forced to accept it. I tried to shake it off as I finally did, in fact, head to the grocery store, buying a few necessities. As soon as I got them home and put away, I dialed Ava's number.

"Silver Girl," she answered on the third ring.

"Hey, it's me."

"What's up?" she asked.

"Busy today?"

"Dead. The wine walk is all weekend." She sighed audibly.

"Think maybe you could get someone to cover for you for a couple hours then?"

"Why?" she asked, a mischievous note lacing her voice. "What did you have in mind?"

I filled her in on my conversation with James. I was almost certain he'd known Heather was cheating on him. Or at least suspected. What I didn't know was if he'd put up with it quietly or done something about it. But I was intrigued by the idea that Heather's poor business practices had upset a client. It was interesting timing that she'd been arguing with him just days before her death. I wondered just how heated the argument had gotten, and if the client had let it go at a phone call, or decided to pursue it in person.

"You think maybe this client killed her over a bottle of wine?" Ava asked when I'd finished.

"I think it all depends on the bottle. I've seen some go for six figures."

Ava whistled on the other end. "So how do we find out who this mystery client is?"

"I say we start with Jennifer Foxton." I paused. "Feel like lunch at the Links?"

"You think Jennifer is there today?"

"The Wine Country Invitational is today," I said, remembering the banner I'd seen on our earlier visit. "I doubt she'd miss that."

"And you think she'll talk to us?"

"I think it's worth a try. As long as you don't mind exploiting Byron, your newfound 'friend at the club,' to get us in?"

"I'll meet you at the Links in twenty."

CHAPTER EIGHT

———

Less than an hour later, I'd just valeted my car when Ava's vintage GTO pulled up to the Links club. As she got out, I quickly checked to make sure that the front of my linen dress hadn't wrinkled beyond socially acceptable limits, that my hair was neat, and that I didn't have panda eyes. The air was reasonably humid, and it often had the effect of melting my makeup.

Satisfied that I would pass inspection, I followed Ava across the paved driveway and toward the foyer. The click-clacking noise of our heels echoed on the marble floor, competing with the sounds of flutes subtly echoing from hidden speakers.

Hoping luck was on our side and Byron the Flirtatious was on duty, Ava had dressed in a miniskirt, an off-the-shoulder top, and heels so high her calf muscles rippled with every step.

Unfortunately, luck was playing a little cat-and-mouse game with us again, as when we approached the reception desk, Byron was nowhere to be seen. In his place was a young woman I didn't recognize.

"What do we do now?" Ava whispered.

I pursed my lips. "Stick to the plan?"

Ava paused. Then shrugged. "Worth a try," she whispered back.

"How can I help you today?" the woman, whose name tag read *Jeannie*, asked, her professional grin firmly in place.

"Um, I was wondering if Jennifer Foxton is here today," I said, eyes cutting to Ava.

She leaned forward on the counter, showing a good amount of cleavage. "We're dear friends," Ava told the Jeannie.

"I'm sorry, but we can't give out any information about our members." Her tone was pleasant but decisive, her gaze going back toward her computer screen.

"Jenn is expecting us," I said, hoping I sounded like one of the Links set even if I didn't quite look it.

"She'll be disappointed if we don't meet up," Ava added, punctuating the statement with an adorable pout that would have had any man melting.

But apparently Ava's charms were lost on Jeannie, as she just turned her slightly-less-pleasant smile on us again. "Sorry. This club is members only. Unless your friend has secured a guest pass for you, I'm afraid there's nothing I can do."

"Maybe you could just issue us a guest pass for a teeny-tiny minute so we can find Jennifer?" Ava pleaded.

Jeannie shook her head hard. "Sorry, club policy. You must be a member or signed in by a member to enjoy our facilities. I'm sorry. There's nothing I can do."

I sighed, only half believing she was sorry. "Okay, thanks."

Ava and I turned away—me hoisting my not-designer handbag higher on my shoulder, and Ava adjusting her top to put away the unhelpful cleavage.

"Well, that was a bust," Ava decided. "I guess I could always call David Allen again."

I bit my lip. The fewer favors I owed David the better. I was never quite sure what he had in mind for cashing them in. My gaze fell on a sign for the restrooms.

"Wait, I might have an idea." I grabbed Ava by the arm, turning back to Jeannie's counter.

"Uh, excuse me," I asked her.

Her smile was forced as she greeted me again. "Is there something else I can do for you?"

"Can I just use the restroom quickly before we leave?" I shot her a grin that was all teeth.

Her gaze went from me to the sign above the door to my left. Finally, she relented. "Sure. But that's it."

"Of course," I promised. "Thanks!"

Ava and I quickly made our way across the foyer before Jeannie the Gatekeeper could change her mind.

"You don't really have to go, do you?" Ava asked once we'd made it safely inside the ladies' room.

I shook my head. "But, if we can wait until Jeannie forgets about us or goes on break or something, we can slip out and into the club."

"How long do you think that will take?" Ava asked, looking around the restroom.

It was pretty upmarket, with real cloth towels, an assortment of soaps and lotions for members' needs, and a couple of leather chairs.

I shrugged, taking a chair. "Hopefully not long?"

Ava sat beside me, and we waited. Several well dressed women came and went, largely ignoring us. I played several rounds of solitaire on my phone, crushed a copious amount of candy, and scrolled through a day's worth of political memes and cute baby photos on social media.

"I'm so bored," Ava declared to the ceiling, leaning her head back in the leather chair. "And the scented soaps are starting to give me a headache. Think the snooty receptionist is gone yet?"

I checked the time. Twenty minutes had passed.

"Worth a shot," I decided. I carefully opened the door a crack and peeked out.

Jeannie was still on duty, but thankfully, she was helping another member. A guy with a ton of golf gear, who seemed to be asking for help with transporting it to the green.

"Let's go," I whispered to Ava.

I opened the door just enough to slip out, eyes on Jeannie the whole time. Luckily, *her* eyes were glued to the several bags the golfer was gesturing to, and we quickly tiptoed, the best we could in heels, out of the foyer and down the hallway.

We speed-walked toward the terrace, the soft classical music being piped throughout the club doing nothing to calm my guilt. I was so not cut out for sneaking.

"I can't believe that worked," Ava said beside me, her eyes practically twinkling. She, on the other hand, looked like she was getting a rush from crashing the club.

"Let's just find Jennifer before someone ousts us," I told her.

We quickly checked the terrace, the lounge, and the club rooms without any sign of our prey. I was starting to think maybe Jennifer had skipped the big club event as concession to mourning, when we passed the bar and I spotted her sipping from a long stemmed glass. I should have known to check the bar first.

She was dressed in another power suit—this one in a pale gray—the pencil skirt skimming just below her knees. I wondered if the politician's wife ever went casual. Did she golf in a suit too?

Ava and I both ordered a Moscato—light *and* refreshing—and took a moment to watch Jennifer chat with a couple of other women, also dripping in gold jewelry and hair extensions. When they left her, with air kisses all around, we took our opportunity to approach.

"Jennifer?" I asked, coming up behind her.

She spun, glass of white wine in hand and her eyebrows raised expectantly. The fake smile of greeting froze on her lips as she faced us, clearly not sure who we were.

"Emmy Oak," I supplied. "From Oak Valley Vineyards. And this is Ava Barnett."

Her eyelashes fluttered as she still tried to place us. "Yes. Well, how lovely to see you both again."

"We met the other night at the Wine and Chocolate Tasting event," I told her.

That jogged her memory, the smile dying in place. "Yes. Of course," she said, her voice tight. Though the grief was short lived as her eyes quickly roved my outfit. "I didn't realize *you* were a member here." The look on her face might have been contempt had the Botox allowed her any expression at all.

"We're here as guests," Ava quickly lied. "Can I offer my condolences on the loss of your friend?"

Jennifer took in a deep breath. "Yes. Thank you. It's been…difficult for everyone." Her hands gestured the room at large, though it hardly held mourners—it was drinks in hand all around, accompanied by smiles and murmured laughter.

"You and Heather were close, weren't you?" I asked.

She nodded, sipping her drink. "Yes, I suppose so. My husband, Senator Foxton," she supplied. Unnecessarily. We were all painfully aware of who her husband was at this point. "He and James golf together. When he married Heather, I took her under my wing, so to speak."

"That was about a year ago?" I asked.

She nodded. "A little over. Last spring. Lovely wedding."

"And James and Heather were happy?" Ava asked.

Jennifer blinked at her. "Uh, yes, I supposed so. I mean, of course they were."

"Heather never mentioned anything to you about leaving James?" I pried.

"L-leaving James?" Jennifer turned her attention toward me, but the surprised blinking continued. If she wasn't careful, one of those false eyelashes was liable to flutter across the room all on its own. "Oh, don't be preposterous. Why on earth would she be leaving him?"

Maybe to be with the hot young golf pro? But I figured the question was rhetorical.

"I understand that you introduced Heather to a lot of the collectors she brokered wine for," I said, switching to a less preposterous subject.

Jennifer nodded, seeming to relax a bit now that we were talking wine and not the possible marital discord amongst her cronies. "Oh, well, yes. Yes, I did. You could say I sort of sponsored her here at the club. You know, vouched for her and all that."

"Do you know what sort of wines she was brokering?" Ava asked. "I mean, how much they might be worth?"

Jennifer scoffed. "*We* do not discuss money. It's vulgar."

I bit the inside of my cheek to keep from laughing out loud at that. Everything about this place was designed to subtly show off how much money you had.

"Anyone in particular that Heather did business with?" I asked.

She shot me a suspicious look that very nearly reached her placid forehead. Hmm…might be time for a refresher on those fillers.

"Why do you ask?"

"I, uh, I have some vintage bottles in my cellar myself. Rare, old ones," I said, remembering my conversation earlier with James. "I was thinking of possibly selling." And now that I thought about it, if the price was right, it might be a good way to drum up some funds. As much as I'd hate to part with our history, if it could save our future, it would be worth it.

"What have you got?" she asked, challenging me.

"We have a 1962 Pinot Noir from our own estate, and a couple of bottles of Cabernet from Grace Family Cellars from 1988, for starters."

She nodded. "I'm impressed."

I took that as high praise. I had a feeling it took a lot to impress *Senator* Foxton's wife.

"Any guesses who might be interested?" I asked.

"Well, I'd start with Frank Torrance. I know he sold a few of his collectible bottles to Heather. She might have even brokered a couple of sales for him."

I mentally filed the name away. "Anyone else?"

"May Vanguard. Ellery Fitzjames. Damon Roe." She ticked them off one by one. "I introduced Heather to a lot of people.

I reached into my purse and grabbed my phone, quickly pulling up the photo of the Man in Black. "Do you know if this man was possibly one of her clients?"

Jennifer squinted at the screen for a moment before shaking her head. "Never seen him before," she commented.

"He's not a member of this club?"

Her lips puckered in distaste. "No. He is definitely not Links material," she said, raising her glass to her lips, giving me the impression she wanted to wash a bad taste away.

"Heather had a disagreement with a client just before she died," I said, putting my phone away. "She didn't happen to mention to you who it might be?"

A hint of a frown broke through her esthetician's efforts. "No. But you're not trying to say that someone *here* would hurt Heather?"

That was exactly what I was trying to say.

"Look," she went on, "I don't know what sort of people you're used to dealing with, but this is *not* that kind of place." She paused, breathing deeply, as if glad that issue had been put to rest. "Now, if you'll excuse me, I see someone I must talk to. Fundraising never stops, you know." With that she spun on the heel of her Christian Louboutins and walked off to greet a group of women by the window with her same, frozen smile.

* * *

Ava and I sat for a moment, finishing our drinks and watching Jennifer work the room.

"She's good," Ava mused, sipping her Moscato.

I nodded agreement. "Smooth as a baby's butt."

Ava snorted into her glass. "I'm sure she'd love that analogy." She paused. "You think she really thought James and Heather were on good terms, or was she covering for Heather?"

I shrugged. "I wish I knew." I sipped the last of my drink. "Either way, though, James is possibly in a much better financial place with Heather dead than divorced."

"And he gets to play the grieving widower instead of the guy whose trophy wife left him for the hot golf pro."

"Good point," I told her, pointing my empty glass her way before setting it on the bar. "Ready?"

She tossed back the last of her glass and nodded.

For fear of being spotted by Jeannie the Gatekeeper, we both put our heads down as we entered the foyer, keeping to the back wall and generally trying to be as invisible as possible.

Which might have worked out better if a loud male voice hadn't shouted, "Ava!"

We both froze, my gaze going to the reception desk, where Byron was hailing us with a big smile and a wave high above his head. Where had he been an hour ago?

"Hi, Byron," Ava said, approaching as I quickly checked behind him to see if Jeannie was nearby. No sign. I gave a sigh of relief that she was MIA.

"Fantastic to see you again," Byron said, eyes riveted to Ava.

She gave him a breezy smile. "Thanks, but we're just on our way out."

"Oh, what a shame." His smile drooped.

"Uh, Byron," I jumped in, "how long have you worked here?"

"Just over five years," he answered, a hint of pride in his voice.

"So, you must know all of the guests who come through these doors?" I asked.

He nodded. "Personal service is part of the package here. I make it my business to know as much as I can, and greeting every member personally by name goes a long way."

I quickly retrieved my phone and pulled up the photo of Man in Black.

"Byron, do you know this man?" I asked.

"We're not allowed to divulge information about our guests," he said apologetically as he took the phone from me. "But as I have never seen this man before, I can happily tell you that he's not a member here."

Another dead end.

"Thanks anyway," I added, sliding my phone back into my bag.

"Anytime. I look forward to seeing you around here," he called after us.

Though again, I was pretty sure who that comment was directed at.

* * *

I parted ways with Ava at the curb, as her car came much faster to the valet station than mine. (Note to self: show more cleavage when visiting the club.) My stomach growled as I waited, reminding me I hadn't yet had a proper lunch. As I mentally ran through the groceries I'd bought and wondered what recipe I could conjure up with them, a couple exiting the building caught my attention.

Caroline Danvers and the hottie golf pro Cole Jackson. They were making their way toward an unpaved path that ran through the gardens. Cole gestured for Caroline to go first, his hand on her lower back. As she followed his direction, his hand slipped much lower than what I thought appropriate for a married woman, and her giggle floated toward me.

Hmmm, that was interesting.

With a quick glance at the valet—who showed no sign of retrieving my Jeep yet—I jogged after them. Nosy? Yes. But curiosity wasn't the only thing that killed the cat—sometimes it was rotting in a jail for a crime she didn't commit.

By the time I traversed the tall hedges that bordered the gardens, I'd almost lost sight of them. Almost. They were just rounding a corner when I caught the flash of Caroline's bright orange golf shirt.

I hurried after them, regretting my shoe choice with every step. Slippery sandals weren't made for grass, especially when you wanted to be stealthy.

Caroline paused as Cole turned to say something to her. They were far enough in front of me that I couldn't hear what it was, so I crept closer, stopping behind a planter box that came just below my knee. The plants within it gave me good cover, and if I strained hard enough to listen, I could just make out hints of the conversation. Not that I really needed to. Their body language was giving me all sorts of clues.

Clearly they thought they were alone. Cole's hand squeezed Caroline's bottom as he guided her toward a utility shed with a door marked *Club Staff Only*. He pushed it open with his free hand, and Caroline let out that giggle again as she entered. The door closed quietly behind them, cutting off my view

Though I had a good idea what they were up to.

Caroline had insinuated that something was going on between Cole and Heather. Silly me, the thought hadn't even crossed my mind that Caroline might be getting *golf lessons* as well. I suddenly wondered how Heather had felt about that—sharing her side piece with her frenemy. Had the two argued about it? Caroline had left the Wine and Chocolate party early…but that didn't mean she hadn't come back and offed Heather in the alleyway in some sort of fit of jealousy. And hadn't it been Caroline who'd made a point of telling me about this mysterious Man in Black she'd seen as she'd left. For all I knew, he was a complete red herring in all this and Caroline had made up the argument she'd witnessed just to throw suspicion off herself.

My head was whirling with theories that this new development offered up as I made my way back to the valet station. I was so engrossed in them that I didn't even see the man standing at the head of the garden path until I rounded the hedge and nearly plowed right into him.

"Sorry," I mumbled, looking up into his eyes.

Dark eyes. Filled with hazel flecks that were, right now, running an active relay as they stared me down.

Detective Grant.

CHAPTER NINE

———

"G-Grant," I said, taking an unsteady step backward in my heels. Unsteady enough I instinctively grabbed a handful of his shirt to keep from falling over as he reached out for my arm and pulled me close.

"Fancy meeting you here," he said, his deep, low, and *so* close voice causing goose bumps to dance over my entire body.

"I could say the same thing," I told him, licking my suddenly too dry lips. I realized that I still had a handful of his shirt and quickly released it, smoothing the fabric and noting his pecs underneath it. I might have smoothed a bit longer and harder than I had intended, but once I started, it was hard to stop.

Grant looked down at me, a questioning smile beginning to crease the corners of his eyes. "What exactly were you doing?" he asked me once I was sure that I could stroke the fabric no more.

"You had wrinkles in your shirt," I explained, clearing my throat. "Can't have you walking around a place like this looking messy."

The smile widened, amusement at my expense clear on his face. "I meant, before you walked into me. What are you doing here?"

"Uh…here? At the Links? I was…having a glass of Moscato." Which was totally truthful, even if it did leave out a few details.

"Really?" he arched an eyebrow my way. "You don't strike me as the country club set."

I crossed my arms over my chest. "Is that an insult?"

He laughed out loud, the sound an unexpected rumble that washed a new wave of goose bumps over me. "On the contrary. I think it was a compliment."

The sexy detective just complimented me. I tried not to let that go to my head. "What are you doing here?" I countered.

"I'm investigating a murder," came the simple response.

I felt a small lift of hope in my chest. "You mean you think maybe a member here had something to do with Heather's death?"

He paused, clearly taking care with his wording. "I think there may be some information to be gleaned here that may be pertinent to her death."

"So, you're looking in a direction other than Leah?" I clarified, that hope spreading.

Grant gave me his blank, unreadable Cop Stare. He sucked in a breath, blowing it out through his nose as his eyes assessed my face. Finally he did a quick glance in both directions and put an arm around my shoulder to lead me away from the walkway, as he lowered his voice.

"Look, Leah was here the day before Heather died."

"What?" Even the heat coming from Grant's touch didn't mitigate my shock at that statement. "What do you mean, here? She wasn't a member."

"No, she wasn't. She came in uninvited. She was turned away at reception, but a witness says she refused to leave and they called security."

A witness at reception. What did you want to bet her name was Jeannie? I suddenly wondered if that was where she'd been when Byron had hailed us—giving a statement to Grant.

"Did you ask Leah why she was here?"

"Not yet," Grant admitted. "But apparently she was asking for Heather."

I licked my lips again, though the nervous habit was for a whole other reason. "Did she see Heather?"

Grant nodded slowly.

"What happened?" I almost didn't want to know.

He blew out a breath again, and I could see a hint of sympathy in the hazel flecks, moving slower now. "The two were involved in an altercation. Security was called, but by the time they arrived, it had escalated to the point of assault."

"Assault?" I repeated, hating how this story was unfolding.

More nodding. "Leah punched Heather, leaving her with a bloody nose."

That hope crashed and burned into a lead ball in my gut. "She didn't!"

Grant sighed. "I'm afraid she did."

"But why?" I asked. "I mean, Heather must have provoked her. Leah isn't violent." At least not that I'd ever seen.

But there was more.

"More than one witness has stated that as security arrived, they heard Leah threaten Heather," Grant went on. "She was quoted as telling Heather to 'watch her back.'"

I closed my eyes and thought a really dirty word. Of all the stupid…

"Look, it was just coincidence, I'm sure," I said, opening my eyes to face Grant again. "I mean, how stupid would Leah have to be to say that and then actually stab the woman in the back?"

Grant shrugged. "I don't know."

"Leah is not stupid," I defended.

"I never said she was."

"But you're saying she's a murderer?"

"I'm saying," he said slowly, as if talking to a six-year-old, "that there is ample evidence of assault and verbal threat from her to the victim just before the victim expired."

"Which are coincidence," I repeated.

Grant ran a hand through his hair, making it fall sexily into his eyes. If I'd done that, mine would have frizzed in all directions.

"Emmy, your loyalty to your friend is admirable."

"Thank you."

"But it's not evidence."

I shut my mouth with a click. Mostly because I had no argument to that. He was right—my belief in Leah wasn't going to sway a jury any more than it was swaying Grant.

"I have to follow the evidence, and as much as you may want to think Leah didn't kill Heather, it's what the evidence says that matters."

I hated his rationale, but I couldn't argue with it.

"She didn't do this," I said again, even though it sounded weak to my own ears. His logic had taken the fight out of it.

"For your sake, I hope not," he said, taking a step toward me, closing the gap our argument had created.

Warmth radiated off of him, and I resisted the urge to reach out and touch that strong, comforting chest again.

"But please leave the investigating to me," he said, his voice low and soft.

"I was just having wine," I protested weakly, my heart pounding at his nearness, making it hard to focus on anything else.

"Okay. Just have wine somewhere where I'm not investigating a murder. Okay?"

"Okay," I agreed. Even though I was mentally crossing my fingers behind my back. As long as Grant was looking in Leah's direction, I owed it to her to keep going in another.

Grant narrowed his eyes at me. "Really?"

Dang, he was a good cop. He could sniff out a lie before it even happened.

Thankfully, his cell phone rang, diverting his attention before he could interrogate further. Because I knew under those intense hazel flecks, I was a goner. I'd crack like a piggy bank when the ice cream man drove by.

My shoe kicked at a pebble lying on the terrazzo tile, and I concentrated on it while Grant *ahahed* and *hmmed* and finally told whoever was on the other end that he was on his way.

"Duty calls," he said, pushing his phone into the pocket of his jeans. "Can I walk you to your car?"

I'd like to think he asked so that he could spend more time with me, but I had a suspicion he just wanted to ensure that I left the premises.

"Sure," I agreed.

By the time we were back at the valet station, my Jeep was, thankfully, at the curb. Grant opened the door for me, ever the gentleman, closing it and leaning on my window.

"Stay out of trouble, okay?" he said, the corners of his mouth turning up in a hint of humor even though I knew he meant it.

"I'm never in trouble," I replied.

He let out a small laugh. "*That* I don't believe for a second." Then he walked away, disappearing inside the country club.

I watched him the entire way, noting the way his jeans molded his backside to perfection and how his shirt stretched across his back, hinting at the muscles underneath.

Down, girl. It was seriously not like me to drool like a teenager over a man. Let alone a man intent on putting my friend in jail. I gave myself a mental shake, making a promise to keep Grant out of my mind. And, unlike the promise I'd made to him to stay out of all of it, this one I intended to keep.

* * *

As I pulled away from the club, I used my hands-free to call Leah. I listened to it ring as I wound down the long drive, flanked by tall cypress trees and stately oaks. Finally her voicemail sang down the line a cheery request for a message.

"...please leave your name and number, and I'll call you back," her voice chirped. She'd obviously recorded it in happier times.

"Hey, Leah, it's Emmy. Can you call me when you get this please? It doesn't matter what time it is. Just ring. Thanks." I tried to keep my tone light, not wanting to freak her out.

Then I drove home and realized I hadn't eaten in hours. After perusing the contents of the refrigerator, I decided on a simple Lemon Artichoke Chicken. Usually I marinated the chicken overnight for a faster cook, but I was in no rush. In fact, the rhythmic chopping, seasoning, and sizzling of the work helped to soothe my mind and get me closer to Zen than the breathing app had. As I popped the chicken and artichoke hearts into the oven to finish cooking, I decided to give the dish a

Mediterranean flavor profile by adding an olive and parsley gremolata on top. Once it was all assembled, I took it into my office, attempting to get a little work done while I ate. Even if thoughts of Heather's murder kept creeping to the forefront of my mind.

While I still liked James's motive as the discarded husband passed over in favor of the hot young golf pro, I had to admit that seeing Caroline and Cole together had thrown a whole new light on the women's relationship. I suddenly wondered if the thinly veiled barbs I'd seen the two exchanging the night of the Wine and Chocolate party were symptoms of a much deeper rivalry. One that might have turned deadly?

Or had Heather's death had nothing to do with her personal life and been about a wine deal gone wrong? James had been sure Heather had rubbed at least one client the wrong way…but just how unhappy had he or she been?

I finished my last bite of tangy, buttery chicken and pushed my plate to the side as I turned to my computer. Jennifer had rattled off the names of a few of Heather's clients, but I wondered just how many there might have been. And how much they'd paid for her services. Brokers usually took a small fee for connecting sellers with buyers, the percentage based on the ultimate cost of the wine. Collectible bottles could go from anywhere in the low hundreds to the mid six figures. Many collectors considered them investments, and buying and selling was much more than just a fun hobby for them.

Unfortunately, there was precious little information about it all online—most collectors preferring private deals to public bidding, for obvious reasons. If it was public knowledge how much you'd paid for a rare bottle, you had a hard time asking much more for it from a seller on the other end.

Which meant if we really wanted to know if something about Heather's deal gone wrong was worth killing over, we needed to look at her private records.

I grabbed my phone, dialing Ava's number.

"Hey, it's me," I said when she picked up two rings in. "Got plans tonight?"

CHAPTER TEN

———

"Black clothing—check. Flashlight—check. Appropriate footwear—check. I think we're set."

Who knew Ava had so much knowledge when it came to breaking and entering?

"I'm not sure that your three-inch wedged heel boot is considered appropriate for what we're about to do," I muttered.

"What? You don't think they're cute?"

"Oh, they're cute alright. Just not what I would have chosen."

"Well, they were all I had."

"Don't you own a pair of sneakers?" I asked.

"Sure, but they're white. Not the favorite choice of cat burglars."

"We're not cat burglars. We're not stealing anything. Just looking around."

"Yeah, well, I'm sure Grant will take that into consideration if we get caught."

Her words caused my heart rate to pick up. "I do not plan on getting caught," I told her.

"Right. Sure. I mean, I just said *if.*"

Her confidence did nothing to slow my pulse. I prayed that the veins in my head could handle the pressure. Having a stroke was not something I wanted to do, but having a stroke while breaking into James and Heather Atherton's house was even less appealing.

"You're sure James isn't home?" Ava asked for the third time as I slowed my Jeep to a crawl down his street, checking house numbers for the right one.

"Positive. Leah told me last week about this thing at Spencer's school. A play."

"What production?"

"*Aladdin,*" I told her as I found the right house, slowly passing it and parking up the street a bit, where a large yew hedge shielded the car from the homes beyond. "Leah said she wanted to take him, but it was James's turn. She did the last school event—bake sale."

"Ah. I remember that. I bought way too many brownies."

"Anyway, he should be gone for a least a couple of hours. Longer if the kids drag it out."

"It's a wonder James didn't cancel," Ava mulled as we exited the car. "What with his wife dying only a couple days ago."

Shoot. That thought hadn't occurred to me. Ava must have picked up on my hesitation as she turned to me and said, "He didn't cancel, did he?"

I shrugged. "I'm not sure," I admitted. I looked back at the Atherton house. "But the lights in the house aren't on, so I'm going for no?" It came out more as a question than a statement.

"Okay, then lead on, Cagney."

I tried not to roll my eyes. "If we're gonna be seventies detectives, can we at least be Charlie's Angels?"

"Ohmigod, I loved that show. I even had the lunchbox," she said, slipping a black baseball cap on her head.

I did the same, tucking my hair under an old SF Giants cap.

James and Heather's home fronted a semi-busy street. It wasn't a thoroughfare, but it wasn't a quiet cul-de-sac either. More than one car whizzed by, its headlights illuminating our path. The upside to that was that we hadn't needed to use our flashlights yet. The downside was that we would look pretty suspicious if the occupants of the vehicles were to look our way.

"Which room is Heather's office?" Ava asked, her attention on the twelve dark windows frowning down on us as we crossed their front lawn.

"I have no idea," I confessed.

"So we search all of them?" Her tone pitched up, and the neighbor's dog started to bark.

"We probably should be keeping our voices down," I suggested.

"Sorry, but I thought you knew the layout of the house."

"How would I? I've never been inside before."

"So what's the plan?" Ava asked.

I sucked my bottom lip in and bit down hard. "Let's find a back door," I suggested as a car drove past, its headlights highlighting the frown etched into Ava's forehead.

We kept close to the hedge surrounding the property until we hit the back gate.

"They don't own a dog, do they?" Ava asked, her hand on my back. The bushes hid the glow of the passing lights, and the shadows loomed over us, dark and eerie. A cool breeze danced across my cheeks, and a chill ran down my spine.

"Let's hope not," I replied, picking up my pace.

My feet sank into the lush grass, and the scent of white evening primrose filled my senses, making me want to sneeze. The neighbor's dog had ceased barking, and now the evening air was peaceful and serene. Had I not been attempting to get into someone's house illegally, I probably would have enjoyed it. As it was, I was starting to sweat.

Luckily, the back gate was unlocked, and as we slipped the latch free, the privacy at the back of the house gave my pulse a chance to drop into slightly less than heart attack range. The tall bushes continued around the perimeter of the property, and no prying eyes from the outside world could see us. So long as I was right in my assumption that James was busy watching Spencer's classmates sing about magic carpet rides, we were now on much safer ground.

"Now what?" Ava asked, her voice slightly louder, obviously feeling the relative security as well.

"Now we cross our fingers."

I lifted a potted plant by the back door, hoping for a spare key. No luck. I tried a second one with much the same results.

"You think James has a hide-a-key somewhere?"

I shrugged, glancing around the spacious yard, complete with swimming pool and outdoor kitchen. "I know Leah always keeps a spare hidden around her condo. I was hoping it was a habit she'd picked up from him."

We tried looking under all the potted plants in the backyard as well as any large rocks. All we found were a few roly-poly bugs and slugs.

"Okay," Ava said, drawing in a deep breath. "I guess I'll have to pick the lock."

"With what?" While I'd seen Ava pick a lock once before, I'd honestly thought the positive result had been kind of dumb luck, all of her knowledge having been gleaned from TV cop shows.

Ava slipped her hand into her pocket and pulled out her wallet. She extracted a credit card.

"Oh, not Nordstrom!" I told her.

"You're right." She nodded, putting it back and pulling out a Chevron gas card. "This is safer." She approached the back door, trying to slip the card into the crack between the door and the frame. She jiggled, wiggled, and coaxed. Her tongue protruded from the corner of her mouth at the effort.

"Any luck?" I asked, shifting from one antsy foot to the other.

"I'm sure this is how they did it on *Midsomer Murders* the other day..." she mumbled, more to herself than to me.

It must have looked easier on TV than it was in real life, as about ten minutes in she stood and shook her head. "Sorry. I don't think this is going to work. It's locked up tight." As if to illustrate her point, she put her hand on the knob to the back door and twisted.

And it turned with ease.

Ava blinked, her eyes shooting to mine.

Mental forehead thunk. "It was unlocked the whole time?"

"Huh," she said. "I guess I never thought to check it."

Honestly, I hadn't either. Let's face it, we were not Charlie's Angels. More like the two stooges.

"Come on. Let's get this over with before James comes home," I said, leading the way inside.

Under-counter lights had been left on, the glow giving us just enough light to make out that we were in the kitchen, and that kitchen was fabulous. The counters were marble, the cabinets high gloss white and glass, and the appliances stainless steel and expensive. I might have salivated just a little bit when my gaze fell on the built-in espresso machine, but Ava grabbed my arm, pulling me along and preventing me from running my hands lovingly over it.

"Emmy, put your gloves on," she hissed.

"What? I didn't bring gloves," I replied.

"What do you mean?"

"You just said to wear black, bring a flashlight and comfy shoes. You never said anything about gloves!"

"I figured you would have known to bring gloves to a break and enter," she replied, rather sarcastically, if I may say so.

"What do I do?" I asked.

"Stay still, and don't touch anything. I'll see if I can find any." Ava made her way across the room as I wiped the door handle clean with the sleeve of my sweatshirt.

The creaking of a cupboard door echoed in the semidarkness before Ava flicked her flashlight on and started a checklist of things found under Heather's sink. "Oven cleaner, dishwasher detergent, scouring pads." Ava huffed. "As if Heather ever used any of this stuff. Ah. Here we go."

She stood and smiled, returning to me with a pair of bright yellow rubber gloves.

"Really?" I asked.

"What else did you think I was going to find under the kitchen sink? Versace?"

I took them from her. "I guess they're better than nothing," I said, pushing my fingers into the rubber sheaths.

"So, where do we start?" Ava asked, eyes going to a hallway that led off the kitchen.

"Your guess is as good as mine. Ground floor?"

Ava nodded in the darkness, swinging her flashlight down the hall and leading the way.

Three doors later we knew that the downstairs of the Atherton home housed a guest bathroom, a home gym, a music room, and a lavish living room. Finally at the front of the house, we entered a pair of French doors that housed what looked like a home office. And from the feminine décor and floral pattern on the drapes, I had a suspicion it was Heather's and not her husband's.

I took a moment to slow my breathing as we closed the doors behind us.

Ava moved toward the desk and flicked the lamp on.

"Should we have that light on?" I asked, eyes cutting to the windows.

"It'll make our job so much quicker," she commented.

"But what if someone on the street notices it?" Anyone passing by on the road could see the light.

"They'll think nothing of it. Our flashlights zipping around might be a different story though."

That was actually a good point. I hurriedly flicked my flashlight off and allowed my gaze to roam the room.

"This is a pretty nice office," Ava commented, her gaze following mine.

She was right. Mahogany cabinets matched the glossy desk, which held nothing but a small desktop computer, keyboard, and mouse. Behind it on the wall was a large framed painting reminding me of a Monet. Several bottles of red wine were displayed on the glass shelving that sat alongside it, and a set of dusty footprints were embedded in the white plush carpet that made their way to the desk, only stopping beneath Ava.

Crap.

"Ava! Your shoes," I almost screamed.

She looked down, and even in the dim light I could see that her face paled. "Oh no. I kind of remember stepping in the flower beds while we were looking for a key."

"What should we do?" I asked, horrified. Here we were trying to be sneaky, and Ava's size sixes would lead anyone to the exact spot we were snooping in.

"You start looking through the files. I'll see if I can find the vacuum." Ava slipped her boots off and retraced her steps. As she opened the door and looked up the hall, I heard her say. "And the mop."

I shook my head as I sidestepped the footprints.

I started with the paper files in a cabinet behind the desk, but all they held were boring insurance and tax forms. A few photos adorned the shelves, but most were of Heather herself. Clearly she was her favorite subject.

I made my way to the computer.

The high-backed leather chair was sumptuous and soft as I sank into it and pulled the keyboard close. Hitting the *Return* button a couple of times, the screen came to life, asking for a password. I tried a few of the obvious choices—her husband's name, Cole's name, *Linkslady*. The rubber gloves made my fingers clumsy, and after a dozen or so attempts, I sat back and tried to think.

The sound of a vacuum cleaner retracing our steps from the kitchen filled the still evening air, and it made my stomach clench. I really hoped that sound didn't travel too far and make the neighbors question why James was doing housework at this hour. As Ava made her way into the room, frantically rubbing the vacuum cleaner head over her dirty footprints, I did my best to ignore her and started opening desk drawers.

Paper clips, sticky pads, stapler. All standard home office stuff. In the third drawer down, I found a small leather-bound book that looked like a diary. I pulled it out, thinking there was no way I was going to get that lucky.

I was right. It was not a diary but a book of passwords. Which was almost as helpful, as I moved back to the keyboard and typed in *WINSTON*. Suddenly the screen came to life, and I was confronted with Heather's cluttered computer desktop.

"Who's Winston?" Ava asked, switching the vacuum off and wiping her forehead with her sleeve.

"No idea." I shrugged, distracted by the dozens of files that appeared. Allowing my eyes to quickly scan their names, I stopped on the one labeled *Client Files* and moved my mouse so that the cursor was over the top of it. Two clicks later I had an array of files in front of me, each labeled with names of clients. I pulled my phone from my pocket and took a photo of the screen. A few of the names were familiar—ones Jennifer had rattled off to us at the Links. Some I'd heard around town. Some were new.

"Check some of the other files," suggested Ava, leaning on the vacuum handle. "I'm sure I saw one marked *Inventory*. Maybe we can see what kind of price tag was on these bottles."

Clicking back, I found the file that she was referring to and opened it.

"Whoa." Scanning the ledger, I noted some of the prices that Heather was selling bottles for, and just how many sales she was processing.

"That's an enormous amount of money," said Ava.

I had to agree. I had a fleeting thought of a career change as I noted the amounts Heather had been selling bottles for. Several were marked as being acquired at Dixons, which I recognized as a local auction house. I quickly took a snapshot of the screen using my camera phone. "But James said he was bailing her out," I remembered.

"These are just the amounts she sold for," Ava pointed out. "We don't know what she acquired for. Or what her commissions were. Maybe her net wasn't making ends meet?"

I nodded. "It's possible." I mean, we had inventory at the winery, but that didn't mean we were making a profit off it currently.

"There's one marked *Bank Statements*," commented Ava, pointing to one of the file icons.

I opened it, and we scanned copies of bank statements that were listed chronologically. I clicked on the latest one.

"Check out that balance." It was well into the six figures. Bordering on seven.

"And check out the name of the bank," Ava said, pointing to the screen.

I squinted at the logo on the top of the statement. The title Cayman Trust was listed above an address in the Cayman Islands.

"An offshore bank account," I mused.

"I've heard of people having those, but I didn't think it was a real thing," Ava said.

"And this account is in Heather's name only," I added.

Ava raised her eyebrows at me. "Maybe Heather's little hobby wasn't doing as badly as her husband thought."

"You think she was keeping this account secret from him?" I asked.

"It's possible. And I imagine he wouldn't be too happy if he found out about it."

"Especially if Heather was talking about leaving him," I added. "But would he be unhappy enough to kill her?"

Ava didn't answer. Instead she gripped my shoulder tightly.

"Did you see that?" she said, her voice suddenly going to a whisper.

"What?"

"Lights. Coming up the driveway."

"Seriously?" I asked, my heart jumping into my throat.

"Seriously," Ava squeaked.

I hurriedly shut down the files that I had open. Trouble was, I had a lot of them, and my fingers had gotten clumsier as perspiration within the gloves was now at maximum saturation. Ava grabbed her boots and clicked off the desk lamp.

By the time I put the computer into sleep mode and darkness filled the room, I heard the sickening sound of the front door opening and two sets of feet entering the house.

Uh-oh.

CHAPTER ELEVEN

———

I listened in horror as Spencer's tiny voice filled the air, talking in an excited chatter about the play. I checked my watch. Dang. They must have left early.

"What are we going to do?" hissed Ava.

I had no idea, but considering Spencer's voice was getting closer by the second, I figured whatever it was, we were going to have to do it soon.

"Try the window?" I suggested, my voice only just above a whisper.

"It's too small," Ava replied.

Shoot.

"Did you clean up all your footprints?" I asked.

"Yes. I mopped the hallway and kitchen. And, might I just add, that it wasn't really that clean to begin with."

Now didn't feel like a great time to discuss the cleaning abilities of James and his housekeeper.

"You put everything away, right?"

"Sure. Everything but that vacuum over there."

"We need to put it back where it came from!" Panic was forming in my belly, making me feel ill.

"How?" she asked.

"We can't leave it there! James'll know that someone has been here."

"Maybe he'll blame the housekeeper. She is pretty bad at her job."

I sighed and tried to slow my thoughts.

"They have no reason to come in here," I said, attempting rationality. "So we should just sit quietly and wait it out."

"That's your plan?" Ava hissed back.

"Dad!" Spencer's voice called. "Can I use the computer?"

My heart actually stopped beating for a moment.

"You need to have a shower first," James's voice boomed. "After that you can have half an hour on it."

I silently thanked the lords. James may have been a terrible husband and maybe even a murderer, but at least he was a half decent father.

"Awww, Dad," complained Spencer.

"Don't whine, Spencer. The faster you have your shower, the sooner you can be playing your game."

I had my ear pressed to the door, when the sound of Spencer's feet came stomping up the hallway toward us. James seemed to be following him. As they passed the office door, I heard Spencer's voice loud and clear.

"Can you smell that, Dad?"

"I can't smell anything," James replied.

"It smells like ladies' perfume."

My gaze shot to Ava. She did a palms-up shrug.

"Are you wearing perfume?" I whispered.

She nodded. "Always."

I closed my eyes. I counted to ten. I tried not to think about how bad I'd look in prison orange.

"You have an overactive imagination, Spence," I heard James answer his son.

"No I don't. It smells like cotton candy."

"Your friend Connor was eating cotton candy at the play tonight. You probably got some on you."

"Maybe," Spencer said, his voice much quieter. "Do you have any candy here, Dad?"

"Nope, I don't. And it's nearly your bedtime. You can't eat candy at this time of night…"

The voices faded as the sound of footsteps on the stairs took their place. Within seconds, Spencer's stomping on the floorboards above my head told me that Ava and I had a small window of opportunity.

"We gotta get outta here," Ava whispered.

Truer words were never said. I opened the door a crack and peered into the hallway. The sound of running water competed with the sounds of Spencer and James arguing about his bedtime routine. Spencer was trying his hardest to convince James that Leah allowed him an hour on the computer every night, but James was having a hard time believing him. I gave Spence full points for trying.

Tiptoeing into the hall, Ava followed close behind me. I had my eye on the entry into the kitchen, hoping to retrace our steps, when Spencer's squeals echoed loud and clear.

"Get back here, Spencer!" James bellowed. "And do as you're told."

"I want to find Winston first. He needs me."

I spun to Ava as the upstairs footsteps pounded their way back toward us, and within seconds Spencer's giggles bounded down the stairs. I grabbed the handle to the nearest room, pushed the door open, and Ava and I flung ourselves inside, just in time.

"Where is he, Dad? Where's Winston?"

Ignoring the commotion that was going on in the hallway, I squinted against the darkness and tried to remember which room this was. Turns out it was the home gym.

Ava had moved ahead of me, making her way across the room, hopefully searching for a way out of there.

"There might be a door leading to the pool," she whispered.

I hurried to follow her, but my toe caught on something metal. I tripped and fell, my hands outstretched into the darkness, willing something to stop my fall. I made contact with what I could only think was a bench holding weights. Momentum had the better of me, and I crash landed, a dozen or so weights rolling off the bench before bouncing off the floor around me. The sound boomed through the darkness, and I held back my scream when one of the weights hit my toe. Sneakers didn't offer much protection against a ten-pound dumbbell.

Even though it was dark, I could feel Ava freeze. "Emmy?" she whispered once the last weight stopped rolling across the floor. "Are you okay?"

I heroically held my tongue as pain shot up my leg. "I think I've broken my toe," I cried, quietly.

"Spencer! Was that you?" James yelled.

"No! It came from the gym."

James's footsteps pounded down the hallway. "Go upstairs and wait in your room. I'll check it out," he commanded.

"But, Dad, I need to find Winston. What if he's hurt?"

"Spencer, go now!" James's voice was panicked as he commanded Spencer to safety.

My heart pounded to a point where stars danced in front of my eyes, but I knew I had only seconds to move. Ava rushed toward me, grabbing my hand and pulling me to my feet.

"Move!" she hissed.

I did as asked and hobbled across the room, where she grabbed my arm, pulling me quickly inside a small wooden sauna that was almost as cramped as my shower.

The sound of the turning handle on the door overtook the pounding in my ears, and we crouched down below the window. I'd just tucked myself into a tight ball when the light flicked on, and the sound of James's deep breathing filled the air.

Through a crack in the wooden slats, I saw him scan the room, the shiny barrel of his handgun reflecting the overhead fluorescent light that he had flicked on.

"Who's there?" he demanded.

For a second, tense silence filled the air.

Then a large black cat with a long tail jumped out from behind the leg press toward James.

I stifled a cry of surprise, not sure my heart could take much more tonight.

"Winston!" James let out a long breath and dropped the gun to his side. "Of course it was only you."

Whoever said that black cats were unlucky were sorely mistaken. James picked up the feline, scratching him behind the ears as he turned back toward the hallway and shut the gym door behind him.

I breathed freely for the first time since I'd heard James and Spencer arrive, and Ava and I tumbled clumsily out of the cramped sauna.

"I found the door to the pool," she whispered, pointing to the far corner.

Thank God for small favors. "Let's get out of here, *Lacey*."

* * *

By morning I could tell my toe wasn't broken, just very bruised. Thank goodness. But that didn't help the pain to be any less. I quickly showered and dressed in a pair of jeans and a couple of layered tank tops, and hobbled to the kitchen in search of food.

"Good morning, Emmy," Conchita sang, already elbow deep in a large ball of dough on the floured counter.

"It might be," I said, peeking over her shoulder. "What's that?"

"It's about to be fresh wild blueberry muffins."

I raised an eyebrow her way. "Where did you get the fresh wild blueberries?" I asked, knowing full well that had not been on my necessities grocery list.

"Eddie brought them!" She smiled at me.

"Eddie?"

"The new wine manager?"

I'd completely forgotten about happy, incompetent Eddie starting today. "Is it Monday already?" I asked, pouring myself a cup of coffee.

"All day!" Conchita confirmed cheerfully.

"So, Eddie brought blueberries. Anything else I should know about our new recruit?"

Conchita pursed her lips together, kneading dough with a force. "He seems very nice. Cheerful. Quite a snappy dresser." She paused. "I think he might be gay," she informed me.

I smiled. "You think?"

She shrugged. "Not that it matters. The world needs all kinds."

I smiled, sipping my coffee. All I hoped about Eddie was that he was the quick-to-catch-on kind.

Two hours later, I'd shown Eddie the bottling line, the barrels, the filtration system, and the ancient labeling machine that was still churning on a wing and a prayer. And maybe a little duct tape.

Eddie chatted nonstop the entire tour, and I felt lucky to get a word in edgewise. By the time we were finished, I knew that Curtis had been sneaking bacon and eggs for breakfast, when the doctors had specifically insisted on oatmeal, that their Pomeranian named Winky was due for a vet visit, and that Eddie's mother lived in Palm Springs and was having cataract surgery on Thursday. Whether Eddie had retained anything I'd said, I didn't know. But he gave me a confident smile and a happy wave as I left, assuring me, "Don't worry! I'm in charge of everything!"

That was *exactly* what I was worried about.

I left Eddie checking the labels as they spat out of the machines, ensuring that each one was straight, secure, and unsmudged. Our new design had been Hector's idea, and I loved it. The gorgeous gold scrolled font of our name and the foiled oak barrel that sat beneath it filled me with pride, almost as much as the contents of the bottle.

We just needed people to buy it.

I held on to that thought as I ducked into my office. First thing I did was try calling Leah again. As with the day before, it went to voicemail. I hoped she was just screening again and not in trouble. Grant wouldn't have arrested her without giving me a heads-up, would he? My fingers itched to call Grant just to be sure, but his standard "stay out of trouble" lecture practically rang in my ears, forcing me away from my phone and toward the pile of orders and receipts on my desk. Unfortunately, the receipts outweighed the orders, and I could just see Schultz's hands doing his infamous seesaw of debts to assets, dipping down low in the assets direction.

Maybe I really should think about selling those vintage bottles in the cellar. My mind wandered back to the prices Heather had been getting for her sales. I didn't think what I had in the cave was anywhere near in the same league, but it could at least help pay for a new bottle washer.

Telling myself it was at least halfway for professional reasons, I pulled up the photos I'd taken the night before of Heather's client lists. I scrolled through, checking each one against the guest list at our Wine and Chocolate party. There were several overlaps, which I checked against the inventory lists, matching bottles to names. It looked like Heather acquired bottles for her clients more often than selling their collections. She must have had some good connections at Dixons, as many of the vintages listed were quite old and rare. I knew private collections and lots came up now and then, but she'd been lucky to acquire so many so fast.

Unfortunately, I didn't see any discrepancies that I could see a client arguing with Heather over. The names of the bottles she'd sold looked like they'd been priced perfectly, according to the info I could find online. Possibly even a bit low, to Heather's credit. I couldn't imagine anyone being unhappy with the deals she'd brokered.

I sat back in my chair, feeling deflated. If Heather had been arguing with a client last week, nothing on this list was giving me a clue as to who it could have been or what it had been about.

Of course, if everything I was seeing here was true, it also meant James had lied to me about how bad Heather was at business. Or, Heather had lied to James.

James had said he'd put up the capital for Heather to start her business. If she'd taken that and turned it into the type of figures we'd seen in her bank account, James might have laid some claim to it. Heck, if Heather had wanted a divorce, the community property law in California meant he'd be legally entitled to half of it. Of course, he'd have to know it existed first, and being in the Cayman Islands would have cloaked it well. But if James had stumbled upon the account somehow and realized what Heather was up to, I could only imagine he might not be too happy. It was great motive to want her gone. Close to seven figures of motive.

I thought of the James-Cole-Heather love triangle and wondered if Heather really had been planning to leave her husband for the hot golfer. Of course, there was the other love triangle of Cole-Heather-Caroline playing out at the Links club. Or, maybe more accurately, in the garden sheds. Which meant we had intersecting triangles? I was never very good at geometry. But I knew it was a mess, and Cole seemed to be at the heart of it. And if anyone knew if Heather was really planning to leave her husband, it would be him.

I closed the photos on my phone, switching screens and dialing a familiar number.

"Hey, it's Emmy. Care for a drink at the Links?"

CHAPTER TWELVE

———

David Allen was in the lounge, sipping on what appeared to be a scotch on the rocks as I approached. "Well, there's my favorite winemaker turned amateur sleuth," he said, giving me a small salute as I took the chair beside him.

"Thanks for putting me on the list again," I said.

"Anytime. Drink?" he asked, raising his own glass.

While that had originally been my cover, I declined. "I'm not really a whiskey before five o'clock kind of gal."

He shot me a lopsided grin then leaned in close. "It's apple juice," he confessed. "I've got a card game later, and I'd like those two gentleman to think I'm sloshed." He gestured to a couple of guys in polo shirts and slacks, chatting in club chairs near the window.

I shook my head. "Sneaky."

"Smart," he corrected, sipping his juice. "Who's your prey today, Ems?"

"Cole. Have you seen him around?"

He nodded. "I have. In fact, he just finished a lesson with a buxom brunette a few minutes ago. If you're lucky, you can catch him before the three p.m. cougar makes her appearance."

I glanced at the clock. I had about five minutes. "Thanks," I said, quickly leaving the lounge for the pro shop.

Luckily, as I approached, it appeared I'd beaten the cougar, as Cole was idly leaning on the glass counter and staring off into space as I walked up.

"Hi, Cole," I greeted him.

It took a moment for recognition to flash, but when it did, he gave me a professional smile. "Right. Ava Barnett's friend."

I tried not to let my ego take a hit at being known as "the friend."

"Emmy Oak," I supplied.

"Of course, Emmy." He shot me his megawatt smile. "How lovely to see you again. To what do I owe the pleasure?"

"I was wondering if I could chat with you about your clients."

His smile faltered for a second, but he quickly pulled it back up. "I'm not sure I can help you. Client confidentiality, you know."

I was pretty sure that only extended to lawyers and doctors, and not golfers, but I let it go.

"Heather Atherton. You spent a lot of time with her, right?"

"She booked several lessons, yes. We've been over that."

We had. And the beating around the bush hadn't gotten me very far then. I decided to try the direct approach this time. "You mentioned before that Heather didn't get along with her husband."

He cleared his throat. "Did I?"

I nodded. "Was she planning to leave him?"

"Why on earth do you think I would know that?" he asked.

"Because she was leaving him for you," I told him point-blank.

He let out a sharp bark of laughter. "That's preposterous."

"Is it?" I challenged. "You were sleeping with her."

"I was her golf instructor," he said, his charming smile growing thin. "Nothing more."

"Right," I said, heavy on the sarcasm. "Just like with Caroline."

The smile died altogether. "I'm sorry. Who?"

"Caroline Danvers," I reminded, though I was pretty darn sure he remembered her. "She is a client of yours, correct?"

Cole licked his lips, holding his gaze steady on mine. "Yes."

"Does she have *daily* lessons too? You know, the kind Heather took?"

His cheeks went just a shade paler under his tan. "I'm sorry. I'm not sure what you mean."

"Oh, come off it, Cole. I saw you with her yesterday."

His expression froze in place. "You must be mistaken. Caroline has lessons on Thursdays."

"You were in the shed behind the gardens." I gave him a knowing grin. "You and I both know I'm not mistaken."

He threw his shoulders back and sucked in a deep breath, flaring his nostrils with the effort. "I think you should leave, Ms. Oak."

"So you're denying it?" I challenged.

"Both Heather Atherton and Caroline Danvers are married women," he said.

"Not for long if Heather was leaving her husband. Was that the plan, Cole?"

"Are you even a member here?" he countered instead of answering.

I jutted my chin forward. "I could be."

"But you're not," he said, all the charm and twinkle gone from his eyes.

Then he leaned into my personal space, his voice suddenly low and taking on a menacing edge. "I'd be careful who you go around accusing of such things, Ms. Oak. You could end up getting hurt."

My heart leapt into my throat, and I sucked in a breath. I was still processing the threat as he stood back, glanced at a point above my head, and his beaming smile returned to his face.

"Mrs. Foxton," he called.

I looked over my shoulder to find Jennifer Foxton standing in the doorway to the pro shop. For the first time since I'd met her, she was not dressed in a power suit—instead sporting a short white skirt and matching polo shirt that almost looked like a uniform. Her eyes went from Cole to me in a way that made it clear she'd witnessed at least part of our exchange. How much, I had no idea.

"Ready to hit the driving range?" Cole asked her breezily.

"Uh, yes." Jennifer's politician's wife smile slipped into place as she approached us, though whether it was for my benefit or Cole's, I wasn't sure.

Cole didn't so much as give me a backward glance as he took her arm and led her out onto the fairway.

I let out a breath I hadn't realized I'd been holding as he stepped from sight. While I knew confronting him head-on with the accusation of his sleeping around was a risk, I'd honestly felt relatively safe in the brightly lit, well populated Links club. That had disappeared the second he'd invaded my personal space. For all his charm and tanned gorgeousness, Cole had a hard side. One I wondered if Heather had been unlucky enough to see. I suddenly wondered how much Cole knew about Heather's business. Did he know she had a fat bank account in the Cayman Islands waiting for her? If he did, I wondered how upset he'd get if, at the last minute, something had happened to change Heather's mind about leaving her husband for him. Had Heather decided to stick with her safe bet, leaving Cole out in the cold?

My mind ran over possibilities as I made my way back through the club, stopping at the bar to say goodbye to David before I left. I entered the cool room, searching for my host among the small smattering of those enjoying an early afternoon cocktail. Melodic piano music filled the air courtesy of a man tapping keys at a baby grand. Servers in pressed uniforms and bow ties circulated silently around the room. But no sign of David. No sign of his two gentlemen in slacks either, so I figured they must have struck up their game.

I did, however, spot someone else I knew sipping a glass of rosé alone at a table near the windows overlooking the golf course.

Caroline Danvers.

While my better judgment—which sounded a lot like Grant, coincidentally—told me to leave it alone, my body drifted toward Caroline's table.

"Mind if I join you?" I asked.

Caroline looked up from the view, staring at me a beat before recognition set in. "Oh, uh, yes. Sure. You're the girl from the winery."

"Emmy." I was going to get a complex if people didn't start remembering my name. "How are you?"

Caroline blinked at me, as if not understanding the question.

"You holding up alright?"

Then it dawned on her. "Oh, right. Yes. Heather." She took a long sip from her glass, not necessarily answering me as her gaze flittered back toward the windows.

I looked out, following her line of sight. It wasn't hard to guess what had her attention, as Jennifer Foxton was just to our left, Cole's arms wrapped helpfully around her back as he adjusted her hands on her club.

"He's very good, isn't he?" I asked, slowly, watching her reaction.

But she just nodded, and sipped (gulped?) her wine again.

"He told me he used to have daily lessons with Heather," I said, eyes still on her face.

She snorted. "Did he?"

I nodded. "How well did you and Heather get along, Caroline?" I asked softly.

She shrugged, tearing her eyes away from the window. "Fine. But really she was more Jennifer's friend than mine." Caroline drained her glass, signaling for a server to bring another.

I watched him nod and retreat without saying a word.

"Jennifer mentioned that she introduced Heather to a lot of you at the club."

"Forced her on us, more like it," Caroline said, starting to sway slightly in her chair. "Of course, that's Jennifer. Jennifer does whatever Jennifer wants, whenever she wants to do it."

I wondered if that was some longtime rivalry speaking or the wine. "She looks like she's enjoying her lesson with Cole," I noted.

"Yes, and that was my lesson! She just took it! My lesson. It was my time with him, not hers." Her words were like bullets, firing hard and fast.

"And Cole gave it away to Jennifer?"

"What?" Caroline turned to me, blinking.

"Your golf lesson. If he gave away your slot, you could take it up with the club."

Caroline visibly blushed, and she attempted to conceal it by turning back to her glass, a bewildered look coming over her face at finding it empty.

Clearly it hadn't been her first. Which made me feel slightly guilty to exploit. "Caroline, I saw you with Cole yesterday," I said softly, so as not to be overheard.

Her gaze lifted to meet mine. "What?"

"I saw you and Cole. In the garden." I left the insinuation hanging.

A host of emotion ran across her features—surprise, embarrassment, and maybe even a little sadness.

"Oh God," she said, burying her face in her hands.

"You've been having an affair with Cole?" I asked, even though I knew the answer.

She uncovered her face, her eyes watery with emotion and too much rosé. And she nodded slowly. "Yes." It was just a whisper.

"How long has this been going on?"

"A few months. Since shortly after he started here."

"Did anyone else know?" I asked. "Heather?"

She let out a bark of laughter through the tears. "Heather." The word was said on a sneer. "You know he didn't care about her at all."

"You mean Cole?" I asked, even though I could guess. "Cole was sleeping with Heather too."

I had to wait for her answer, as her new glass of wine came, the server silently replacing the empty one before walking away with it.

Caroline took a fortifying sip before continuing. "He didn't love her," she repeated. "He didn't. She wasn't special to him. Not like what we have." A tear slid silently over her skin, running off her chin and landing on the polished wood table.

I reached for a cocktail napkin and handed it to her as she gave an unladylike sniff.

"He loves me. Me! I'm the special one."

I had the feeling Cole Jackson had a lot of *special ones*, but now didn't feel like the time to raise that point.

"All of the others, they're just income to him. I don't even pay him anymore, and that's how I know how he really feels for me. Heather had to pay. In fact, everyone else has to pay for his services. Not me. That's how I know he loves me," she finished quietly, delicately dabbing at her tears.

"He gives free lessons?" I asked.

Caroline paused. "What?"

"He gives you free golf lessons?"

She blinked wet lashes at me. Then to my surprise, she laughed. "Oh, you really are slow, aren't you?"

I stared at her, my mental hamster trying to catch up on his wheel before it hit me.

"Wait—are you saying that these women have been *paying* Cole for *sex*?"

"Shh!" she hissed, her eyes whipping around the room. "Discretion," she warned.

I found that ironic, considering it had been Cole grabbing her giggling behind that had led me on this Easter egg hunt.

"How long has this been going on?" I asked.

"I told you. We've been seeing each other for a few months."

"I meant, how long has Cole been charging the women here for sex?"

Caroline's eyes darted around the room again. "Look, don't judge. Some of our husbands just aren't really there for us. Trevor travels so much, and…well, women have needs just as much as men do, and Cole is very good at what he does."

I'll bet he was.

"How many people know about his sideline business?" I asked, wondering which job was really the sideline—the golf instructing or the gigolo gig.

Caroline shifted in her seat, fiddling with the stem of her glass. "Cole is very discreet, and his clientele very select."

"Like Heather Atherton?" I asked.

Caroline nodded.

I glanced out the window. "And Jennifer Foxton?"

Caroline's eyes flickered to the pair. Cole was standing beside Jennifer now, laughing at something the woman had said.

"I doubt it," Caroline finally decided. "Jennifer is besotted with her husband." She paused. "Or at least his political aspirations. She'd never do anything to jeopardize that."

"But Heather would jeopardize her marriage?" I pressed, steering back to the dead woman.

Caroline shrugged. "Heather was bored. James is a good fifteen years older than she was. And, well, little blue pills can only do so much, you know?"

Ew. I did not want to think of James and his need for little blue pills.

"Anyway, she got tired of him," Caroline finished.

"Enter handsome Cole," I said, unable to keep the disdain for the man out of my voice.

Caroline must have picked up on it, as she shot me a look. "Look, Cole is a good person. Life has been hard for him. He wasn't born with a silver spoon in his mouth, you know?"

I hesitated to point out that most people weren't. But we didn't all become gigolos to the rich and lonely.

"Anyway, this is all hush-hush," Caroline warned, sipping her drink again. "Seriously. Cole could get fired if this came out." She paused. "Possibly arrested. It might even be illegal."

"Gee, ya think?" I blurted out. "Caroline, it's prostitution!"

"Shh!" she shushed me again. "That's such a dirty word."

It was a dirty situation. Then a thought occurred to me. "Caroline, what lengths do you think Cole would go to in order to keep this secret?"

She swallowed a sip of rosé with a little hiccup. "What do you mean?"

"I mean what if, say, one of the women was so enamored with Cole that she was going to leave her husband for him," I said, thinking of Heather. "Maybe she told Cole, he rejected her as just a paying customer, and she threatened to expose him?"

Caroline stared at me for a moment, her expression unreadable. "That's ridiculous. No one here would do that."

Maybe no one *here*. But I was starting to wonder about the woman who had been found behind the dumpster.

CHAPTER THIRTEEN

———

Warm air washed over me as the automatic glass doors swished open, and I stepped outside to hand the valet my ticket. Though, I was beginning to realize there was a hierarchy to this getting-your-car-back thing, and I didn't think my Jeep ranked very high, as my wait was, as usual, longer than most. I took the few moments to let my mind wander over the new info Caroline had imparted on me. It wasn't hard to believe Cole was a gigolo, and it sadly wasn't hard to imagine the bored housewives of the Sonoma elite being interested enough to pay a small sum for his attention. Somehow, though, Heather hadn't fit that mold in my mind. Heather had looked like a model—and not a past-her-prime one either. Had she really been paying for Cole's services…or had she, like Caroline, had a *special* arrangement with the golf pro? On the other hand, I wondered if Heather's husband knew she'd been paying for extracurricular activities with the allowance he'd given her. I could only imagine he wouldn't be happy to find out.

As if on cue, I spotted a familiar face walking through the glass doors—James Atherton. He handed a valet ticket to the guy in the blue blazer who, I noted, moved a lot faster to get Atherton's car than he had mine. Clearly he ranked better in the pecking order. As he waited, James turned my way, his pleasant smile turning to a frown of confusion when he recognized me.

"Hi." I did a lame little wave in his direction.

"Emmy Oak."

Well, at least one person remembered who I was around here.

"Nice to see you again," I told him politely.

"What are you doing here?"

I cleared my throat. "Uh, waiting for my car."

He shook his head. "No, I mean here. At the Links. You're not a member."

I tried to tell myself he was so sure because he'd been here so long—not because my shoes were from Macy's instead of Gucci.

"Guest of a friend," I said.

"What friend?" The frown between his brows that had formed at seeing me hadn't decreased any, and I felt like I was getting the third degree from my elementary school principal.

"Just...a friend," I answered, not necessarily wanting to put David Allen in anyone's crosshairs.

He shot me a hard look. "First my office, asking questions. Now my club. If I didn't know better, I'd say you were stalking me."

"Stalking?" I managed to cough out. "No, I would never stalk you." Okay, so I broke into his house, but we all had to draw a line somewhere.

"Then what, exactly, are you doing here?"

"I was...having a drink with Caroline Danvers," I told him. Which was, incidentally, true.

His eyes narrowed. "You never mentioned being friends with Caroline."

Probably because I wasn't. "You never asked," I countered.

He shut his mouth in a thin, hard line, eyes still narrowed. He looked like he had more to say, but at that moment my phone chirped from my purse, giving me a lovely excuse to step away from his death glare.

I pulled it out and seeing Leah's number, quickly swiped to accept the call.

"Hey," I said.

"Hey," came Leah's voice over the line.

I took a couple more steps away from James, just in case he could hear it.

"Sorry I didn't get back to you yesterday. It's just been crazy."

"No, I totally understand," I assured her. "How are you?"

I heard her swallow. "Good."

"Liar."

She laughed, though it was far from a hearty chuckle. "Okay, so I've been pretty crappy. The police were here again."

I figured as much, after my encounter with Grant. "You okay?"

"I'm not in handcuffs, so I guess that's something," she replied.

"I'm so sorry, hun." I watched James get into a bright red sports car and peel away down the drive. I shook my head, thinking how unfair life was. "Hey, I was wondering if I could chat with you about something," I said. "Are you at the Chocolate Bar right now?"

"Yes, and it's pretty quiet. The afternoon hangries won't come in for another couple hours."

I grinned. I had to credit Leah's strength of spirit that she could still have a sense of humor. "I'll be right over," I promised, finally seeing my Jeep pull into view.

* * *

The Chocolate Bar smelled like home-baked goodies and warm coffee, a combination that instantly soothed me as I stepped through the doorway. The place was deserted, but as the bell over the door jangled, Leah appeared quickly from the back in her signature pink apron.

"Wow, you really meant you'd be right over," Leah said, grabbing me in a hug.

It might have been my imagination, but she felt skinnier and more bony than the last time I'd hugged her.

"Yeah, well, I was in town when you called," I told her, not necessarily wanting to say exactly where.

"I've got a batch of brownies just out of the oven," she said, moving away toward the glass counter. "Why don't you take a seat on the couch and I'll bring it out."

My stomach growled as I followed her gaze and looked at the plate of brownies stacked high on top of the glass bakery cabinet.

"Coffee?" she asked, retrieving them.

"Do you have to ask?" I replied as I sidestepped three empty tables and chairs to make my way to the well-worn leather couch.

While things were quiet, Leah had obviously kept herself busy by cleaning. This shop was always spotless, but today it glistened like no other. The polished concrete floor reflected the overhead can lights; the windows were so immaculate that if it hadn't been for the signage, they could have been nonexistent; and the timber tables and metal chairs were lined up precisely, waiting for a hopeful rush of customers.

Leah made her way toward me, sitting in the lounge chair opposite and placing a tray on the coffee table. She handed a steaming mug of goodness to me, which I accepted, inhaling deeply.

"Tell me things haven't been this quiet all day," I said, looking around the empty shop.

"We had a few people in earlier." She sipped at her cup.

I could tell she was trying to keep up appearances. Leah usually had more than a few customers—*droves* would have been the word I'd use. Clearly people were still staying away from the shop.

"How's Spencer?" I asked, helping myself to a brownie.

"Fine. He stayed at his dad's last night."

"I know," I said automatically around a bite.

She paused. "You do?"

I swallowed the brownie, feeling it stick in my throat like mud. "You, uh, told me. Remember. A couple weeks ago?"

Leah frowned. "Oh. Yeah, that's right. I probably did." She smiled. "Wow, you have a good memory."

I did an internal sigh of relief, my guilt receding into a corner like the bad dog it was.

"Anyway, he said he had a good time. Kids bounce back. At least that's what they say, right?" She shot me an unconvincing smile.

"How's James taking it?" I asked.

Leah gave me a questioning look. "James?"

"I, uh, ran into him the other day. He didn't seem all that shaken up."

Leah shrugged, grabbing a brownie herself and playing with the edges until crumbs formed on her plate. "I don't know. James never was one to show much emotion. But honestly, I haven't talked to him. We share Spence—that's it."

"Gotcha." I nodded, shoving more brownie into my mouth. "Thish ish delish," I said, enjoying every morsel.

A genuine smile broke through her melancholy. "Glad you like them."

I swallowed, washing the chocolaty heaven down with a sip of coffee.

"Leah, there was a reason I called you yesterday," I admitted.

She raised her eyebrow in question. "Okay, shoot."

"I heard about the fight you had with Heather. The day before she died."

Leah froze, staring at me.

I sighed. "Leah, why didn't you say anything to me?"

She licked her lips. "What would I have said? 'Hey, guess what I did today, Emmy? I punched my ex's new wife.'"

"I would have understood," I told her.

Leah shook her head. "I doubt that."

"So try me. What happened?" I reached out, putting a hand on her knee.

She stared at it for a second before licking her lips again. "Look, it's not like I set out to hit her. I just…she got me so mad. And it wasn't just this one time, you know?"

The brownie sat like a rock in my stomach. So she and Heather did have a history of not getting along. "What happened this time?" I pushed again.

She took a deep breath. "She was pressuring James. Saying he was paying me too much. She resented the alimony. Especially since I opened this place. I guess she thought I should stop taking his checks now that I was making money of my own."

"But James wouldn't do that?" I asked.

She shook her head. "No, the alimony is set in the terms of our divorce. James isn't stupid enough to violate that. Besides, you know how much we've been struggling here." She gestured her arms wide, as if the empty benches could attest to that. "If we didn't get James's payments every month, I don't know what would happen."

"If you knew James wouldn't give in, why did you go see her at the Links?"

"Well, there was more." She paused, sipping her coffee.

"Tell me," I prompted.

"James pays child support too. Which, of course, Heather hated." She rolled her eyes. "But unlike the alimony, that number can change."

"How so?" I asked.

"It's based on how much time James spends with Spencer. The more time Spencer stays at his house, the less money he has to send me to care for him." She paused again and did more lip licking. She was really going to need some ChapStick after this conversation. "Heather was pressuring James to sue for custody."

"No way!" That felt like a low blow even for Heather.

Leah nodded. "Way."

"But he never would have gotten it, right?"

She shrugged, moisture building behind her eyes. "I dunno. I mean, for all his faults, James isn't a bad father. And he can certainly provide for Spencer more than I could."

"Yeah, but can he bake a brownie?" I asked, only halfway joking as I held up the confection.

She attempted a smile through her building tears.

"Look, I'm sure no court in the world would take Spencer away from you. He's obviously a great kid, raised well, and adores you."

"Thanks." She let out a shaky breath. "But I wasn't as confident as you, and when I heard what she was trying to pressure James into, I confronted her."

"At the Links."

"Yeah. I told her to stay away from my son, and she laughed in my face—saying soon he'd be *her* son."

"Ouch."

Leah nodded. "You see why I snapped and hit her?"

Honestly? I did. "Witnesses heard you tell her to watch her back."

The wet tears spilled over Leah's lashes, and she swiped at them with the back of her hand, making my heart squeeze. "I didn't mean it like that. I just meant that if she could play dirty, then so could I," Leah cried. "I didn't mean that I would literally stab her in the back."

I reached out and grabbed her free hand in mine. "You know I totally believe you, right?"

"Do you?" she asked, her eyes big and watery.

I nodded vigorously. "Of course! Look, we've all had a mean girl like Heather in our lives at one point or another."

"If only I could turn back time, I would just have walked away. It was so stupid." Her shoulders heaved as she covered her face with her hands and dissolved into crying in earnest. "They searched my house," she sobbed. "They even went through Spencer's room."

"Who did?"

"The police." Her head came up, her eyes meeting mine. "I'm sure they think I did it."

"They won't find anything," I reminded her. "You didn't kill Heather, so how can they?"

"But what if..." Leah couldn't finish the sentence.

"They won't," I said sternly. "There is no evidence linking you to the murder."

She let out a shaky breath. "Right."

"Look, why don't you and Spencer come out to the winery tonight?" I asked, handing her a napkin from the tray. "Bring some pj's, and I'll cook dinner for you both. I'll invite Ava too, and we can make it a girls' night in. Spencer can sleep in the guest room, and we can relax with a bottle of wine and some chick flicks."

"Chick flicks?" she asked, scrunching up her nose.

I shrugged. "*Thelma and Louise* is my go-to, but I'm open to suggestions."

She grinned. "I don't think I could watch a romance without throwing up right now. Let's see some guys blowing stuff up instead."

I laughed, happy to see her smile in earnest in response. "Blowing stuff up it is," I promised. "It's a date."

* * *

I left Leah's with another half dozen cupcakes, which I gave at least 50-50 odds at surviving the drive back to the winery, before texting Ava about our impromptu girls' night. She texted back immediately, saying she was in.

I stopped briefly at the grocery store to pick up a few items and, on impulse, grabbed a dozen daisies as well. To paraphrase Meg Ryan, it was hard to be unhappy with a bunch of friendly daisies staring you in the face. And Leah could certainly use a little friendly right now.

I glanced at my dash clock as I got back into the car and put the AC at full blast to ward off the summer heat. I still had a couple of hours before I needed to start dinner. I decided to take a quick detour before heading home, typing the address for Dixons into my GPS. Whether Heather was killed for personal or professional reasons, money seemed to be at the heart of it all. It was possible it was a jealous husband, rejected lover, or jealous frenemy that had finally snapped. But if James had been telling the truth about the argument with a client, it could also have had to do with her wine business. The dollar amounts she was dealing with were vast, and it still bothered me that James had thought her business was failing. Maybe someone at the auction house she'd done so much business with could shed some light on the subject.

I'd never been to Dixons before, and I'd admit to not knowing very much about it. The only time Oak Valley Vineyards and an auction had ever been mentioned in the same sentence was when Schultz warned of bank foreclosure if we didn't get that seesaw higher on the assets hand.

An elegant brass sign alerted me that Dixons was on the right, and I pulled into their parking lot, taking a moment to study the building. It was older, harkening to an era when architecture was as much for decorative purposes as practical, sporting white molded pillars, a high stone façade, and copper trim with lush green ivy growing up the sides.

The lot was nearly full—a sure sign that an auction was currently going. I crawled the lanes, looking for an empty slot. As I zigzagged my way through the lot, I nearly missed a black

SUV tearing through. And when I say I nearly missed it, I meant just that.

Hitting the brakes hard, I just managed to swerve out of the vehicle's way, narrowly avoiding an impact. Cursing under my breath, I death-stared the driver of the SUV as he turned the corner.

It was only then that I got a look at the bad driver in question, as his face became visible through the open window.

I froze.

Dark hair. Weathered features. Scar cutting through his eyebrow. Wearing a dark cowboy hat.

The Man in Black.

CHAPTER FOURTEEN

I blinked, feeling adrenaline rush through me at the recognition, even as the Man in Black pulled out of the lot, clearly not caring who I was. It took a second for my instincts to kick in, but when they did, I pressed down hard on the accelerator, maneuvering my way back to the road. I managed to stay a few cars behind the SUV and follow him as we wound our way through town. At one point, when two other black SUVs pulled into traffic between us, I thought I might have lost him. It was like that game where the magician places a ball under one of three cups and then moves them around so quickly you lose track of which cup was which. But happily the correct one made a left turn, and I caught sight of the driver just in time.

My tires squealed as I took the corner at speeds usually frowned upon, but the Man in Black didn't give any indication of noticing me. A few blocks later, I watched him pull into the lot of a storage facility with a sign outside that read *A1 Personal Storage*. I drove past, made a U-turn at the next light, and parked on a side street behind the facility. I got out of the car and followed the fence along the perimeter of the property, my sandals slapping against the pavement, until I found an open gate at the front. I quickly stepped inside, finding myself in a maze of small warehouses housing dozens of storage units with metal rolling doors.

I tried to seem as inconspicuous as possible as I quickly traversed the grid, hoping for a glimpse of the Man in Black. The heat coming up from the dark pavement in unrelieved waves was just starting to melt my eyeliner, when I caught sight of a cowboy hat disappearing inside the unit marked *J26*.

With a totally unnecessary look over both shoulders, I stepped closer, hoping to at least get a peek inside the unit. I kept close to the buildings, painfully aware that there was nowhere to hide—the buildings were laid out in long rows on flat pavement. Nothing to duck behind, no corners to hide around. I took a couple of steps closer, feeling way too exposed.

Then the Man in Black stepped out of J26.

My heart leapt up into my throat as I pivoted on my sandals and walked the other direction as quickly as possible, hoping he didn't notice me. Or would think I was just another customer there to store some of grandma's treasures.

My breath came in audible pants as I heard him close and lock the rolling door behind me, his footsteps echoing as loudly as mine as they followed my same path. I swear I felt his eyes boring a hole into my back. But I just kept walking, quickly following the same route I'd taken to get there. I was almost to the gate before I dared turn and look behind me.

No sign of Man in Black.

I let out a deep sigh, power walking the rest of the way back to my car. Sweat had collected at the back of my neck by the time I closed myself in the safety of my Jeep and powered on the AC. I quickly pulled away from the curb, wanting to put as much distance between myself and the Man in Black as possible.

I was dying to know what was in the storage unit. Sure, it could just be a couple of innocent old Harleys. But Man in Black had been at the same auction house where Heather had gotten the bulk of her inventory. And he'd gone straight from there to the storage unit. Had he been storing something for the auction house? Did he work for them? But then why had he crashed our Wine and Chocolate event, and what had he been arguing with Heather about? If, in fact, he had been?

My thoughts were interrupted by my cell ringing through my car speakers via Bluetooth. I hit the button to accept the call.

"Hello?" I answered.

"Hello, my lovely Ems," came the familiar voice of David Allen. "It's me."

I wasn't sure how I felt about David thinking we were on an "it's me" basis, but I let it go.

"What's up?" I asked, still trying to get my heart rate back to something akin to normal.

"I thought you might be interested to know about a little snafu here at the club."

"Snafu?" That sounded promising. "What happened?"

"Apparently, security had to come remove a certain young lady from your Cole Jackson."

"Remove her?" I asked. "Like, she was throwing punches at him?"

"Quite," he said. "Like a featherweight champ. I daresay she got a couple of good ones in to the face too."

Ouch. I would imagine Cole's distress at any damage to his charming moneymaker.

"Who was she?"

"Well, that's where it gets good, babe," he said, clearly enjoying drawing this out.

"Tell me."

He paused. "Okay, but you owe me a favor now, wine lady."

Against my better judgment, I sighed out, "Fine. Who hit Cole?"

"Caroline Danvers."

"Get out!" I shouted in the interior of my car.

David chuckled on the other end. "I thought you'd like that."

"What was the fight about?"

"Beats me," he said. Then laughed again at his own pun. "You'd have to ask poor Cole that one."

"Is he still there?" I asked, changing lanes at the light and turning toward the Links.

"That he is. Nursing a black eye and a bruised ego with a strong whiskey."

"I'll be right there."

*   *   *

Thankfully, David had added my name to the guest list, and fifteen minutes later I found Cole Jackson laid out on a lounger that overlooked the 18th hole, alone. He had a cushion behind his head, an ice pack over his left eye, and a glass of amber liquid in his right hand.

I approached, standing over him. "I heard you had a little disagreement, Cole."

He lifted the ice pack and narrowed his eyes to glare at me. Quite a feat when one of those eyes was already starting to swell shut.

"You again," he mumbled.

"Ouch. That looks painful," I commented, though I didn't have it in me to lace it with any real sympathy.

He sighed, turning his attention back to the green and placing the ice pack back over his eye.

"What happened?" I asked, perching on the edge of the lounger beside him. "Lovers' spat?"

"Hardly," he shot back.

"Really? Because I heard that Caroline was a bit upset with you."

"A bit upset?" he spat out, lifting the ice pack from his eye again. "I think this is a lot more than a *bit* upset."

Good point. "What did you say to her?"

"Nothing!" he protested. "She just attacked me! In front of my eyes she morphed into a psychopath. The woman's crazy." He glanced down at his glass, swishing the contents before taking a sip.

"Cole, Caroline told me everything," I said, hoping to get him to open up.

He glanced at me with his one good eye, assessing my face, as if trying to figure out what "everything" consisted of.

"I know about your little racket here," I told him.

He worked his jaw back and forth before responding, and I wondered if Caroline had landed a punch there too. "Yeah, well, like I said. Caroline's crazy. You can't believe half of what she says."

"I believe she's been sleeping with you. And that you told her you loved her," I added.

Cole let out a laugh on a short breath of air. "She said that? What a psycho bi—" He paused, his good sense catching up to his instincts just in time. "I never said I loved her," he said emphatically. "That's the truth."

"Okay," I said, shifting my weight on the lounger. "Lay some more truth on me. What set Caroline off today?"

He glanced over his shoulder, as if making sure we were alone. "Look, Caroline and I had...an arrangement."

"Go on," I prompted.

"She was lonely. Her husband's out of the country a lot. I...comforted her."

Ick. "Gloss over the details, lover boy," I told him.

He scowled at me. "Fine. Let's just say, Caroline took our arrangement too far."

"How so?"

"She was talking crazy about leaving her husband."

"Which you didn't want her to do?"

"Hel—" He paused, catching himself again. "Heck no. Her husband is loaded, and she's one of my biggest clients. Why would I want that cash flow to stop?"

I tried really hard not to let my distaste for the man show on my face. "Caroline told me she doesn't pay you anymore."

His eyes shot up to mine. "She told you that?"

I nodded. "Like it was the proof that you loved her."

"Geeze, that woman's nuts."

"So she *was* paying you?"

"Look, her husband left for London one time and forgot to transfer some money to her spending accounts or something. She didn't have the cash, so I let her have a few sessions on credit."

"How generous."

He looked up at me and scowled again. Clearly I hadn't been able to keep the disdain at bay that time.

"You said Caroline was *one* of your biggest clients," I said, digging as much as I could before I lost him. "Was Heather another?"

He gave me a *well duh* look. "You figure that all out on your own?"

"Humor me," I prompted. "What was your arrangement with Heather?"

He shrugged. "Same as any other woman here."

"But she was here a lot."

He grinned. "I'm very good at what I do. The things I can do to keep a rich cougar satisfied would make your toes curl." He waggled his eyebrows suggestively.

"That would be a hard pass," I told him.

He shrugged. "Your loss." He gave me an up and down. "I'd even give you a discount."

I wasn't sure if he was intentionally trying to squick me out or if it was just second nature to him.

"What was Caroline and Heather's relationship like?" I asked.

He leaned his head back on the lounger again, sipping from his whiskey glass. "About what you'd expect. All air kisses and backstabbing." He let out that short bark of a laugh again. "Sorry. Poor choice of words, huh?"

His sympathy was overwhelming. But it was an *interesting* choice of words. Perhaps a Freudian slip? "Did Caroline harbor some animosity toward Heather?"

He nodded. "She was crazy jealous."

"Of Heather's time with you?"

"Of everything. Look, Heather was younger, prettier, and smarter than half the women here. Caroline didn't like it. She especially didn't like it when Heather was with me. Caroline would show up on the green when we were having a lesson, pop up in the lounge when we were having a drink. It was like she was stalking us."

"You don't think she'd go from stalking to actual violence, do you?"

Cole took the ice off his swelling eye, staring up at me with a *well duh* look in his one good one again.

* * *

I left Cole nursing his wounds and was just pulling back up to the winery when I got a text from Leah saying she was just closing the bakery and would be over in twenty minutes.

I pulled some fresh shrimp from the refrigerator, deciding on a simple, savory Shrimp Scampi with Angel Hair Pasta for our girls' night. Light, luscious, and fast, since I'd bought the shrimp already shelled and deveined. I got the water boiling for the angel hair while I melted together butter, garlic, wine, and spices in to a fragrant sauté. The shrimp took just a quick bath in it, turning a lovely pink as the angel hair cooked up to a perfect al dente.

I was just adding the finishing touches of lemon juice and a sprinkle of parsley on top when I heard Leah's car pull up. I set down the platter and went outside to greet her.

"Hey," I said, giving her a big hug, which she returned, if slightly less heartily. I glanced behind her at her empty backseat. "Where's Spence?"

She sighed. "He wanted to go to his dad's again tonight."

"Oh." I paused. "You okay?"

"Yeah, yeah, I guess so." She shook her head, negating the actual words. "Spencer's worried about his dad being lonely without Heather." She laughed, though it was more sadness than joy. "I guess I should be happy he's such a compassionate kid."

"Very," I agreed. "He's got a big heart. That's a good thing."

She nodded, attempting to smile again. "Give me a glass of wine, and maybe I'll see the bright side in all of this."

I laughed, leading her inside and doing just that, pouring her a Pinot Blanc that I knew would pair well with the garlic in the scampi dish.

Ava arrived shortly after, and we took our plates out to the terrace, enjoying the cool breeze as the sun began its descent that bathed the landscape in beautiful hues of pink, orange, and purple. It was like a painting and a million miles away from thoughts of smarmy gigolos, catty socialites, and murder.

"You'll never believe who came into the shop today," Ava said, twirling pasta on her fork.

"Who?" I asked, taking the bait.

"Byron!"

I chewed, trying to place the name.

"Our friendly neighborhood country club concierge," she supplied.

Oh. That Byron.

"He works the front counter at the Links," Ava said, turning to Leah to fill her in.

"Ah" was all Leah said, eyes going back to her food.

"Anyway, he asked me out for Friday night."

"What did you say?" I asked.

She shrugged. "I said sure. I mean, why not? He's kinda cute."

I rolled my eyes. In Ava's world, just about every guy was "kinda cute."

"Did you just roll your eyes at me?" Ava said.

"Maybe," I told her playfully.

"Tell me you didn't dig those biceps on him," Ava teased back. "And those big hands. I can only imagine what he could do for a girl with those hands…"

"Ugh," Leah cut in. "I thought we agreed—no romance tonight." There was a smile on her face, but I could tell she was only half kidding.

"Well, I had an eventful day," I said, changing the subject.

"Oh, do tell?" Ava prompted, stabbing a prawn with her fork.

"I met the Man in Black."

"Shut the front door!" Ava said, her fork clattering to her plate.

"Who's the Man in Black?" Leah asked, her gaze going from Ava to me.

"The Johnny Cash look-alike from the Wine and Chocolate Tasting," I explained, jogging her memory.

"That photo you showed me?" she asked.

I nodded. "That's him." I filled her and Ava in on finding him at the auction house and following him to the storage unit.

"So, what was in it?" Ava asked when I'd finished.

I shrugged. "I didn't get a chance to look inside."

Ava let out a dramatic sigh and draped her body over her chair. "You're killing me, Emmy."

"Sorry! He saw me, and I panicked."

"That sounds dangerous," Leah said, frowning at me.

"It was broad daylight," I assured her. "I was fine." Though, in all honestly, I'd been freaking out at the time.

"*That* is the problem," Ava said, stabbing her fork in the air as she chewed.

"What?"

"The broad daylight. We need to go back when it's dark."

"That sounds like a bad idea," Leah hedged.

"Very bad," I agreed. "Especially the *we* part."

"Well, how else are we going to find out what he's hiding in there?" Ava asked.

"We don't know that he's hiding anything," Leah reasoned.

"Or that it has anything to do with Heather's death," I added.

Ava looked from me to Leah, shaking her head. "You two are no fun." She stabbed another prawn as if it were his fault I wouldn't agree to breaking and entering with her. At least not a second time.

"I'd rather be safe than fun," I told her. Even though she was right on one point—it was kind of killing me too that we didn't know what was inside the storage unit.

I was contemplating that though, imagining all manner of salacious items, when a pair of headlights cut through the falling dusk.

We all followed their trail up the winding oak-lined drive toward us.

"Expecting company?" Ava asked, eyes cutting to me.

I shook my head.

We didn't need to wait long to find out who it was, as a few minutes later the sound of a car door slamming was followed by footsteps on the gravel drive, coming around to the side of the property where we sat.

I was halfway holding my breath when a tall, broad frame rounded the corner, his face shadowed by the twinkling fairy lights hung from the roofline.

Detective Christopher Grant.

"Grant," I said, trying to cover my surprise.

"Hi, Emmy," he returned. "Sorry to interrupt like this." He nodded toward the table where we were just finishing the meal.

"Uh, no, it's fine," I told him, pushing my chair out and standing. "Would you like a plate?"

He took a deep breath, letting it out slowly. "I'm afraid I can't stay."

A small niggle of anxiety started to grow in my belly. "Oh?" I asked. I took a few steps toward him. "Well, what can I help you with?"

But he looked past me to the table. "I'm actually here for Leah."

Leah set her wineglass down on the table. "Me?" she squeaked out.

He nodded slowly.

"Why?" I pressed. "What's going on?"

Grant's eyes went to mine, and I could clearly read regret in his hazel flecks. There was also a generous amount of sympathy, though whether it was directed at me or the scared woman at the table behind me, I couldn't tell. But I could tell what he was going to say almost before the words left his mouth, the anxiety in my stomach ratcheting up a notch.

"Leah Holcomb, I have a warrant for your arrest."

CHAPTER FIFTEEN

———

I watched in horror as Grant stepped toward Leah, reading her the Miranda rights. Leah's eyes shot from me to Ava, filling with fearful tears. Ava jumped up from the table, throwing a few choice words toward Grant—none of which could be repeated in polite company.

"Wait, you can't arrest Leah," I protested, finding my voice as the initial shock wore off.

Grant paused in his list of ways Leah could incriminate herself. "I'm sorry, Emmy, but—"

"But nothing!" I interrupted. "You have no evidence she did this."

"Actually, I do."

That froze the argument on my lips.

"What evidence?" Ava demanded. She placed herself just between Grant and Leah in a protective gesture.

Grant's gaze went from me to Ava. "I'm sorry, I'm not at liberty to share that."

"Bull!" Ava spat back at him.

"Ava," I said, putting a hand on her arm to restrain her. The last thing I needed was two of my friends in handcuffs this evening.

I turned to Grant instead. "Please," I told him, "maybe there's a logical explanation for it." In fact, I knew there was. Because Leah did not do this.

Grant did that slow breathing thing again, which I knew was as close to displaying emotion as he got. "Alright," he said, cracking his neck from side to side, as if I somehow gave him stress. Go figure. "The CSU found something at the crime scene that belongs to Ms. Holcomb."

"What did they find?" I asked.

"A gemstone. It's small and yellow."

"Citrine," Ava said automatically.

I turned to her, our eyes locking. The good luck necklaces she'd given Leah and me before the party.

"How do you know it belongs to Leah?" I asked.

"During a search of her home, we found the piece of jewelry it came from. A necklace."

I turned to Leah.

Her hand went to her bare neck, as if feeling the absence of it right now. "I-I realized that the stone fell out. I didn't notice until after the party." She looked to Ava. "I was going to tell you later and see if you could fix it, but then Heather..." She trailed off. Clearly after the body had been found, the gemstone had been forgotten.

Until now, that is.

"So what," Ava said, countering Grant's so-called evidence. "So she lost a gemstone in her own bakery. That's not a crime."

"It was in the alleyway," Grant said, his expression unreadable, the hard lines of his jaw clenching any emotion back.

"Maybe she lost it when she took out the trash," Ava countered again.

I had to admit, she might have missed her calling as a defense attorney. She was thinking a lot more quickly and clearly on her feet than I was.

But Grant shook his head. "The gem was found on the victim's body." He paused, his eyes going to Leah again. "We believe it was left there after the victim was dead."

The ball of anxiety in my belly turned into a lead weight. I looked from Leah to Grant again, feeling desperation bubble up inside me. "Th-there has to be another explanation," I said, almost as much to convince myself as him. No way was Leah guilty.

Only right now, she wasn't offering up any other explanations, and she wasn't putting up much of a fight either. Her head hung low, her eyes on the ground, her entire posture one of defeat.

"I'm sorry," Grant said softly to me. Then he pushed past both Ava and me, and he gently took Leah by the elbow, leading her away from the table and toward his waiting car.

Ava and I followed, trailing after the pair, even though I knew there was nothing we could do. Even if Grant wanted to let her go, he couldn't. He had a warrant. One way or another Leah was going to jail tonight.

My heart squeezed, picturing poor Spencer's face. I prayed James did his best to shield his son from this.

Grant carefully helped Leah into the backseat, then shut the door behind her.

"I'll call a lawyer," Ava assured Leah through the open window. "We'll get you out on bail in no time. Don't worry."

Grant took my elbow, leading me a step away from the vehicle to relative privacy. "Emmy, I know you're upset, but—"

"Darn right I'm upset," I told him, some of the fight coming back to me.

"But you need to stay out of this," he warned, sounding tired.

"You don't get to tell me what to do," I returned.

"I do if it's illegal."

Good point. I tried to read his expression to see if he was thinking of any illegal acts in particular—like minor B&E at the Atherton house—but he wasn't giving anything away.

"Look, I have to follow the evidence, Emmy," he said, his voice softening.

"Well, you of all people should know that sometimes the evidence is wrong," I shot back.

The soft look in his eyes shifted. "What do you mean 'of all people'?"

"Haven't *you* been the focus of an investigation? Before you transferred?" I reminded him. The truth was I knew little about the incident other than what was public record—an arrest had gone wrong, a man had died, and Internal Affairs had eventually dropped it, and Grant had been reassigned from SFPD to the Sonoma Sheriff's Office.

But clearly there was more to the story, as Grant's jaw went granite hard, his eyes flat and dark, and his voice low, deep, and holding an edge of danger to it. "*That* was different."

"What? Because you're a cop?" I asked, sticking to my guns even under his hard glare.

"No. Because the evidence was right that I killed him. I was guilty."

That took the wind out of my sails. "Oh" was all I could think to say. "I-I'm sorry."

He swallowed, his jaw loosening its death grip on his back teeth a little. "Don't be," he said. He took a deep breath, letting it out slowly through his nose. "I don't regret it."

I wasn't sure which was more unnerving—the thought of Grant guilty of killing a man or the thought that he'd do it again. Though, as the little gold flecks peeked through the darkness in his eyes again, I wasn't sure I totally believed his macho façade. There was emotion running through them, and it didn't feel like pride. It felt a lot more like sadness.

"Leah isn't guilty," I said softly.

Grant sighed, his gaze going up to the sky that was just starting to hint at the first twinkling stars of the night. "I wish it was all that simple." When his eyes came back to rest on mine, they looked tired, like the emotion had been drained out of him. "This isn't my call, Emmy. The evidence was enough for a warrant. I'm just doing my job."

"Your job sucks," I told him.

"Yeah, some days it does," he agreed. He sighed again, reaching a hand out and gently tucking a strand of my hair behind my ear.

I froze in place, the intimate gesture catching me off guard. I hated how my traitorous body heated at his soft touch.

"I have to go," he said, his voice so low it was almost a whisper.

He turned and walked back to his car, slipping into the driver's seat without a word.

Ava stepped away from the vehicle, still reassuring Leah that everything would be okay. We watched them drive away, my cheeks tingling from his touch even as anger collected in my chest on Leah's behalf.

"Poor Leah," Ava said as the taillights disappeared down the road.

I nodded, feeling tears of frustration for her back up in my throat. "Grant told me to stay out of it."

Ava snorted. "As if we take orders from him."

I smiled. "That's what I said."

"You know what this means, right?" she asked, turning to face me in the shadowing light.

I wasn't sure. But I had a bad feeling as I saw the determined fire in her eyes. "What?

"We're the only ones looking in the right direction for Heather's killer."

I licked my lips. "You might be right."

"I know I am!" She paused. "Which means we need to keep looking."

I took a deep breath. "Which means we're going back to A1 Personal Storage tonight, doesn't it?"

Ava gave me wicked grin in the evening glow. "Grab your cat burglar boots, Cagney."

*   *   *

To say I was becoming a pro at dressing the part for the crime might have been a slight overstatement, but not far off. I donned the same black skinny jeans I'd worn the night before, this time pairing them with a long-sleeved black turtleneck and, learning from my mistakes, a pair of black leather gloves. I capped it off with a small backpack in lieu of a handbag and loaned Ava a similar outfit. I tried not to take it personally that she looked much better in it than I did. If anyone could make breaking and entering look chic, it was Ava.

By the time we were pulling up to the facility in Ava's GTO, night had fallen, and the only light came from sparse streetlamps placed at odd intervals. We parked two streets away, making the rest of the journey on foot.

Fortunately, the parking lot of A1 was empty as we came around the perimeter of the gated complex. Unfortunately, the gate that had been welcomingly open before was now closed and securely locked.

"Uh-oh."

"What 'uh-oh'?" Ava asked.

"The gate. It's locked."

"Well how did you get in before?"

"It was open," I said dumbly. Clearly we hadn't thought this plan out ahead of time.

"Oh. That is an uh-oh," Ava agreed. She looked up and down the deserted street. "We could try to climb over."

I glanced up at the six-foot-tall fence surrounding the facility, complete with spiky wires on top. "That sounds like a terrible idea."

"Do you have a better one?" she asked, putting her hands on her hips.

I bit my lip. "I don't suppose you can pick that?'" I asked, gesturing to the padlock on the gate.

Ava shook her head. "Let's face it, it was probably dumb luck I ever got one open before."

I was afraid of that. "Okay, let's climb the fence."

I pulled my leather gloves on and checked the surroundings for security guards. This area of town was mostly industrial buildings—small warehouses, car repair shops, and commercial buildings. At this time of night, it was a ghost town.

However, I did spot security cameras mounted on the front office. A couple were trained on the parking lot, and one was staring us directly back in the face.

"Maybe we should see if there's a less conspicuous spot to climb," I suggested, nodding toward the device.

Ava followed my gaze. "Agreed."

The moonlight was helped along by the dim streetlamps lighting our path as we walked the perimeter, looking for a better spot. At that moment, we were just two women who had a thing for black out for a late night stroll. But if anyone saw us trying to scale a fence, we'd be toast.

Knee-high grass stuck up in tufts of unloved patches near the fence until we got to the very back of the block, where the storage facility faced a heavy machinery lot. There were no streetlamps on this block, giving the large, dormant construction equipment the look of shadowed beasts in the lot across the way.

"This looks good," Ava said, turning on her phone's flashlight and shining it up at the fence.

Good was the last thing it looked to me. But it was a lot better than spending the night in a jail cell like Leah was doing, so I sucked it up. "Let's do it," I said resolutely.

Ava stuck a toe in the slats of the fence, hoisting herself up to the top with ease. I was a bit slower, but with a few false starts, I managed to follow her to the top, where she'd thrown her jacket over the wires as protection.

Which might have done its job if my backpack hadn't caught on the jagged fence slats, making me lose my balance as I threw a leg over. I grabbed at whatever my hands could connect with to save me from falling, and sharp wire tore my gloves, digging into my hand. I said a few silent curse words as I fell the last three feet, twisting my ankle beneath me as I landed.

"You okay?" Ava asked, standing over me.

I nodded, biting my lip to keep from crying like a baby. "Uh-huh," I said. As I stood up, favoring my right leg, I found a tissue in my pocket to wrap around my now bleeding fingers. Putting the glove back on was much more difficult, but I managed it as I sucked up my pride and hobbled across the cracked cement after Ava.

"Which unit is it?" Ava asked.

"J26," I told her.

"Where is that?"

I looked around. The darkness coupled with our back entrance had me all turned around. I'd done a lot of zigzagging through the maze of warehouses when I'd been there before, and I had no idea what direction our target had been in.

"I don't know," I told her honestly.

"No matter," she said, shrugging off the minor detail. "We'll just check them all."

"Swell," I muttered, only slightly limping as I followed her.

We wandered the facility for what seemed like an hour before we finally found the J building, with unit 26 sitting near the far end. Like all the other units, this one held a metal rolling door that was padlocked shut on the right. My ankle throbbed as I contemplated it.

"Now what?" Ava asked, eyes on the padlock as well.

I really should have thought this through. Of course the facility would be locked at night. Of course the storage unit would be secure. We'd gotten into James Atherton's place on dumb luck. Cat burglars, we were not.

I reached out to turn the padlock over, hoping maybe it was a combination style that we could guess in less than a hundred attempts. But as I touched it, the arm fell out of its slot, coming apart easily in my hand.

"It was unlocked!" Ava hissed in the darkness.

I shrugged. "Maybe he left in a hurry last time?" I asked. I wondered if the Man in Black had seen me earlier in the day and cut his visit short. Maybe forgetting to lock up properly?

"Or maybe the breaking and entering gods are on our side," Ava said, winking at me.

That, I doubted. But at the moment, I didn't care. All I cared about was getting a quick peek in the unit before anyone caught us.

The doors rolled upward with a noisy clatter that I was positive carried into the next county. I instinctively looked around, making sure we were still alone as Ava pulled out her phone again.

"Whoa. Look at that," she said, shining her flashlight into the unit.

The room was about ten feet wide and several degrees colder than the air outside. Stacks of cardboard boxes filled the space, going all the way to the ceiling. It was hard to see how deep the room really was, but several shorter rows of boxes were stacked near the entrance. I walked to the nearest one, opening it to find it was filled with wine bottles.

"There must be hundreds of them," Ava mused, her light going around the room.

"Thousands," I decided, seeing that each box could hold 24 bottles. I could easily count ten boxes in the first row alone.

"What kind of wine is it?" Ava asked, coming to look in the box I'd found.

My heart actually missed a whole series of beats as I pulled out a bottle and looked at the label. A 1972 Latour that I knew retailed for well over a thousand dollars a bottle.

"It looks old. Is it good?" Ava asked.

"Very," I told her, quoting the price tag.

My hand shook as I put it back and lifted the next bottle in line. This one was a 1982 Margaux. Cheaper but still four figures. I placed it back where I found it and continued inspecting the contents of the box, calling out the names of several similar bottles to Ava.

"Whoever stored these bottles like this should be shot," I mused out loud.

"Wow, envy much?" Ava asked, teasing me.

I shot her a grin over my shoulder. "I just meant wines this rare should be stored properly. They should be in a temperature controlled environment." While the room was cool enough now, I hesitated to think what it would feel like at noon during a heat wave.

I moved on to the next box, checking the bottles held there. This one was only half full, but the first bottle I lifted was a 1979 Haut Brion Bordeaux. I paused. I'd seen that name before.

"Hang on," I said, taking my backpack off and pulling out my phone. I handed it to Ava. "Check the photos we took of Heather's inventory list."

She did, scrolling as I held up the bottle until she found what I was looking for. A 1979 Haut Brion, a 1982 Margaux, and a 1972 Latour were all listed in her stock. It was too much to be coincidence.

"You think this is where Heather stored her inventory?" Ava asked.

"It has to be," I decided. I also decided that James was right about one thing—Heather knew nothing about the wine business. These bottles were in dire trouble if they weren't put into a temperature controlled room pronto.

"Let's check the other boxes," I suggested.

Ava opened the one closest to her. Only, unlike the two I'd opened, this one held two dozen empty bottles. Ava pulled one out, comparing the label to the list on my phone. "It's not in her inventory." She paused. "Why would she keep the empty bottle though?"

I shrugged. "What are the rest of them?"

Ava pulled out several more empty bottles, all with labels of older wines, some European, others local. I didn't know them all, but the ones I did felt collectible. Only the contents had apparently already been enjoyed.

"Is there a market for old, empty bottles?" Ava suggested. "Just, like, for decorative purposes maybe?"

"Maybe," I decided. Or maybe Heather had thought she could create one.

"Well, I definitely think—" But Ava paused mid-thought, her body freezing in place. "What was that?" she whispered.

Adrenaline hit my belly. "What?"

"I heard something," she whispered again, shutting off her phone light.

We both sat silently, listening in the dark. I was about to chalk it up to Ava's imagination, when I heard it too.

Soft footsteps.

Heading our way.

"Someone's coming," Ava said urgently. "Does this place have a security guard?"

I shrugged. "I don't know."

"We gotta get out of here."

We both moved at once, a bundle of unfocused limbs all aimed at getting out the warehouse door as quickly as possible. Ava grabbed my arm, practically hauling my limping self along as we ran toward the back of the facility. But we only got a few paces outside the rolling door when I realized I still had the bottle of Haut Brion in my hand.

I stopped, practically knocking Ava over it the process. "I have to put this back," I whispered to her.

"What?!" she whispered back. "Are you crazy?"

"What if they notice it's missing?" I hissed back.

"What if the security guard catches us!"

Good point. I shoved the bottle into my backpack, vowing to return it to James at a later date.

Ava pulled me along, both of us running as fast as we could from the storage unit and toward the shadowing safety at the back of the facility.

My ankle was on fire as I struggled to keep up, but halfway there, I knew it was a futile effort, as it gave way altogether.

Ava got a couple paces ahead of me before she noticed. "Whadda ya doing?" she whispered, urgency slurring her words together.

"I can't," I confessed, pointing to my ankle.

Ava tried to pull me to a standing position and bear my weight, but we only got a couple feet before we both realized my size eight was probably pushing more toward a ten at this point. No way could she carry me the two blocks to my car.

"I'll pull the car around," she decided. "You wait here. Don't make a sound. I'll be right back."

While the idea of being possibly found by the roving security guard was not one I relished, I realized she was right. It was the only way we were getting out of here. I nodded.

"You sure you'll be okay?" she asked.

"Go." I glanced around. "I'll hunker down behind that dumpster," I decided, spying a couple at the end of the row.

Satisfied, she gave my hand a quick squeeze then sprinted into the darkness.

I hobbled to the dumpster and crouched down beside it. I leaned my head back on the cool metal, closing my eyes and letting my breath even out as I listened for those footsteps again. Nothing. Luck was on my side—he seemed to be patrolling the other side of the facility now. I wondered how long it would be before he realized someone had broken into unit J26.

A soft noise sounded to my left.

My eyes shot open, and I listened in the dark.

Nothing.

"Ava?" I whispered quietly. Could she be back already?

I struggled to a standing position, ears perked for any sign of life.

But none came to me.

I hobbled to the edge of the dumpster, only daring to peek out when I'd done a ten count without any other sounds than my own ragged breathing.

Only I probably should have counted higher.

As soon as I ducked around the corner, something large and heavy flew toward my face.

Then all I saw was darkness.

CHAPTER SIXTEEN

———

My mother was calling me in for dinner. Her voice floated across the grass like the lush scents of growing grapes and summer jasmine, wafting down to me on a warm breeze as I hid just inside the cellar door.

"Emmy?" she sang out. "Where is my little Em?"

I couldn't help a giggle escaping me as my mother came closer, her voice booming through the heavy oak door.

"Now, where could my little Emmy be hiding?" she asked, her voice playful and young. "Is she in...here!" She threw the door open, grabbing me in a fit of tickles and giggles that had us both dissolving to the cool tiled floor of the cellar.

I reached a hand up to touch her face, thinking she looked so young. The skin was smooth beneath my fingers, her eyes sparkling and clear, her mind sharp and not a jumble of memories that often overlapped each other.

A sadness washed over me, which she must have felt, as her soft brows drew together in concern. "Emmy? Are you alright?"

I tried to tell her. To warn her what lay ahead. To let her know I wanted to keep her just like this, right here. But somehow, my voice wouldn't work. I couldn't force sound out.

"Emmy? Emmy can you hear me? Are you alright?"

And suddenly it wasn't my mother's voice, but someone else. Female. Worried.

"Emmy? Em!"

My mother's face faded even as I longed with all my heart to hang on to it, and it was suddenly replaced by another woman as I blinked my eyes.

"Oh, thank goodness, you're alright." It was Ava. She was hovering over me, her head haloed by a streetlamp behind her.

I shut my eyes against the harsh light, trying to get my fuzzy head to make sense of where I was. Pain throbbed at my temple, and my jaw felt funny.

"Emmy. Can you hear me?" someone else asked.

This time the voice was male. I knew I recognized it, but the pain was stopping me from thinking straight.

"Hey? You okay?" he asked again. This time the question was accompanied by a warm hand gently going to my hair, smoothing it back from my forehead.

I opened my eyes with difficulty again, willing them to focus on the face in front of me. Beside Ava, Grant knelt on the ground, his eyes darting around my face, as if looking for signs of life. They found mine and held, a small smile coming to his full lips, hovering just inches above mine.

"Hey," he said softly, infusing the one word with a whole range of emotion.

"Hey yourself," I croaked out, lifting myself up on my elbow. A new wave of pain seared through my head, but I tried to focus through it. "What happened?"

"You were attacked with a wine bottle is what happened," Ava said hotly.

I tore my gaze away from Grant's with difficulty. "What?" I spied shattered green glass near my feet. I attempted to pull myself to a sitting position, but Grant stopped me.

"Don't get up," he commanded, gently touching my shoulder. "An ambulance is on the way."

"No," I protested. "I'm fine." Plus, I didn't have any insurance.

"You're not fine. You were unconscious. And probably concussed."

I relented, lying my head back down on what felt like a piece of clothing that had been put between me and the pavement. Mostly because he was right—I did not feel fine. I felt like I'd been hit by a truck. My hand reached around to touch my forehead, where I felt the warm trickle of blood on top of what I could only describe as a massive goose egg erupting from my skull. Nausea rumbled in my stomach.

"How did you get here?" I asked, trying to concentrate on anything but the throbbing in my head.

"A silent alarm was tripped when someone breached the perimeter of the facility."

"Silent alarm?" That was one Ava and I hadn't thought of.

Grant nodded. "The security company dispatched a guard to investigate."

I glanced to his right and for the first time noticed the man standing a couple of feet away. He was wearing a gray uniform and had a chin that blended seamlessly into his neck and a belly that muffin-topped over his belt. I had a hard time picturing him running anybody down. Though the gun on his hip told me that it was very possible he never had to actually run.

"Apparently security found you unconscious, just as your partner in crime here"—Grant gestured to Ava, who had the good graces to at least look sheepish at the moniker—"pulled up in her convertible."

"He called 9-1-1, and I called Grant," Ava admitted.

"We were just looking around," I told Grant, wondering how much Ava had confessed. Though, I figured it didn't really matter at this point. We were as busted as we could be.

"Yeah. I put that much together," Grant said. Some of the softness fell out of his tone, the cop in him cutting through.

"But there was someone else here," I said. Clearly, or I wouldn't be lying spread out on pavement that was so icky I planned to burn these clothes when I got home.

His eyes darkened. "Did you see who it was?"

I shook my head, instantly regretting the movement, as pain flared again. "No. It happened too fast." I paused, thinking of our "dumb luck" at finding the storage unit unlocked. "But I think maybe they'd been in the storage unit too," I decided.

"Was it a man? Or a woman?" Ava jumped in.

I pursed my lips together, trying to bring up a mental image. But all I'd seen was the flash of something coming toward my head before the picture faded to black. "Sorry. I really don't know."

"Well, I can tell you one thing—it wasn't Leah." Ava crossed her arms over her chest to emphasize her point.

"Why would Leah hit me?" I asked. My mind must have still been foggy.

"She wouldn't. That's the point, because she's not the killer."

"You think this had something to do with Heather's death?" Grant asked.

"Well, of course," Ava said, throwing her hands up in the air. "Hello? Why else would someone hit Emmy?"

"Maybe they thought she was breaking into the facility," Grant reasoned.

Which would have been a good thought, because I was.

"Or," he went on, "maybe someone else was here who didn't want to get caught. Kids drinking. Vandals."

"Or maybe it was the Tooth Fairy," Ava added sarcastically.

Grant shot her a look. To her credit, she shot him one right back.

"Enough," I said, trying to put a halt to their banter before I had World War III on my hands. "My head hurts."

Ava was instantly at my side again. "Sorry, hun. Hang in there. The ambulance is on its way."

I hung, closing my eyes again and trying to calm the myriad of thoughts in my brain. I heard Grant stepping away, talking in hushed tones to the security officer. Sirens sounded, growing from a faraway echo to filling the night air.

The next hour was a blur as the EMTs arrived, followed by more security people, followed by uniformed officers in squad cars, followed by the facility's manager, who was completely up in arms about all the law enforcement swarming his facility in the middle of the night.

I tried to ignore the general commotion as the EMTs peeled me off the ground and I was poked, prodded, pressure checked, and examined until they suggested I come with them to the hospital just to be sure I was okay. Then I told them I had no insurance, in which case they said to ice, Advil, and watch for signs of a concussion. I had a feeling they still would have liked me to see a doctor, but I appreciated their sympathy toward my uninsured plight as they cleared me to go home.

"I'll drive you," Grant said, suddenly at my side again as the activity died down.

"It's fine. I came with Ava."

"That was not a suggestion," he told me. "I'm taking you home."

For a moment I feared the Big Bad Cop really cared. Then he ruined it by stating, "I don't trust you enough to let you out of my sight."

I rolled my eyes, which only minimally hurt. "It was one little break and enter."

"One?" Grant pinned me with a hard look. "You sure about that?"

I bit my lip, wondering if James Atherton had a silent alarm that had recently been tripped too.

"Yep," I lied.

"Hmm." His eyes said he knew I was hiding something, but thankfully he let it go. "Come on. Let's get you home."

Nothing in the world sounded better.

*　*　*

Grant loaded me into a black SUV, and we drove through the quiet night. I closed my eyes against the bright traffic lights as we made our way through town, grateful when the relative darkness of the winding lanes to the winery gave me reprieve.

"So, want to tell me what you were doing at the storage facility tonight?" Grant's voice filled the space between us.

So much for reprieve.

But I didn't see any point in lying to him now. "We went to check out a storage unit."

"J26," he stated.

When I sent him a questioning look, he added, "You left the door open."

"Right. We, uh, left in kind of a hurry."

He made a noncommittal sound in the back of his throat. "So what were you doing at J26?"

I took a deep breath and spilled. I told him about Caroline having seen the Man in Black arguing with Heather, about me tailing him from the auction house, and about the rare, expensive bottles we'd found in the storage unit.

"You're sure they were Heather's inventory?" Grant asked.

I nodded in the dim light from his car dashboard. "Positive. They all matched the bottles on Heather's inventory list."

Grants' eyes shot momentarily to mine before going back to the road. "You have Heather's inventory list?"

Oops. Had I let that slip? "Uh, yeah."

"Should I ask how you acquired that?"

"No. Definitely not."

More indistinguishable grunting. "Okay, so the bottles were the same as the ones on Heather's list."

I did a mental sigh of relief that he was willing to let that last bit go. "They were," I agreed. I thought back. "At least the full ones."

"Could be coincidence."

"That would be a heck of a coincidence," I argued. Then I paused. "You didn't happen to get any information on that storage unit while you were there did you?"

He worked his jaw back and forth for a second before answering. "Yes. I did."

"Want to share?"

"No. Definitely not."

"Touché."

His eyes left the road to meet mine again for a second, and I could swear they were crinkled at the corners with amusement this time.

"Just tell me that the unit was in Heather's name?" I pleaded.

He sighed, shifting in his seat so that a waft of his aftershave floated toward me. It was subtle yet spicy in the confined space. "Actually, her name was not on the lease."

"Whose was?"

"Black Market Wine Group." He glanced my way again. "The name mean anything to you?"

"No." I shook my head, and regretted it as a wave of dizziness caused nausea to bubble in my stomach. "I've never heard of it." I paused. "And Heather wasn't connected to the unit at all?"

Grant shook his head. "Not that the manager of the facility knew of." He paused. "Who, by the way, I convinced to generously not press charges against you and your Nancy Drew sidekick."

"Ava," I corrected. "But thank you."

"You're welcome," he said.

We were silent a moment, him driving and me mulling over the new info. "Maybe Black Market was the name of Heather's wine broker business?" I mused out loud, though I'd yet to hear anyone call it that.

"I couldn't say," Grant answered. "All I know is that the facility records indicated that the unit has been rented by Black Market for the last eight months. Prepaid in cash for another four."

"Cash?" I asked. "Doesn't that seem suspicious?"

Grant shot me another look—this one easily readable. If I knew what was good for me, I should drop it.

"Just saying," I mumbled, letting my gaze fall out the window as we pulled up the tree-lined drive to Oak Valley.

The gravel crunched under Grant's tires as he drew to a stop and cut the engine. The sudden stillness in the air had me feeling every minute of the late hour in my muscles, making them heavy and weak.

Grant walked around to help me from the car, which I was grateful for. I'd like to say I could have made it up the pathway to my cottage all on my own, but if it hadn't been for him carrying half my weight, I would have been hard pressed to even crawl it.

I unlocked the door, pushing inside, and was instantly enveloped in the comforting scent of home.

"Thanks," I told Grant, stepping inside. "For everything tonight."

"You're welcome." He glanced around, eyes scanning the room.

I had a feeling it was a habit for him, assessing every situation the moment he walked into it. I wondered if he ever allowed himself to just relax.

"I, uh, think I can take it from here," I said. As much as I wasn't hating the heat from his nearness, I was beyond tired. And my bed was calling me like a beacon.

But Grant shook his head. "I think not."

"Excuse me?"

"EMTs said you might have a concussion." He took a step toward me, looking down at me through his dark lashes. "I'm not leaving you alone tonight."

My head was suddenly dizzy for a whole new reason as a rush of hormones flooded my system.

Down, girl.

"Y-you're staying here?" I managed to get out.

He nodded slowly, his eyes not leaving mine.

I licked my lips. "I'm fine," I protested. "I don't need you to do that."

"You can't even stand up on your own."

"Sure I can," I argued. I held my arms out and stood, as if to prove it.

And it might have been great proof if another wave of nausea hadn't hit me, making me sway so that his hands quickly reaching out to catch me were the only things keeping me from the ground.

"Sorta," I added weakly.

His arms were strong and warm, and I briefly wondered why I hadn't feigned dizziness before in order to be held in them. His face was so close to mine that I could smell the faint hint of evening coffee on his breath. And his voice was low, deep, and laced with emotion when he spoke.

"Let's get you up to bed."

I think my hormones just died and went to heaven.

* * *

After depositing me upstairs in the cozy master bedroom, Grant left me alone to sleep in the guest room, acting like a perfect gentleman. Much to my body's dismay.

I wasn't sure if it was the sexy detective waking me every hour to be sure I wasn't concussed or the images of the Man in Black wielding a wine bottle, but sleep eluded me once again. By the time the sun came up, I was more exhausted than I had ever been. My head pounded as I rolled onto my back and spread-eagled myself to the four corners of the mattress. I was just considering getting up, when a text came in on my phone. I fumbled around on the nightstand and checked the readout. It was from Ava.

You alone?

I paused, listening for sounds from the guest room. When I realized I wasn't sure if I'd heard any, I reluctantly got out of bed and hobbled the few paces to the guest bedroom door. It was ajar and Grant-less, though there was a page torn from his notebook, with a message on it.

Had to go. Feel better. I'll call you later.

Short and sweet, but at least he hoped I felt better.

I quickly texted Ava back.

Alone.

On my way over. I have Half Calf.

Bless her. The Half Calf was the coffeehouse next to Ava's place that had a cute logo of a cow jumping over the moon and the best caramel flan lattes on the planet.

I hobbled back to my room and took a quick shower and a couple painkillers. The knot at the side of my head was starting to turn a brilliant shade of purple. I tried covering it with concealer, but I wasn't sure it was actually an improvement. I'd just thrown on an asymmetrical skirt in a flowy peach organza and a slim white T-shirt, when I heard Ava at the door.

"Coffee delivery," she called.

"Be right down," I answered as she let herself in.

I took the stairs slowly, and found Ava shaking her head at me as I came into the room. "You poor thing," she mumbled, her eyes going from my ankle to my head.

"I tried to cover it with concealer. Does it look that bad?" I asked.

She made a face. "Well, it doesn't look *good*."

"Gimme the latte," I demanded. At least I could be caffeinated if I had to look like I'd lost a boxing match.

Ava plopped herself down on my sofa. She was dressed today in a long, flowy maxi-skirt, Grecian sandals, and a formfitting cami tank that showed the fact her cup size was significantly higher up the alphabet than mine.

"So, how was your night with Grant?" she asked, moving her eyebrows up and down suggestively.

"Uneventful," I emphasized, sitting beside her as I sipped my coffee. "He slept in the guest room."

"Well, that's just plain sad."

I swatted her on the arm. "I'm not interested in Grant."

She raised both eyebrows. "Wow, look at that nose of yours grow, girl."

I rolled my eyes. "Okay, not *that* interested."

She shrugged. "I almost bought that."

"Have you talked to Leah yet this morning?" I asked, doing my best to change the subject.

Ava nodded. "She called earlier. Her divorce attorney gave her the name of a good defense lawyer. Bail arraignment is later today."

"What time?" I asked.

"She didn't know yet. But she thinks if she puts up the condo for collateral, she has a chance at making bail. And hopefully, the judge won't think Leah is a flight risk because she has Spencer."

"I'd like to be there," I said.

Ava nodded. "So, did Grant divulge anything about the storage unit during your *super-platonic* sleepover?"

I shot her a look, but instead of harping on her matchmaking ambitions, I filled her in on what little Grant had known about the unit. "Have you ever heard of the Black Market Wine Group?" I asked.

She pursed her lips, thinking, but eventually shook her head. "Sorry. Doesn't ring a bell."

"Yeah, me neither."

Ava pulled out her phone, googling the name. "Wow. I never knew how many people had a sense of humor about wine. There's, like, fifty different companies using some variation of the name Black Market."

"I'm wondering if it was something Heather put together for her brokering business," I suggested. "You know, like an LLC for tax purposes?"

"If Heather was stashing cash in the Caymans, I doubt she was a stickler for tax laws," Ava pointed out, putting her phone away.

"You're right. But it still could have been her business."

"Well, I think this was too much of a coincidence that the inventory lists matched all the bottles we found. Whatever or whoever Black Market is, it's definitely Heather's wine in their storage unit."

I nodded, tending to agree.

"What did Grant say about the wine bottle?" Ava asked.

"Huh?" I'll admit I was lost in my own thoughts there for a minute.

"The Haut Brion?" Ava prompted. "The one you had in your hand when we left the unit?"

I blinked at her.

"You *did* give it back to Grant last night, didn't you?"

Mental forehead thunk. "I forgot."

"Ohmigod, Emmy!" Ava shrieked, setting her coffee cup down with a thump on my end table. "We stole evidence from a crime scene!"

"I didn't know it was going to be a crime scene when I took it," I reasoned.

"Yeah, I'm sure Grant will totally give us a pass on that." There she went with that sarcasm again.

"Really, I'm the victim in the crime," I pointed out.

Ava shot me a look. "Which crime? The breaking and entering, the trespassing, or the theft of a thousand -dollar bottle of wine?"

I bit my lip. Okay, so the lines between victim and perpetrator were a little blurry.

"I was concussed," I protested, walking to the door, where I vaguely remembered dropping my backpack before Grant led me upstairs. "I wasn't thinking clearly."

"A thousand dollars. Is that still a misdemeanor theft?" she asked, pulling out her phone to google again.

"It's not theft. It was an accident," I protested, pulling the bottle from my backpack.

"Geeze, put that thing away," Ava said, glancing over her shoulder as if Grant might pop up from behind my sofa with an arrest warrant.

"I'll just return it," I told her.

Ava blinked at me. "There's no way we can get in that storage unit again unnoticed."

"I-I'll give it to James," I decided. "With Heather gone, it probably belongs to him now anyway."

Ava's eyebrows went up into her hair again. "And tell him what? That we accidentally stole it?"

Yeah, that wasn't likely to go over well. "I'll say that…that Heather left it at the Wine and Chocolate event. By accident."

Ava shook her head. "And why would Heather have a bottle of wine with her there?"

"She could have been meeting a client?"

"But she wasn't."

"But James doesn't know that." I gently set the bottle down on the coffee table between us. "Look, it doesn't matter if I fib a little about how I got it—the important thing is that it's back with its rightful owner."

But Ava was still giving me a look like I was sporting a birch branch where my nose once was. "This is a terrible idea."

"Stop judging and help cover this goose egg well enough to go out in public," I pleaded with her.

Her eyes flitted to the bump on my head. "Got any hats?"

CHAPTER SEVENTEEN

—————

We parted with Ava promising to do more digging into the Black Market Wine Group, and me promising to let her know the second the wine was back with James and we were off the hook for at least one crime. (Which, as she found out, was not a misdemeanor but felony grand theft.)

I pulled up to Bay Cellars and parked in their lot, which was not quite as full as before. Apparently weekdays were slower for business. The same dark haired woman I'd seen on my last visit stood behind the stone reception counter. "May I help you?" she asked pleasantly.

"I'm here to see James Atherton," I told her. I held up the cardboard box I'd found to transport the Haut Brion in safely. "I have a bottle of wine for him."

"And your name?"

"Emmy Oak."

She nodded, turning to her telephone. "I'll just let him know you're here."

I waited in the quiet, cool air conditioning as the woman spoke in hushed tones. I didn't have to wait long as James Atherton appeared only a moment later, a frown etched on his face.

"What are you doing here?" he asked in a tightly restrained voice.

"I have something for you," I said, holding up the box.

James looked at it, then back up at me, clearly confused as to why I'd be bringing him a present.

"Maybe we could talk in private?" I suggested.

He glanced toward the receptionist, who was doing her best to look like she wasn't listening to our conversation. Then he nodded, motioning for me to follow him up the stairs to his office. I did, only slightly limping in the soft ballet flats I'd chosen as a concession to my ankle.

As soon as we got to his office, he closed the door behind me. "So what are you doing here? And don't pretend it's to sell me your winery again."

I cleared my throat. "No, I came to give you this." I opened the box, extracting the wine.

Surprise was evident in his eyes as I set the bottle down on his desk. "What is this?" he asked, picking it up gently with the reverence it deserved.

"It's a 1979 Haut Brion," I told him.

He frowned in irritation at me again. "Yes, I can see that. What I mean is, what are you doing with it in my office?"

"It was Heather's."

The frown deepened as James turned the bottle over, almost as if inspecting it for some sign his wife had owned it. "You must be mistaken."

I shook my head. "I'm not. I fou—uh, she left it at the Wine and Chocolate Tasting."

He let out a bark of laughter and set the bottle down. "Now I know you're lying. What on earth would she be doing bringing this to your little tasting?"

I ignored the *little* part with no small effort.

"She must have been meeting a client?" I said. Which would have been more convincing if I hadn't phrased it as a question. Ava was right. I was a terrible liar, and this was not going well.

"She was doing no such thing," he told me emphatically. "And I don't know what this is you're playing at." He waved his hand in the direction of the bottle. "But I'd like you to leave."

"Wait!" I bit my lip. "Okay, the truth?"

"That would be preferable," he agreed.

"I found this in a storage unit. Along with a lot of other collectible bottles. They're all Heather's."

"A storage unit?"

I nodded. "A1 Personal Storage."

He shook his head. "No, you're mistaken. Heather kept her wine in our cellar at home."

"Maybe some of the bottles, but not all of it. There are at least a thousand bottles sitting in a warehouse off seventh."

"A thousand... No. Heather's hobby was not that big. Or lucrative."

I hesitated to tell him about her account in the Cayman Islands that said otherwise.

"Besides," he went on, "a warehouse? Not a wine storage facility?"

"No," I told him sadly. "No temperature control. No moisture control. Just some cardboard boxes on concrete."

"No. It wasn't Heather's," he reiterated. "There is absolutely no way she would store something like this in a warehouse."

I had to agree—it was a rookie mistake. "You said she didn't know much about the wine business. Maybe she just didn't realize? Or thought it would stay cool enough?"

"Heather had no head for *business*, but she definitely knew better than to store something like this somewhere like that. You are mistaken. It's not Heather's."

"Look, every bottle I found in the unit matched Heather's inventory."

His expression changed. "How do you know what Heather had in stock?"

Let's face it, I sucked at the espionage thing. I might have graduated from the CIA, but I was a terrible spy. "She, uh, told me about them at the Wine and Chocolate party," I tried.

He didn't look convinced, but it was hard to refute. "Look, I don't know where you really got this or what you're game is—some sort of pathetic attempt to plant evidence on me maybe?"

"W-what?" I asked, my turn to be shocked.

He narrowed his eyes at me. "I know who you are now. My son told me you're friends with my ex-wife."

I pursed my lips. "I am. And she's innocent."

He scoffed. "And this is some weird way of proving it? Sticking me with this bottle? What, is it stolen?"

Technically? Yes.

"I'm telling you the truth," I protested. "This bottle belongs to you."

But he wasn't having it. He grabbed it off the desk and shoved it toward me with such vigor that I feared for its life.

"Take this and get out. Now. Before I call security."

What could I do? I grabbed the bottle and got out. It still felt like stolen goods in my hands, making me feel guilty and nervous as I walked back out to my car, mulling over my next move.

James had been so certain the storage unit wasn't Heather's. But I felt certain it was. I glanced down at the bottle in my hands. How to prove it? Heather had noted the name of the auction house, Dixons, in her inventory next to several bottles. I pulled up the photos of the list again, and sure enough, it was noted next to the entry for the bottle in my hand. Maybe if I could prove some sort of chain of custody for the wine, I could prove that it—and the other bottles languishing in unit J26 at A1—were Heather's.

I carefully nestled the bottle in my jacket, setting it directly in the blast of the AC as I pulled out of the lot and drove toward Dixons again.

* * *

As with most auction houses I'd been in, this one had a hushed feel to the air, like a museum. I was instantly filled with the notion that I should just look and not touch…mostly because I knew just about everything in the place was worth at least double the balance in my bank account.

An older woman in a loose blouse and ankle length skirt greeted me at the reception desk. "May I help you?" she asked, blinking up at me behind a pair of bifocals.

"I hope so," I told her truthfully. "I was hoping I could speak to someone about a chain of custody for an item."

Her sparse brows formed a frown that sent wrinkling ripples throughout her face. "Is it an item you believe was purchased at auction here?"

I nodded. "Yes, I'm almost certain it was."

"And the previous owner didn't provide you with any paperwork?"

I pursed my lips, hesitating to tell her that the previous owner was dead and technically I'd stolen the item in question. "Uh, no. I was hoping maybe you had a copy?"

"What is the item?" she asked, turning to a computer that looked about as old as she was. I wouldn't have been surprised to find a small hamster on a wheel running it beside the huge square monitor.

"It's a bottle of 1979 Haut Brion Bordeaux," I said, pulling it out of my bag and gently setting it down on the reception counter.

If the woman was impressed, she didn't show it. However, I had to guess that she dealt with dozens of such rare and expensive items on a daily basis. She gave the label a cursory glance, then plugged the name into some database—typing, scrolling, and squinting at the screen.

"Do you know approximately when the bottle might have been purchased?" she asked.

I shrugged. "I don't have a date. But it would have been within the last year," I told her, knowing Heather had only been doing business that long.

"That helps some," she told me, switching to a new screen and repeating her type/scroll/squint routine.

"Was this sold as part of a larger collection or as a stand-alone item?" she asked.

Great question. "Sorry, I have no idea. But the buyer's name would have been Heather Atherton," I supplied. "Or possibly Black Market Wine Group."

She nodded. "Many of our collectors like to remain anonymous, but I'll try searching those names."

Which she did as I waited agonizing minutes in the hushed atmosphere, the woman's clicking keyboard the only sound.

Finally she turned to me, shaking her head. "I'm sorry to say that this Ms. Atherton must have been mistaken about where she acquired it. This bottle has never been through our auction house."

I blinked at her, trying to process that statement. "Are you sure?"

She nodded, eyes going back to her screen. "Positive. Even for anonymous auctions, we keep a very accurate record of all items. For this very reason," she added. "Too many people try to fake provenance these days."

"What about Heather Atherton?" I asked. "She is in your system as having purchased wine here before?"

But she shook her head. "Sorry. I have no record of her either. But like I said, many buyers prefer to remain anonymous."

I thanked the woman and left, feeling deflated. Once the bottle was back in the relative safety of the AC in my car, I pulled up Heather's records on my phone again, thinking maybe I'd been mistaken. Nope, *Dixons* was clearly listed beside it. I was suddenly questioning everything. No one seemed to claim this bottle as theirs. I'd never had such a hard time unloading a $1000 bottle of wine before.

I was contemplating what exactly I should do with it when a text came in.

It was from Ava.

I may have a lead on our Black Market! Meet you at the winery in an hour?

Well, at least someone was having some luck. I quickly texted her back that I would meet her there and headed back to Oak Valley.

* * *

The first thing I did when I got there was put the Haut Brion in the cave for safekeeping. Until I could find someone to claim ownership of it, at least I could ensure it was properly cared for. Then I made my way into the kitchen, where I found Conchita excitedly slicing cured salami and prepping what looked like a Wine Tasting Charcuterie Board.

"Ay, Emmy!" she said as she caught sight of me. "We have a crowd!"

I perked up. "A crowd? I didn't see any cars in the lot."

"They came on a wine bus," she said, her eyes sparkling. "German tourists. Thirty of them."

"Thirty?" I choked out. It had been months since we'd seen that many in the tasting room. Maybe my luck really was turning. "Do you need a hand?" I asked, jumping in to help arrange meats and cheeses on the large wooden board. I grabbed a wedge of brie, which I knew would pair well with our Chardonnay, and some pork pâté, which would complement the creaminess in our Pinot Noir.

"They look like they have money," she said, rushing to the cupboard and pulling out some dried apricots and salted almonds to add to the mix. "Jean Luc said one of them already ordered a case of the Pinot Blanc to be delivered to his hotel."

Be still my beating heart. "Then let's wow the other twenty-nine," I told her.

Between the two of us, we got together a good sampling of cheeses, meats, fruits, and a few veggies, to make an artful display that would make our wines sing to their fullest potential for our guests.

The tasting room was buzzing with activity, and Jean Luc was playing the master entertainer, pouring with flair and even exchanging a few German phrases here and there. I roved the room, chatting, answering questions, filling glasses, and generally trying to be the hostess with the mostess.

I'd just sold another two cases to a lovely couple from Hamburg, when I spotted Ava peeking her head into the tasting room.

I gave her a quick wave of acknowledgment before politely excusing myself from the jovial group.

"Wow, quite a crowd today."

"Totally unexpected. But I just sold three cases," I told her, unable to keep it in.

She gave me a high five. "There's a good Tuesday."

"Tell me about it."

"Want more good news?" she asked, her eyes twinkling mischievously.

"Black Market Wines?" I asked, remembering her text.

She nodded, glancing over my shoulder at the drinking tourists. "Let's go into your office."

I agreed, leading the way down a short hallway. As soon as I had the door closed behind us, Ava pulled out her phone.

"Well, you know how I said there were like a hundred companies calling themselves Black Market?"

The number had doubled since I'd last seen her, but I nodded for her to go on.

"I thought maybe I could weed that down a bit. I started by checking out each company's website. Then social media presence, local press, you know, all that stuff."

"And?"

"Well, it took me a while, as business has picked up today now that the weekend wine walk is over. So I had to do it between customers."

"What did you find?" I asked, not able to handle the suspense much longer.

"I found a Black Market Wine Group that is actually a larger corporation that owns several smaller labels. One of their holdings is a place where they produce a line of wines labeled *Nifty Dollar-Fifty*."

"Nifty?" I asked.

Ava nodded. "They sell for—you guessed it—a buck-fifty a bottle"

I scrunched my nose up. "That can't taste good."

"Agreed," she said. "But it gets better. The winery is in Los Banos." She watched my reaction as the punch line sunk in.

Having lived in California all my life, I knew that the town of Los Banos was a small, farming community located smack in the middle of the state, surrounded by pretty much nothing for miles.

It also meant "the bathrooms" in Spanish.

I couldn't help it—a burst of laughter escaped me. "Dollar-fifty wines made in the bathrooms. Oh wow, I can't wait to taste that."

Ava joined me, and soon we were both giggling like teenagers.

"I'm no wine snob," I continued, tears starting to form. "I've had some inexpensive wines that taste better than some of the more expensive ones." I tried to stifle more laughter. "But I've never had wine from the bathrooms."

"It's not very appealing, is it?" Ava got out between laughs. She handed me her phone, with the company's website up on the screen.

I got myself under control, breathing deeply and wiping away the tears. "So, what does this esteemed winery have to do with our storage unit? It feels like their offerings are a million miles away from the bottles we found there."

"Well, I didn't actually see anything that connected them to collectible or vintage wine. Or Heather."

I felt the hope I'd cultivated before dissipating. "So another dead end?"

"Not exactly." She held up a finger for me to wait as she switched to another screen on her phone.

"Black Market is owned by a conglomeration—if I had to guess, none of the owners actually does much on the day-to-day. Especially not in Los Banos. But, I did find one short blurb on the manager of the Nifty Dollar-Fifty winery." She paused for dramatic effect. "A friend of yours?"

She turned her phone in my direction.

Her screen held an image of a man standing with his arms crossed over a black shirt. His eyes were hidden behind his dark glasses and shadowed by his black cowboy hat, but even through his Johnny Cash impression, I could see the tail end of a scar running through his right eyebrow.

The Man in Black.

CHAPTER EIGHTEEN

"The Man in Black's real name is Max Ford," Ava explained. "I tried searching it, but not much came up." She paused. "Well, that's not true—there are dozens of Max Fords, so a lot came up. Just not a ton that felt like it was our guy."

"What is 'not a ton'?"

"Well, he's been the manager of Nifty Dollar-Fifty for nearly two years now. I couldn't find his name associated with any other businesses, nor could I find what his previous employment history was. I did find an address for a Max Ford in Los Banos, but it looks like it's an abandoned building."

I raised an eyebrow her way. "How could you tell that?"

She shrugged. "Google Earth. The images of the place look like it's been a while since anyone lived there."

"So fake address?"

"Possibly."

"People who are innocent don't usually lie about where they live."

Ava nodded. "Agreed, but I didn't come up with any criminal record, at least not with that name."

"Which doesn't mean he hasn't done anything criminal. It just means that he hasn't been caught," I added.

"That's true."

"Find any phone number or other way to contact him?"

She shook her head. "Nifty Dollar-Fifty has a number on their website but nothing about Max Ford personally."

I thought back to the guy I'd seen. What had the manager of a bargain winery been doing at Dixons? And what was his connection with Heather?

"I hate to say it, but I can't come up with a single reason this guy would have any connection to Heather," Ava said.

"Except that he has her wines," I reminded her.

Ava paused. "Maybe he stole them?"

"All of them?" I asked. "And from where? Where had she really been keeping them?"

Ava shrugged. "I don't know." She glanced at her watch. "But I do know I need to get back to the shop. After the cruddy sales weekend I've had, I don't want to be closed too long."

That, I understood. I walked Ava out to the parking lot, giving her a hug goodbye and thanking her for all her hard work. Even if we still did have more questions than answers.

I watched her pull down the tree-lined drive, enjoying the feel of the sunlight on my face for a moment as I breathed in deeply the mixture of scents nature brewed under the warm sunshine—fragrant pines, musk sage, and the sweet tang of grape leaves drying on the vine.

Reluctantly, I went back inside, stopping in the kitchen to see if Conchita needed anything else as our tourist party wound down.

Only it wasn't Conchita I found in the kitchen, but my new recruit, Eddie.

And I almost had a heart attack when I saw what he was doing.

He had the Haut Brion in his hands, the foil at the neck cut and lying in a pile on the counter. A wine corker was in his left hand as he twisted and pulled with all his might.

"No!" I screamed.

Too late. The sickening sound of the cork popping as it released from the bottle echoed in the kitchen.

"No, no, no, no, NOOOOO!" I yelled, rushing toward him.

I stared in horror at the bottle of Haut Brion in Eddie's pudgy hands. The *open* bottle.

"Emmy?" Eddie asked, setting the bottle on the counter. "You okay?"

"What are you doing?" I cried.

He blinked at me. "What?"

"The bottle. Why did you open it!?"

More blinking. "I-uh, thought I was helping." He paused. "Am I not helping?"

"Noooo," I moaned, unable to keep my eyes off the cork sitting on the counter next to the Haut Brion.

"Jean Luc asked me to get another bottle from the cellar. I mean, this one does look kinda fancy, I guess, but we serve fancy wine to guests, right? Or, yeah, maybe no?"

His words flew over me in a blur, my thoughts consumed by how I was going to explain *this* to James Atherton when I had to write him a $1000 restitution check. *Gee, remember that bottle I accidentally stole after breaking into and entering your wife's storage unit? Yeah, now I've accidentally opened it.*

"You don't look so good, Emmy," Eddie told me. "Can I pour you a glass of wine?"

"No you can't pour me a glass—" I paused. What the heck? The damage had been done. "Fine. Pour."

It wasn't like I could just put the cork back and return it now. I might as well enjoy what a $1000 forty-year-old wine tasted like. And I could so use a drink right about now.

Eddie poured a generous amount in a glass for me and a small taste in a glass for himself.

"Here's to bad decisions," I told him, taking my glass from him.

"Huh?"

"Nothing," I mumbled, thinking I was going to have to give him a detailed tour of the cellar before our next tasting.

Moving the glass under my nose, I inhaled deeply. I detected floral notes, but they weren't as deep or strong as I might have guessed. I placed the glass to my lips, anticipating a glorious velvety texture hitting my palate.

I took a small sip.

And nearly spit it out. Bitter, acid liquid covered my mouth, practically burning as I managed to swallow it. "Ugh," I couldn't help saying.

"Thank goodness. I thought it was just me," Eddie said.

I looked up to find him pursing his lips together like he'd just sucked a lemon.

"It's maybe turned, huh?" he suggested. "Old wines sometimes go bad, right?"

I sniffed at the glass, swirling its contents. No legs ran down the glass—no trails of liquid slowly falling back down. While sitting in a storage unit hadn't done the wine any favors, something about the color as I tilted the glass and let the light filter through the wine was off. Too purpley and not enough ruby red. If it had simply oxidized and gone bad, the color would have a more rust hue.

"It tastes like..." I paused, daring to take another small sip again, cringing as the tangy bite rolled on my tongue.

"Like the stuff at my niece's wedding," Eddie finished.

I glanced up at him. "What?"

"Oh, my niece. She got married last month. Really good kid, but my brother is such a cheapskate. Plastic silverware, buffet meal, tiny little slivers of cake. And he wouldn't spring for anything over five dollars a bottle to drink. I mean, really? It's a wedding. Live a little. Am I right?"

But my mind was a million miles away from weddings right now as it latched on to that one keen observation—what was in my glass tasted like cheap wine.

And there was our connection.

Suddenly puzzle pieces started falling into place. The empty bottles in the storage unit. Why Heather was keeping everything so hush-hush from James. Heather hadn't cared about properly storing her wine bottles, because they weren't filled with rare, collectible wine—they were filled with Nifty Dollar-Fifty. Cheap wine supplied to her by Max Ford.

"Eddie, you are brilliant!" I told him, dumping the contents of my glass into the sink.

"I-I am?" he asked.

I picked up the cork from the counter. "Look at this cork," I said. "It's supposed to have been in this bottle since 1979. Does it look like it's been in contact with red wine that long?"

Eddie accepted the cork and studied it. "I-I don't know. I guess not. I mean, it looks pretty new to me."

"Exactly. Only no one would ever know that unless they opened this bottle. They'd never know it was filled with Nifty Dollar-Fifty!"

"Nifty...what?" Eddie asked, trying hard to keep up with me.

But I was lost in my own thoughts, on a high of having it all fall into place. "And collectors would never open these. They're investments. Or conversation pieces at best. And even if one did, he might just chalk the bad taste up to the wine having turned."

"Like I did!" Eddie said.

"Right. And I might have too, had I not had all the other clues staring me right in the face."

"So, why would someone fill nice bottles with bad wine?" Eddie asked.

"Money," I answered. "Heather was making boatloads of it by taking old empty bottles and filling them with new cheap wine. If I had to guess, they were corked and sealed at the Nifty Dollar-Fifty winery by the Man in Black."

Eddie frowned. "Johnny Cash?"

"Max Ford," I corrected. "He was in on it with Heather, probably splitting the profits when she sold them as the real deal to collectors."

I paused, processing the implications of Heather's scheme. If any of her collectors had found out she was selling them fake wine at real prices, I couldn't imagine they'd be too happy. Then again, there was her rough-around-the-edges partner, Max Ford. He had been seen arguing with her at the party. Maybe something had gone wrong with their scam? Or maybe Max was getting greedy, wanting a larger cut of Heather's profits to continue to keep quiet and supply her with cheap wine. Or maybe Heather was the one who'd gotten greedy, trying to cut Max out.

"So what do we do with this?" Eddie asked, gesturing to the open faux Haute Brion on the counter.

I stuffed the cork back in the top. "We take it to Detective Grant."

* * *

The Sonoma County Sheriff's Office was located about forty minutes north of the town of Sonoma, in a large, imposing building made of glass and brick. As I pushed through the glass front doors, the inhabitants of the building were just as imposing as the structure itself—both the officers in crisp uniforms, wearing gun holsters, as well as the tattooed, pierced, and angry looking visitors sitting on plastic chairs in the main lobby. The floor was polished concrete, and the walls were rendered cement that were covered with posters alerting me to the many organizations that I could turn to if I needed help.

The civilians were separated from the police force with a large counter and glass window, keeping them on the inside and me on the out. Two officers in khaki uniforms sat behind the desk. A young woman with a tight bun at the back of her neck was frantically clicking her computer mouse and scowling at her screen. Whatever she was attempting, it appeared her computer was not cooperating. The second officer was older, male, and honestly looked no happier about his position than his technology challenged coworker.

He watched me approach and slid back a small glass pane. "May I help you?" His tone was bored and anything but helpful.

"Hi," I said, suddenly feeling apprehensive now that I was in a police station about to confess to a theft. Granted, now that we were talking about a $1.50 bottle of wine, I was pretty sure we were back in misdemeanor territory. "I, uh, am here to see Detective Grant, VCI." I gave the officer a smile, hoping that I didn't look like a criminal.

"Is he expecting you?"

I shook my head. I'd tried to call before leaving the winery, but his number had gone to voicemail. And I didn't want to wait. This felt too important.

"What is this in regard to?"

"A murder investigation. I, uh, I have some evidence that I think he needs to see."

"Name?" he asked in the same monotone, as if people came in with evidence in murder investigations all day long.

"Emmy Oak."

"Take a seat Ms. Oak. I'll see if he's available."

I did as asked, choosing one of the hard plastic chairs that was closest to the counter. You know, just in case some of the other people waiting in there actually *were* criminals. I watched Officer Monotone pick up the phone and press a few buttons.

I searched for a magazine or something that would take my attention from the three large, bearded men sitting opposite me. Self-consciously I tugged on the hem of my skirt, hoping to make it at least two feet longer, but in the end I settled for the inch that I could get.

"Ms. Oak," the officer behind the counter called.

I jumped up and moved toward him.

"Detective Grant is out of the office. I can have the evidence clerk take whatever you have and hold it for him."

Which was not ideal, but it was better than nothing. I reluctantly waited for the evidence clerk and handed over the opened wine bottle with a message for Grant to call me ASAP. I wasn't sure he'd know what to do with the bottle without the explanation to go with it.

Thanking the officer, I made my way back through the lobby and immediately tried to call Grant again, just to make sure that he understood how important this was. Unfortunately, it rang a few times and then diverted to his voicemail. I redialed only to have the same thing happen again. I left a brief message to call me as soon as he got it.

My flats clicked softly against the polished concrete as I made my way toward the exit, and I'd just stepped outside when I heard a familiar voice call my name.

"Emmy!"

I turned to see Leah hailing me from the other side of the building. It looked like she'd just come from a side door, and she quickly jogged the distance between us, enveloping me in a hug that was so tight it almost knocked me over.

"Leah!" I cried, surprised. "What are you doing here? Are you okay?"

"Just had the bail hearing," she explained, drawing back. "I didn't think anyone would be here, but here you are."

I felt guilt creep into my cheeks. While I had meant to find out when her hearing was, I'd been here for an entirely different reason. "So you made bail?"

She nodded. "Barely." She paused. "I had to put the condo and the Chocolate Bar up as collateral."

I felt a pang of sympathy for her. I knew the shop was all she had left. Not that she was planning to skip town and lose it, but it still must have hurt to sign that paperwork.

"I'm so sorry," I told her.

She shook her head. "No, it's okay. I'm just happy to be going home."

"Come on. I'll give you a ride. My car's just down the street," I offered, sliding my phone into my bag before guiding her to my Jeep.

The sunlight settled on Leah's tired features, making her look much older as we walked the short distance.

"You okay?" I asked.

"Oh sure. Jail was like a day at the spa," she joked.

I grinned back, but I could tell she'd been through a lot. "Meet anyone interesting?"

"A lovely but unfortunate hooker named Denise?"

I laughed. "Sorry."

"Well, at least I'm not Denise. Denied bail."

"Ouch. They hold a prostitute and let a suspected murderer out on bail?" I cringed even as the words left my mouth, wishing I could just suck them right back into the den of insensitivity they'd escaped from. "Sorry."

"No, really, it's okay." Leah shrugged, smiling, though her eyes looked tired and far from filled with humor. "It's true. I'm going on trial for murder."

A sniff escaped her, and I grabbed her in another fierce hug before depositing her into my car.

"You mind if we stop by the Chocolate Bar first?" she asked, buckling in.

"Sure. Why?"

"I just wanted to check on the bakery cases. I have a bad feeling a lot of the food needs thrown out at this point, but I'd like to salvage what I can and freeze it."

"No problem," I told her, pulling out into traffic and making a U-turn at the light.

The Chocolate Bar wasn't far from the police station, so I wound the windows down and allowed the afternoon air to filter in. We rode in companionable silence for a few blocks before Leah finally broke it.

"Grant asked me about you," she said.

That took me by surprise. "Really? What did he say?"

"Just wanted to know how long I'd known you and Ava. Where we'd met. That kind of thing."

While there was a 99% chance it was all about the case, I felt my cheeks heating at the 1% possibility that he was just interested.

"He asked about the necklaces Ava gave us," Leah continued. "If you still have yours."

"I do," I told her. Unlike Leah, I hadn't immediately put mine on at the event. Guests had arrived, and I'd deposited it in my purse for safekeeping. After Leah's arrest, I'd been sure to check that my citrine was still in its home. It had been.

"Leah, how do you think your gemstone got on Heather's body?"

She sighed audibly in the interior. "I've had a lot of time to think about that."

"Come to any conclusions?" I asked, making a right at the light.

She shook her head. "Like I told Grant, I didn't realize the stone had fallen out until the end of the party. I could have dropped it anytime. Anywhere."

I glanced over at Leah. She was staring out the front window, her face blank. But her eyes kept cutting to me in a sideways motion. Almost as if making sure I was buying her story. Leah was lying.

"But you didn't drop it just anywhere." I paused, making an educated guess. "You dropped it on Heather's body."

Leah continued to stare straight ahead, but her breath came faster, and her eyes began to tear up.

"Leah?"

She sniffed loudly, a tear falling down her cheek. "Yes," she finally admitted. "I-I went outside to take the trash out as the party was winding down and…and I found her." She turned to me, her eyes big and full of watery tears. "But she was already dead! There was nothing I could have done for her."

"What did you do?" I asked softly, trying to keep my eyes on the road.

Leah took a shaky breath. "She was crumpled over. At first I thought maybe she just drank too much and passed out. Which, I found kind of amusing at the time." She gave me a dry smile.

"Go on."

"Well, I leaned down to rouse her. But as soon as I touched her, I knew something was wrong. She was cold and limp. And, that's when I saw…" She licked her lips, and I could tell she was envisioning the same bloody scene I'd come across. "Then I knew she was dead."

"Why didn't you tell anyone?" I asked.

"I-I panicked! I ran. I got almost to the end of the block before I came back to my senses. And then I realized I had some of her blood on my hands. I came back inside and went to the restroom to wash it off. By the time I came out, you were screaming that she was dead." Leah paused. "I-I figured it didn't matter at that point who had found her first."

"Did you tell all of this to Grant?" I asked

She shook her head. "What's the point? He wouldn't believe me now anyway."

"He might," I protested. "Look, just tell him the truth and…and…and we'll figure it out from there," I finished lamely. Honestly, I had no idea how to get her out of this jam any more than she did.

Thankfully, the Chocolate Bar came into view then, saving me from any more false comforting words, and I navigated the car to a stop in the alleyway behind it. By the time I had unlatched my seat belt and made my way around to Leah, she was already out and at the back door.

"It's so good to be home." She smiled, retrieving the key from her handbag.

Only she didn't need the key. As she slid it into the lock, the door swung open on its own.

Her eyes went to mine.

Someone else had gotten here first.

CHAPTER NINETEEN

———

In a heartbeat, I was standing beside her, the two of us surveying the mess that was her kitchen. Pots, pans, flour, and sugar all competed for floor space with broken plates, mugs, and glass. The freezer door had been left open so that the contents were spoiled. Recipe books were torn, and drawers were upturned.

Leah's gasp was audible, and horror froze in her eyes as she took it all in.

"Oh no," she whispered.

I had a few other choice words, but that about summed it up.

Shock settled in as I carefully stepped over the mess, glass shards crunching under my feet. Coming into the main room of the bakery, it was even worse.

Leah covered her mouth with her hand, making choked sobbing sounds as we took in the upended tables and broken chairs. Leah's chocolate creations were smeared across the counter, and coffee beans were tossed across the floor.

The scene was sickening, but what made my stomach churn the most was the word *murderer* spray painted in red across the wall.

"Who would do this?" Leah asked, her voice so quiet I almost couldn't hear her.

I had no idea, but what I did know was that we needed to call the police.

I took Leah's arm and led her back the way that we'd come, carefully stepping over the debris, not wanting to disturb anything. Once outside, I helped her to sit in the car and dialed 9-1-1 to report the crime.

"Why would someone do something so awful?" Leah asked, the shock wearing off as tears filled behind her lashes.

"The police will find them," I reassured her, squeezing her hand as I sat on hold with the dispatcher, waiting on the arrival of help.

"The Chocolate Bar is all I have," she cried, the tears quietly gliding over her cheeks and falling into her lap.

"You have me and Ava." I gave her a reassuring smile, but I wasn't sure she even saw it through her grief.

"This shop is the first thing that I did on my own without a husband to help me. Now it's destroyed."

"I'm sure it's not as bad as it looks," I soothed.

"Liar," she accused.

Guilty as charged. It looked bad and probably was.

I rubbed her shoulders, trying to be as comforting as I could. Which wasn't much, given the circumstances. I was grateful when we saw red and blue lights flashing against the wall of the Chocolate Bar as a patrol car pulled into the alleyway.

After we filled the two uniformed officers in on what we'd found, I placed an arm around Leah's shoulders, preventing her from following them into the shop. I knew Leah well enough to know that if she followed the police, she would be cleaning up the mess behind them. Just entering earlier had probably done enough damage, and I didn't want to take away from anything that might be useful in finding who had vandalized her shop.

After what seemed like forever, one of the officers came out and let us know they'd called forensics to come dust for prints. The lock had been jimmied open on the back door, but as it didn't appear anything was taken, he suspected average vandals.

I bit back a retort that there was nothing average about having your livelihood destroyed. Instead, since there was nothing else we could do there—clearly any baked goods in the shop were beyond salvaging now—I drove Leah home, practically carrying her weight as I helped her up her condo steps.

"Spencer is still with his dad?" I asked.

Leah nodded. "My mom is picking him up in a bit and bringing him home."

"Good. I'm sure he'll be excited to see you." Though, I thought it was good she had a little time to get herself together first. I'd never seen her look so frail and beaten down. I hoped the sight of her son would cheer her some.

"I, uh, I can make coffee?" Leah offered, gesturing inside the condo.

I was about to agree and offer to make it for her myself, but I was interrupted by the sound of my phone ringing from deep within my handbag.

"You go ahead. I'll just be a second, and then I'll be right behind you," I told her, fishing it out, hoping it was Grant getting back to me.

Only the name on my readout was not Grant but David Allen.

"Hello?" I answered.

"Hello yourself, Ems," came David's slow drawl on the other end. "How's my girl today?"

"I'm a grown woman. Not girl."

"Ouch. Touchy."

"And I'm not *your* girl."

"Did someone forget to take their princess pills today? Because you sound a bit on edge, babe."

I took a deep, cleansing breath. "What is it that you wanted, David?"

"It's not what I want, but what I can give you," he promised, his voice low.

"Please tell me this is not another euphemism."

His laugh was genuine on the other end. "No. I called to tell you that the photo you've been showing everyone? The one of the guy who looks like Johnny Cash?"

"What about it?"

"Well, the guy just showed up at the club."

Now he had my attention. "At the Links?"

"Yep. I'm certain it's him. Black shirt, black pants, cowboy hat. Nasty little scar. It's your guy."

"I'm on my way."

* * *

By the time that I had hung up the call, Leah had made her way up the stairs and had disappeared into her apartment. I didn't like the idea of leaving her alone, so I quickly called Ava, who said she'd come sit with her until Leah's mom and Spencer arrived. I relayed the offer to Leah, leaving out the minor detail of whom I was rushing off to meet, and jumped into my car, hoping that whatever Max Ford was doing at the Links, it kept him there for a few more minutes.

By the time I arrived at the Links, late afternoon was now making its way toward evening, and the heat of the day was finally dissipating. After signing Byron's guest book again, I texted David, who responded right away saying he was on the south lawn, where an evening cocktail party was in full swing.

After asking Byron for directions, I followed a corridor down the length of the main building, ending in a pathway that was flanked by flowering shrubs and subtle uplights. Sounds of the party floated toward me as I neared the open lawn—glasses clinking, soft laughter, the smooth strains of jazz music being piped in through hidden speakers.

As I neared the party, I could tell the group was generous in size, a large sign above reading *Wine Country Invitational Mixer.* Though the attire appeared to be casual summer cocktail wear, I still felt I stood out a bit in my T-shirt. I tried not to be self-conscious as I did my best to look like I belonged there, accepting a glass of champagne from a passing waiter. The twinkling lights strung above us danced in the evening breeze, and the sunset cast a pink glow, bathing everyone in a flattering light. If I hadn't been looking for a murderer, then I would have enjoyed the occasion. Instead I was scanning every face for the Man in Black.

But it was another familiar voice that came hot and angry in my ear.

"What are you doing here?" James Atherton demanded.

I spun to face him, finding a scowl on his features, his mouth drawn into a thin, angry line.

"Enjoying the champagne," I told him, raising my glass as evidence.

The frown deepened. "What is it about me that you are so obsessed with?" he hissed.

"You?" I tried not to laugh. "I'm not here for you."

"You show up at my office under false pretenses, you follow me to play golf—"

"I did not follow you," I protested, though it fell on deaf ears as he continued.

"—and then you try to plant evidence on me and stalk me here at this cocktail party!"

I shook my head. "I'm here as a guest. I have no interest in you." Which wasn't 100% true if he had, indeed, killed his wife, but at the moment he wasn't my immediate prey.

"You don't belong here," he said, pointing a finger in my face.

I glanced around, hoping we weren't making a scene, but no one was paying attention.

"I-I have every right to be here. I'm a guest—" I started.

But James took a menacing step forward, cutting me off. "And you'll always be a *guest* in this town. You and your pathetic little winery. You're a side note, you know that? Just waiting to be crushed by the main story."

He was drunk. The anger I'd seen carefully masked by the slick salesman in my previous encounters with him was unleashed and on full display. And it was intense enough that I felt myself involuntarily taking a step back, wondering exactly what that unfettered anger might do if we were alone together in a dark alley and not in the midst of a well-lit civilized party.

"Is there a problem?" David Allen was suddenly at my side, his height looming over me.

I'd never been so glad to see him in my life.

James's eyes went from David to me, contemplating how much of a problem I was and just how much of a problem he wanted with David. Finally some bit of good sense must have made its way through the alcohol and anger, as he shook his head.

"No, no problem. As long as she"—James pointed that finger my way again—"stays away from me."

"Gladly," I shot back as James spun and threaded back through the crowd to the bar.

As soon as he'd put some distance between us, I took a couple of deep breaths to calm my suddenly too-high pulse.

"What was that about?" David asked.

I noticed he'd stuck with his casual, nonconforming artist look this evening, opting for jeans, Vans, and a dark sweater rolled at the sleeves. I thought I detected a faint hint of marijuana coming off him as he stood protectively close to me still.

"Nothing," I said, trying to shake the whole incident off. "He's just on edge."

David raised one dark eyebrow my way. "'Guilt is the rope that wears thin.'"

"Poe?" I guessed at the quotation.

He shook his head. "Ayn Rand."

He never ceased to surprise me.

"So where is Max Ford?" I asked, refocusing on my reason for being here.

"Ford?" he asked.

"The Man in Black," I added.

"Ah. Well, last I saw him was over by the bar."

I scanned the area now, though I saw no sign of him. In fact, during my argument with James, the size of the crowd seemed to have doubled, making it harder to pick out any particular faces in the crowd.

"So we have a name for our mysterious cowboy now?" David asked, grabbing himself a champagne glass from a passing tray as we walked through the minglers.

I nodded and quickly filled David in on what Ava and I had found out about the man and my unintentional stumble onto what he and Heather had going on. "My best guess is that he and Heather were partners of some sort."

David nodded. "That's quite a racket they had going on."

"Puts yours to shame, huh?"

"No need to insult me," he said with grin. "So what do we think the esteemed purveyor of Nifty Dollar-Fifty is doing here?"

I'd had some time to wonder the same thing on the drive to the club. "Heather must have been the face of the business to buyers—Ford made the product, and Heather sold it. Only now

Heather is gone, and Ford is left with a bunch of his fake inventory to unload."

"So you think he's trying to sell it here himself?"

I nodded. "Why not? It worked for Heather. All Ford would have to do is make the right connections."

"And this would be the place to do it," David mused. "Especially if he already had Heather's client list."

"Let's face it, if he's not above fraud, he's not above crashing a country club party."

"It's a good theory," David told me. "If you can prove it."

Which meant we had to find Ford first. "Look, let's split up," I suggested. "Text me if you see Max Ford, okay?"

He nodded. "I aim to do your bidding, my lady." He raised his champagne glass my way then disappeared into the crowd.

I declined canapés from a passing tray and tried to keep an eye out for any sign of a cowboy hat. I ambled around the south lawn, smiling at people I recognized and pretending to enjoy the festivities.

I noticed that Cole was once again on the job, whispering something into a middle-aged woman's ear that had her giggling more like a middle schooler. I had to admit, he was very good at what he did. The woman looked thoroughly smitten, his grin was disarming, and his hand roamed to places it shouldn't, considering many husbands were in viewing distance. But he was discreet, only touching the woman briefly. If I hadn't known what his side business was, I would have just considered him a harmless flirt.

I moved on, and I spied Jennifer Foxton in another power suit—this one a tasteful navy for an evening event— standing next to an older man with a full head of white hair. He was in a dark suit himself, and his bright veneer-filled smile dazzled even from where I stood. With the way Jennifer was beaming up at him and hanging on his arm, I figured him to be the famous Senator Jonathon Foxton. I watched the power couple for a moment as he worked the crowd, shaking hands, smiling, nodding in feigned interest. I had a feeling he'd go far as a politician.

After making a full circle of the partygoers, I was beginning to think that if Max Ford had been there, he was gone now. I found Caroline Danvers at the bar, looking slightly unsteady as her eyes followed Cole from woman to woman. I hoped the bartender was keeping track of her alcohol consumption that evening, because the look in her eyes threatened another fist fight if Cole didn't watch himself. I was about to approach her and ask if she'd seen the Man in Black, when I spotted something that stopped me in my tracks.

A black cowboy hat.

I scooted around a couple sipping red wine to get a better look. He was chatting with an Asian man I didn't recognize. Though, from the cut of his suit and the gleam on his Bruno Magli loafers, I could guess he was a member of the club and not a party crasher like Ford. Or me.

Ford leaned down, saying something in low tones that seemed to impress the other man. Then he put a hand on the guy's shoulder, leading him away from the crowd.

On impulse, I followed.

Keeping close to the manicured hedges, I grabbed my phone and put it to my ear, keeping my demeanor nonchalant so that any onlooker would just think I was chatting to a friend. I kept an eye on the men as they moved toward the fairway. Ford's hands were gesticulating as he excitedly spoke, and the other man nodded enthusiastically. I felt hope lift in my chest that my theory was right—Ford was looking for a buyer for his fake rare wines. And it looked like maybe he'd just found one.

I lowered my phone and sent a quick text to David that I'd found my guy. The two moved farther from the crowd, and I did an eeny meeny miny moe about following. The last thing I wanted to do was be alone in the dark with Ford, who I was reasonably sure now had killed Heather. But on the other hand, I wasn't really alone. The other guy was there too, and I doubted Ford would kill me in front of a prospective client. And proof that he *was* a prospective client would go a long way toward convincing Grant that my theory was correct.

I kept to the shadows and continued to tail the two until they stopped below a small grouping of trees situated about a hundred yards away from the cocktail party. Ford's head was lowered, and he scanned the area as he spoke. Probably to make sure he hadn't been followed. Good instincts.

Moisture from the lawn licked up at my ballet flats as I tiptoed closer, staying as low as I could to avoid being seen. Sounds from the party faded into the distance as I neared the pair, hoping to catch some snippets of their conversation.

"...business...friend at the club...broker..."

I was catching every few words, but it wasn't quite enough to pull it all together.

I took a few steps closer, keeping close to the shadows as I swiped the video app open on my phone. I was just about to hit *Record*, when I heard sound behind me.

I spun.

Too late.

Stars danced behind my eyes as something large and heavy connected with my head. I felt my phone slipping from my fingers, the wet ground rushing up to meet me.

Then everything went black.

CHAPTER TWENTY

———

Cool grass tickled my ankles, a dampness had sunk into the seat of my skirt, and my arms were being stretched above my head so far that my shoulders ached in protest. I blinked, my vision fuzzy and my mouth dry. The green grass of the golf course seemed to span forever around me as pale moonlight illuminated the fairway. I heard grunting behind me. I blinked, my body taking a moment to focus and realize what was happening. Someone had both my arms and was dragging me across the lawn.

I twisted my head, but at that angle all I could see was a shadowy figure.

Who must have realized I was conscious again, as I was unceremoniously dropped onto the grass, my head hitting the ground with a jarring thud.

"Good. You're awake. You can walk."

I blinked toward the voice, trying to make out features as the person stepped around to face me.

I felt confusion mix with the dull hammering of pain in my head as I took in the features hovering over me.

"Jennifer?" I asked.

She smiled, showing off a row of white teeth that gleamed in the moonlight. "So you're awake *and* coherent."

Sort of. I still had no idea where I was or how I'd gotten there.

But as Jennifer Foxton pulled a shiny silver gun from the Louis Vuitton handbag slung over her shoulder, one thing became clear—I was in serious danger.

"Get up," she ordered.

I swallowed, willing my body to comply as I slowly peeled myself off the ground, swaying only slightly with dizziness as I stood.

"W-what's going on?" I asked, unable to tear my gaze from the gun.

"I'm tidying up," she answered, her voice hard and devoid of emotion. "Move," she commanded, motioning to her left with the gun.

I glanced around, hoping to find Max Ford and his companion nearby. No such luck. In fact, I didn't see any other warm bodies around. It seemed while I was out, Jennifer had pulled me far onto the green. I could hear the faint sound of the party still going in the distance, the lights from the main building distinguishable on the horizon. I wanted to scream for help, hoping to get their attention, but I knew they were much too far away to hear. I'd be a goner before anyone could get to me.

With little choice, I slowly moved in the direction Jennifer indicated. Panic heightened my senses as I felt the cool grass against my toes and caught the light evening breeze bringing the scent of Jennifer's Chanel No. 5 toward me. "Where are we going?" I asked.

"Somewhere no one will hear us," she said simply.

I licked my lips. "You mean, hear you shoot me?" I squeaked out.

"Oh, you are a clever little pain in the rear, aren't you?"

Not so much. In fact, my not-so-clever little brain was whirling, trying to figure out why the socialite had a gun on me. "You killed Heather?" I surmised.

"Of course I did," she stated simply again. Almost as if discussing her manicure or the price of caviar. "She had to be stopped."

"Stopped from what?" I asked. Not that it really mattered now. What mattered was keeping Jennifer talking until some groundskeeper or caddie sneaking a couple rounds in at night found us. The farther we walked from the clubhouse, the more distant that hope was becoming, but I clung to it with all my might.

Jennifer sighed in answer to my question. "I know someone like you wouldn't understand," she reasoned. "But my husband is about to be elected to Washington. *DC*," she added for emphasis. "John has worked hard all his life for this. He deserves a place in the senate. And then…who knows? Maybe even the White House one day."

That was some fancy dreaming. But what I didn't get was what it had to do with Heather's murder. "I still don't understand. Where does Heather come into that?"

I slowed, looking back at Jennifer.

Her eyes had taken on a dilated look that betrayed the mania bubbling just below her calm surface. "You know what Heather was doing, don't you?"

I paused. "The fake wine?"

She let out a laugh, her lips curling into a sneer. "I knew you knew too much."

Oops. Me and my big mouth. "Was the senator involved in her wine scheme somehow?" I asked.

"Of course not!" she spat out, anger suddenly transforming her features. "How dare you even suggest such a thing!"

I held up my hands in a surrender motion as the gun bobbed close to me. "Sorry. I-I'm just trying to understand."

"Well, understand this—without me, Heather would have been nothing. You know she was a cocktail waitress when James met her?" she scoffed. "Trash. *I* made her into Heather Atherton. *I* introduced her to all the right people, vouched for her character, sponsored her to society."

"All those right people…who Heather then sold wine to," I said, the picture becoming clearer.

Jennifer's mouth went into a thin, hard line. "Yes."

"Fake wine. You vouched for someone who was bilking your friends for thousands of dollars."

"That greedy, ungrateful thing," Jennifer went on. "How shortsighted and stupid could she be? One little thing like that and you're in the midst of a scandal. You *cannot* have that kind of thing follow you to Washington. You have to be above reproach. It would have ruined John."

I could think of a few current politicians in Washington who were well below the reproach line, but I didn't argue. "You were afraid someone would find out what Heather was doing and blame you?" I clarified.

"How would that have looked for John?" she asked. "*I* have to be above reproach. And good heavens, think of the disaster it would be to his fundraising! You think any of those people would contribute to his campaign after that? We would be ruined. But did she care?"

I was guessing not, but I didn't answer, letting Jennifer go on with her tirade.

"This was all just temporary for her," she said, sweeping her arms in a wide gesture that encompassed the entirety of the golf club and momentarily took the gun off me. She must have noticed her mistake, as she quickly straight armed it back, the shiny muzzle pointing right at my heart.

Which might have stopped beating for a second.

"Temporary? So she *was* planning to leave James?" I said, honestly pretty impressed I could even find my voice. I was having a hard time remembering to just breathe as I stared down the handgun.

"Yes," Jennifer confirmed. "She was playing him. Using him. Using me! She didn't even care if she got caught. She was milking our crowd for all they were worth. Then she planned to leave town with the proceeds."

"Tucked away in the Cayman Islands," I mused.

Jennifer narrowed her eyes. "What? How did you know that?"

I shrugged off the minor details. "Lucky guess. And Heather told you all of this?"

Jennifer sucked in her already thin cheeks, seemingly contemplating how much to tell me. But considering she was walking me on a slow hike to my death, she must have decided to indulge me.

"Not at first, no. Cole let something slip."

"Cole?" I asked.

"The man has this thing for pillow talk," she said, waving the idea off as ridiculously romantic.

I paused. "So *you* were sleeping with him too?"

Jennifer laughed. "Wasn't everyone?"

I guess they pretty much were. Eww.

"What did he say?" I asked. Though, in all honesty, I was less interested in the golf pro's pillow talk than in keeping *her* talking while I conjured up some escape route from thin air. I glanced to my left—lots of well-tended lawn, a small pond, a sand trap. To the right—more flat lawn. No buildings, no trees. Great for making sure your ball didn't encounter obstacles but terrible for trying to hide from a murderer with a gun.

"What did Cole tell me?" Jennifer went on. "Just that Heather had mentioned leaving James. Which I thought was ridiculous—we all know they had a prenup and she'd get nothing. Heather was too used to the lifestyle to leave it."

"So you knew she had to have money put aside," I said.

She nodded. "That's when I started asking around about how much business she was doing. You know the definition of *rare* wines is that there aren't very many of them. And yet, it turned out that this amateur was finding them hand over fist. I wondered how she could get her hands on so many bottles so quickly. So, I did some digging of my own. I followed her to find out what she was up to."

"Where did she go?" I asked.

"Dixons."

I frowned. "But she didn't get her wine from there," I said, genuinely confused.

"Didn't she?" Jennifer raised an eyebrow my way, a smile creeping along her lips that said she knew something I didn't.

I thought back to the notes on Heather's inventory list. They'd all said Dixons, but I knew for a fact that none of the bottles had gone through there. However, I had seen Max Ford pulling out of their parking lot...

"I can see you're trying to put it together," Jennifer said, almost gloating that she'd figured it out faster.

In my defense, she hadn't just been knocked unconscious and had a gun pointed at her.

"So help me out. What did you see at Dixons?"

She smirked. "Her partner."

"The Man in Black."

She blinked at me. "Who?"

"Max Ford."

"Ah." She nodded. "Yes, I saw Heather meeting up with that cretin in the parking lot of the auction house. He was handing off a case of full counterfeit wine bottles. They were only using Dixons as a drop off point. Great cover, really, if anyone ever saw Heather there. It would just look like she was picking up bottles she'd bought in an auction." She paused. "She wasn't stupid, I'll give her that. And it really was quite the clever little scheme."

"What tipped you off that the bottles were fake?" I asked.

She smiled. "The empty bottles I saw when I looked in her trunk the next day. I borrowed her keys while she was having a 'lesson' with Cole," she went on, doing air quotes with one hand, "and took a peek in her trunk. I just wanted to see what sort of bottles she was moving. Imagine my surprise when I found not only the case Ford had handed off to her but another case of old empty bottles. I put two and two together, and they added up to Heather passing off fakes."

"Did she know you were on to her?"

Jennifer frowned. "Of course not," she said, as if I'd insulted her intelligence. "She didn't have the slightest clue that I knew until the night of the Wine and Chocolate party."

"Where you confronted her?"

"She was getting sloppy," she said, her voice going louder, hinting at emotion.

"Oh?" I asked, my eyes darting to the green behind me. I could just make out a gathering of trees several yards to our left. If I could get to that for cover, I might be able to attract enough attention for help to come...

"Yes, sloppy," Jennifer went on. "That partner of hers showed up at the party. I mean, she couldn't even keep him in check?"

"He argued with Heather there," I said, retelling what I'd heard from Caroline.

"He approached her, and I told them to take the discussion outside. People might start to stare."

"What was the discussion about?"

Jennifer frowned at me. "Well, I don't know. What would I care?"

I mentally rolled my eyes.

"All I cared about was that she was going to get caught. Someone was going to find out. And I told her as much as soon as that man left."

"And what did she say?"

Jennifer's expression went cold and dark. "She laughed and said she didn't care. That by the time anyone figured it out, she'd be on a tropical island spending their cash." Her eyes cut to mine. "And I'd be left holding the bag as the scandal broke." She practically snarled that last bit out, looking more animal than human in the dark shadows.

I swallowed hard. Jennifer had always struck me as slim and slight, but with the menacing edge to her voice and the predatory gleam in her eyes, I realized she was stronger than I'd given her credit for. More dangerous.

"I couldn't have that," Jennifer went on. "You understand. Imagine what that would do to my husband's campaign? Elections are in November!"

"So you killed her?"

"I couldn't afford for a scandal like that to kill the dreams that my John and I have worked so hard for. So I saw an opportunity, and I took it."

"The cake knife," I surmised.

She nodded. "Who better to kill the pretty new wife than the jealous old one? I slipped it into my handbag when no one was looking. Then I told Heather that odious man was outside again, waiting for her in the alleyway. Of course, she believed me. I followed behind her, and it was just too easy to end it all right there."

I felt nausea in my stomach, reliving the scene I'd found that night. Thinking that this polished woman in front of me had been the one to create it.

"You framed Leah," I said, anger starting to mix with the cocktail of fear that was already brewing in my belly.

Jennifer shrugged. "It wasn't all that hard. I mean, the woman practically framed herself. The fight at the club, the way she was avoiding Heather all evening."

"Did you vandalize the Chocolate Bar too?" I asked.

"Oh God no."

Well, at least there was that.

"I had a couple of teenage caddies do it."

Of course. "But why?" I asked.

"That woman was let out on bail. I had to keep the police focused on her and not the club." She paused. "You know that detective had the gall to actually question members here? On club grounds? I don't even know how they let him in."

I thought it probably had to do with his badge and gun, but I didn't think now was the time to point that out.

"Of course, then they let *you* in too, didn't they," she added.

"I'm a guest of a member," I squeaked out. Why did everyone have such a hard time believing I should be there?

She just snorted back. "And you just had to keep picking at Heather's death, didn't you? Had to go asking questions, waving that picture of that man around to anyone who would stand still."

"Sorry?" I tried on. But I didn't think it was very convincing.

"Yes, me too. I'm sorry you didn't just leave it alone. Sorry you had to keep digging. Sorry you had to show up here tonight."

So was I. More than she knew. I glanced around. No magical escape route had suddenly opened up. No weapons appeared from nowhere, no flash of inspiration from the sky. I was on my own.

And I was running out of time, I realized as Jennifer took a step forward, her perfect pointy-toed pumps sinking into the freshly watered ground.

"And now, you need to disappear," she decided. "Move."

"What are you going to do?" I asked as she prodded me on, walking me farther from the main building.

"I'm not going to do anything. You are going to trip into the pond and drown."

"And if I don't want to trip?" I asked, the bravado in the words sounding false even to my own ears.

"Then I'll shoot you."

Okay, at least drowning gave me options.

My mind buzzed between the confession she'd just made, the murky water awaiting me, and anything that possibly stood between me and it to prevent my "trip" as we walked silently across the grass toward the ninth hole pond. The evening song of the crickets competed with the drumming of my heart, which pounded like mad in my ears. As we rounded the sand trap, moonlight trailed across the surface of the small pond, guiding the way to my apparent death.

"Get in," Jennifer commanded.

"I-in there?" I asked, looking at the dark muddy water.

"Yes."

"But it's gross," I protested. Yes, I was totally stalling. Because I thought I had seen a flash of something across the lawn. It was low to the ground and could have just been a shadow or light playing across the green as a cloud rolled over the moon.

"Are you kidding me with this?" Jennifer said, clearly at her wit's end. "You'll only feel it for a second. Then you'll be dead."

I pursed my lips. "But it looks really cold," I said. No, it was definitely not a shadow. I saw it again. A figure moving low across the grass in the darkness. I felt the tiniest bubble of hope in my chest, even as I reminded myself it was more likely a raccoon than the cavalry.

"Oh for goodness' sake, fine. I'll just shoot you," Jennifer decided.

I swallowed hard as my attention shifted to the gun in her hand. I heard my breath in my ears, felt my heart beating inside my rib cage as the shiny metal gleamed in the soft light. I should have seen my life flash before my eyes, but honestly my mind was a total blank. Every thought I had, every muscle in my body, all focused on that gun barrel.

A scuffling noise sounded in the distance to the right.

Jennifer heard it too, her eyes flitting from me to the sound.

Which was all the invitation I needed.

I shot forward, tackling Jennifer in the middle. I heard a loud scream, which, in hindsight, might have come from me, as we both fell to the ground and the gun went off. The loud crack of the shot cut through the stillness of the night like thunder.

Jennifer cursed, grabbing a handful of my hair with her free hand. I cried out, gripping her right arm and slamming it into the ground over and over until the gun broke free from her grip.

I dove for it at the same time Jennifer did, our hands colliding and pushing it down the muddy banks of the pond and into the murky waters.

"Look what you've done!" she cried, her anger coming out in a primal scream as she jumped on my back, flattening me to the ground.

The taste of grass filled my mouth as I spat out a wad of it. I bucked up, pushing her off me.

"This is not how it's supposed to happen!" she screeched, her eyes big and wild.

I tried to stand, but Jennifer was quicker. She grabbed another handful of my hair and dragged me toward the lake on my hands and knees. I was crawling at an intense pace, stuck between holding my scalp, trying to keep up, and listening to Jennifer yell obscenities. She only stopped dragging as my knees hit the water.

I tried to get my feet under me, but she jumped on my shoulders, forcing my face into the murky pond. Inhaling a lungful of water, I panicked, kicking out and using my hands to try to get her off me.

My face hit the muddy bottom, and time stood still. Everything moved in slow motion as oxygen became limited and she held my head down. The light from the moon above permeated the dirt suspended in the water around me, and reeds slowly danced against my cheeks. My chest squeezed with panic, and tears stung as I became lightheaded. My hands stilled and my mind slowed.

I couldn't die like this. I still had so much to do. I had to let Grant know that Jennifer was the killer. I had to save the winery. I had to make my father proud. I had to be there for my mother.

Finding a renewed strength from some forgotten store, I pushed my hands into the dirt and forced myself up, gasping for much needed air. Jennifer tried to push me back, but I rolled over, forcing her into the water, splashing and cursing. As she tried to gain her footing, I clawed my way back to the grass, gasping as I got my feet under me.

And ran.

Jennifer was a second behind me, sloshing from the pond as I took off toward the lights of the clubhouse. My breath was loud in my ears, my ankle throbbed, and my lungs screamed for air. I heard Jennifer behind me, getting closer with every step. I had no plan. I was running blindly, praying I got to someone before she got to me.

Only she was closing in fast. I could almost feel her breath behind me as we neared the outcropping of trees I'd spied before the hole. She was gaining distance. No way was I going to make it to the clubhouse.

Digging deep, I propelled my feet forward, picking up speed.

Which would have been helpful if my foot hadn't caught on a fallen branch.

I launched forward, hands splayed in front of me as I fell to the ground.

Jennifer was a step behind me. She'd be on top of me in a split second.

Without thinking, I grabbed the fallen branch, turned, and swung as hard as I could, channeling my one-season stint on the girls' pony softball league in sixth grade.

I heard the crack as the branch connected with Jennifer's face, and she fell to the ground, silent.

CHAPTER TWENTY-ONE

My breath came in hard pants. Adrenaline that had kept me alive faded, leaving me suddenly too weak to hold the branch up anymore.

The sound that had diverted Jennifer's attention emerged from the darkness as I stood staring at her prone form.

"Emmy!"

I looked up to find David Allen running toward me. I could have kissed the idiot.

"Are you okay?" he asked, stopping just short of me, eyes going from my grass stained clothes, to my wet hair, which I was sure was embedded with chunks of dirt, to Jennifer Foxton, lying bleeding on the ground, her nose at a slightly crooked angle.

I shook my head. "No. Not okay."

"Ems." He took my hand, squeezing hard. I could see some of the fear still coursing through me mirrored in his eyes, and I decided maybe David Allen wasn't such a bad friend to have at the club after all.

"Wow, remind me never to cross you," he said, eyes going to Jennifer again.

I swallowed hard. "Is she dead?" I asked, still hearing the fear in my voice.

He let go of my hand and leaned down, feeling for a pulse. "She's breathing," he decided. "What happened?"

"She tried to drown me. She killed Heather."

He raised an eyebrow my way. "Whoa."

"How did you find us?" I asked.

"I got your text about the Man in Black, but I didn't see you anywhere near him. I tried to text you, but you didn't answer, and I got worried. Caroline Danvers said she saw you take off toward the fairway, so I came looking."

I shuddered to think what might have happened if he hadn't.

"We need to get help," I said. I'd lost my handbag and phone when Jennifer hit me. I glanced toward the main building, wondering if I had it in me to crawl there.

But as if magically summoned, I spied a figure running toward me through the darkness. For a moment I thought maybe I'd been concussed again and was hallucinating.

"Emmy!"

I squinted toward the figure. Was that Grant's voice I heard?

"Emmy!" Within seconds the figure reached me, and I was engulfed in warmth as
Grant pulled me into his arms. His strong hands came around my back and pulled me close, so close I could feel his heartbeat through his shirt. His lips rested on the top of my head, and his breath whispered over me.

I wanted to be a strong woman, one who didn't need a man, but his arms holding me tight undid me, and I collapsed against him. His embrace was warm. Strong. And tight enough that it felt like it could keep me safe from anything—even homicidal socialites.

Suddenly two security guards appeared from nowhere, one dropping to his knees to assess Jennifer, and another calling for an ambulance. I heard David Allen filling them in, voices over the security guard's radio, and several more sets of feet pounding toward us from the main building.

But I tuned it all out, the only sound that mattered the steady, comforting beat of Grant's heart against my cheek.

"You're safe now," he whispered softly. "You're safe."

"How did you find me?" I asked as Grant finally pulled back.

"I got your message," he said. "It sounded urgent, but you weren't answering your phone. So, I tried your partner in crime."

"Ava?"

He nodded. "She told me you were going to the golf club. Apparently she'd been trying to call you as well, with no answer, and she was worried. I arrived just..." He paused, his jaw tensing. "Just as I heard a gunshot."

It felt like hours had passed since that moment, but in reality it had probably all happened in a matter of a couple of minutes. "I grabbed her gun away," I explained.

Despite the tightly reined emotion in his eyes, the corner of Grant's mouth curved upward. "You're one tough chick."

I smiled, though I could feel the emotions I'd been holding at bay all evening starting to leak from my eyes. "Not that tough. I almost peed my pants when I saw the gun," I confessed.

He laughed, pulling me in close again. As the rumble in his chest died down, I looked up and could see the hazel flecks dancing in his eyes in the moonlight as they stared down into mine. "You scared me," he whispered, his deep voice husky and low.

I licked my lips. I had a feeling Grant didn't do scared very often. Let alone admit to it. "I scared me too," I added.

He sighed, and I could tell he was about to say something more, but paramedics arrived then, and Grant handed me off to be treated. Uniformed officers followed the EMTs, and suddenly the entire fairway was swarming with law enforcement.

After a thorough exam, the paramedics finally declared that I had a good bump on the head and possibly some water in my lungs, but I'd live.

There had been a moment that evening when that had seemed like an impossibility.

Somehow during the arrival of police, David Allen had drifted away into the night. I didn't blame him. He didn't have the best record with law enforcement. Though, I had wanted to thank him for saving my life. If it hadn't been for him coming to look for me, I might have been at the bottom of the ninth hole pond by now.

"It looks like I'm going to be tied up here for a bit," Grant told me, suddenly at my side again. "I'll have one of the officers drive you home."

I nodded. Home sounded like the best place I'd ever been in my life.

* * *

The sun was high in the sky and streaming in through the open curtains when I opened my eyes. While sleep had come in restless fits of visions of Jennifer's gun and the taste of fear that the bottom of that pond had instilled in me, exhaustion had finally won over, and I'd slept in late. Later than I remembered doing in recent years, I decided as I looked at my bedside clock telling me it was closing in on noon.

I dragged my body from the bed, every muscle aching as if I'd run a marathon the day before. But the hot water of the shower helped work out some of the kinks, and by the time I'd thrown on a pair of sweats, a comfy gray sweater, and my favorite worn-in Ugg boots, I felt almost human again.

I left my cottage, heading toward the scents of coffee coming from the kitchen. Though, as soon as I got there, I knew a calm, quiet cup of coffee was out of the question. Conchita, Eddie, and Ava were all huddled around Ava's electronic tablet. As soon as I stepped into the room, heads lifted and a cacophony of voices erupted.

"Ay, my baby!" Conchita cried, crushing me to her ample bosom in a fierce hug.

"I'm okay," I mumbled into her breasts before she let me go.

"Curtis and I couldn't believe the news this morning," Eddie said, his perma-smile beaming at me over a cup of steaming something. "I mean, you've had quite a night, huh, Boss?"

"Forget night—she's had a week!" Ava said, grabbing me in another hug.

"Coffee," I pleaded with her shoulder as she crushed me to her. "I need coffee."

Eddie complied, handing a steaming mug to me. Conchita pulled out eggs and brioche to make her famous French toast, and Ava read the latest news from her tablet.

Jennifer had been arrested, and as of the latest edition of the *Sonoma Index-Tribune*, she was conscious and expected to make a full recovery. Though, the prison system probably didn't have plastic surgeons on hand to straighten out that broken nose to country club standards.

Senator Foxton had given no comment to the press about his wife, though he had already officially withdrawn himself from the November ballot. Apparently murder was even more of a career killing scandal than fake wine.

James Atherton had admitted to reporter Bradley Wu to being shocked to find out what his wife had been up to, though how much he knew about her Cayman Islands account, I still wondered. There was no mention of the money in Bradley's blog, and I silently wondered if James would be able to keep it. It was in an offshore account, making it darn difficult for the authorities to get their hands on it. I only hoped James used it for a good cause—like possibly helping Leah put the Chocolate Bar back together. I wondered, as I sipped my coffee, if another visit to his office and a promise to keep my lips sealed about the account might tip the scales in her favor.

Speaking of Leah, according to an official statement by the district attorney's office, all charges against her had been formally dropped, and she was a free woman now. I had a feeling it was going to be a while before she fully recovered from the ordeal, but at least she and Spencer could start rebuilding their new life together. Ava even told me she was planning to help Leah paint a mural over the vandalism on the wall at the Chocolate Bar that weekend.

Ava also said she'd talked to her Links friend Byron, who said Caroline Danvers had been back at the club bright and early that morning to head the gossip mill. From what he'd overheard, Caroline claimed she'd "always known" there was something a bit off about Jennifer and that she'd "highly suspected" that Heather had been up to something illegal. I barely restrained my eye roll at how insightful she was in hindsight. Though in all honesty, if she hadn't come to me about the Man in Black in the first place, it was quite possible Jennifer Foxton could have gotten away with murder, and dozens of the

Links club elite would be still proudly displaying bottles of Nifty Dollar-Fifty in their wine cellars.

Luckily, my part in all of it had been downplayed by the press, though as I checked my voice messages while I finished off a second helping of French toast, I noticed quite a few calls from past clients who'd seen my name in the paper, which had reminded them how lovely our winery was. Two requested event bookings, and another wanted to order several cases of wine for a corporate event. So, I guessed there was an upside to almost being drowned on a golf course by a senator's wife.

After completely gorging ourselves on French toast and downing at least three cups of coffee each, Ava finally said she had to get back to the shop but promised to check in on me later. Conchita tried to stuff one more helping into me, but I staved her off with a promise that I was full up with comfort food and feeling much better. I gave Eddie the rest of the day off to go give Curtis all the inside dirt, and I declared I was taking a Meg Ryan day and binging as many nineties rom coms in a row as I could.

Which I did, snuggling under my favorite afghan, which my grandmother had crocheted, as I watched Meg fall in love with Tom Hanks, Alec Baldwin, Andy Garcia, and Tom Hanks again. I was just cuing up Kevin Kline, when a knock sounded at my door, which I took for Ava making good on her promise.

"Come on in," I called from the sofa. "I'm just getting ready to *French Kiss*."

"That's good to know," a deep, husky voice returned as Detective Christopher Grant walked into my cottage.

"Oh. It's you," I said. Heat suddenly infused my cheeks at how that last statement could have been misconstrued.

"Well, don't sound so excited," he joked.

I shook my head. "No, I-I just thought it was Ava." I shot him a sheepish smile, keenly aware I was in sweats and sans makeup today.

A smile he returned, clearly amused by me. "I, uh, don't mean to interrupt," he said, gesturing to my afghan and booty-dented sofa.

I felt my blush deepen. "No, it's fine. I was just…taking a Meg Ryan day. What's up?"

He grinned again, even if the meaning was somewhat lost on him. "I just wanted to see for myself that you were doing alright," he said, his footsteps soft on the area rug as he crossed the room.

The concern in his voice swept over me like a blanket. If Bad Cop made my heart flutter, Soft Cop made it melt.

"I'm totally fine." I paused. "Ish," I amended, my hand going automatically to my temple where Jennifer had hit me.

Grant's mouth curved up again, his head shaking. "You have got to be more careful with that head of yours." He reached out and gently touched the second goose egg I'd had that week.

"I'll work on that," I murmured, my brain momentarily on pause as my entire body focused on the softness of his touch. I looked up into his eyes, intent on my face as he examined the bump. The hazel flecks were calmer, almost at rest. His jaw was unshaven, and I suddenly noticed a slight Eau de Pond Water about him. "You look tired," I blurted out. "Have you been to bed yet?"

He shook his head. "We're still running down witnesses from last night."

"What's going to happen to Jennifer?" I asked.

He sighed, taking a step back as he reverted to Cop Mode. "She'll be taken into custody when she's released from the hospital. She's got a good lawyer already filing motions to suppress evidence, but considering we have her caught in the act of attempted murder, it will be a hard case to win on his side."

Hearing the words "attempted murder" put the whole night into perspective.

"What about Heather's partner?" I asked, trying to cover the images of the evening rushing back to me. "Max Ford?"

"He's been charged with fraud. We could have pressed for more, but he accepted the lesser charge in exchange for talking. He's admitted to helping Heather fake the rare wines. When she died, he thought he could unload the rest of them himself. He started at Dixons, thinking a wine auction of the lot would be the fastest way,"

"That day I saw him pulling out of the lot."

Grant nodded. "He and Heather had been using the auction house as an exchange point, but when Ford tried to sell the bottles, they asked too many questions about provenance."

"So, he crashed the cocktail mixer, hoping to go direct to the buyers Heather had been working with."

"Correct. He apparently bribed the receptionist on duty to get into the mixer."

Bribery—that was one trick to get into the Links that Ava and I hadn't tried yet.

"And it almost worked," Grant went on. "When we picked him up, he was brokering a deal for a 1982 Margox for five hundred dollars."

"Geeze, I would have gone at least seven."

Grant grinned. "That's because you know your wine." He paused. "Ford also admitted to hitting you the night you were found in the warehouse."

"So it was him?"

"It was. He said he was there looking to move some inventory when no one would see."

Hence the unlocked door of unit J26. "We must have almost caught him in the act," I reasoned.

He nodded. "He said he heard someone coming, closed the door, and hid. He was afraid you were looking to steal his inventory, so he waited until you were alone and hit you over the head."

My hand went up to the other temple, where that bruise was, thankfully, fading.

"He said that's when the security guard showed up, and he ran." Grant paused. "I don't know what he might have done next if the guard hadn't arrived."

I licked my lips. I didn't either, but I had a feeling it would not have ended well for yours truly.

Grant must have had the same feeling, as he took a step closer and shook his head at me again. "Promise me you will leave the criminals to me from now on."

I nodded, in that moment truly meaning it. "You should go home," I told him softly. He really did look tired.

He nodded, his face so close to mine that I thought he might kiss me. Instead, he stepped back. "I plan to."

"Good."

"But I, uh, wanted to see what you were doing later first?"

"Later?" I asked, not sure I understood.

"Yes. Later. Dinner specifically. I thought maybe you'd like to celebrate with a meal and some wine."

A whole host of emotions bubbled up in my belly, all of them pleasant and some of them warming me in places good girls didn't talk about. "You mean...like a date?"

If Bad Cop did sheepish, I figured it would look a lot like the face I was seeing now as he ran a hand through his hair. "Yes," he said, taking a deep breath. "A date."

I couldn't help the grin that I felt taking over my face. I nodded. "Okay. It's a date."

His smile matched mine, showing off teeth and everything. "Good. I'll pick you up at seven and make reservations for Ashton's. I know it's your favorite."

"Wait—how did you know that?"

"I'm a detective." He winked at me.

"That's quite a skill," I shot back, wondering who he'd shaken down for that nugget of info. My matchmaking romantic of a house manager came to mind.

"Trust me," he said, his eyes boring into mine. "I have other skills too."

Oh boy. I'll just bet he did.

RECIPES

Chocolate Molten Lava Cake

1 stick of butter
6 ounces bittersweet chocolate
¼ cup sugar
2 whole eggs
2 egg yolks
1 teaspoon vanilla
½ cup all purpose flour

Preheat the oven to 450°F.

In the microwave or in a double boiler, melt the butter with the chocolate. In a medium bowl, stir in the sugar, then whisk or beat in the eggs, egg yolks, and vanilla. Stir in the flour.

Grease four custard cups or ramekins. Spoon the batter into the ramekins and bake for 12 minutes. You want the edges of the cake firm but the center still soft. Let them cool for 1–2 minutes, then invert them onto small dessert plates and serve warm.

Makes 4 lava cakes.

Wine Pairings
Best served with red blends that combine a range of varieties. Some of Emmy's suggestions: Ménage á Trois Silk Soft Red Blend, Frey Natural Red Wine Organic, Conundrum Red Wine.

Mexican Chocolate Scones

2 cups all purpose flour
1 teaspoon cinnamon
¼ cup unsweetened cocoa powder
⅓ cup sugar
1 teaspoon baking powder
½ teaspoon salt
¼ teaspoon baking soda
1 stick unsalted butter, cold, cut into small pieces
¾ cup buttermilk
1 teaspoon vanilla
½ cup chocolate chips

Preheat oven to 400°F.

In larger bowl or mixer, combine flour, cinnamon, cocoa powder, sugar, baking powder, salt, and baking soda. Cut in the butter just until the mixture resembles coarse crumbs. Stir in buttermilk, vanilla, and chocolate chips, just until it mixes—do not overwork it!

Gather the dough and pat into a roughly 7" circle. Then cut the circle with a knife into 8 triangular pieces. Place the triangular scones on a greased cookie sheet and bake for 15–18 minutes.

Makes 8 scones.

Shortcuts!
You can use premade scone mix and just add cocoa power and cinnamon to the dry mix. Don't have buttermilk on hand? You can substitute ½ cup sour cream instead.

Wine Pairings
Best served with a full bodied red wine, like a Zinfandel or Syrah. Some of Emmy's suggestions: Layer Cake Shiraz, Spellbound Petit Sirah, Ravenswood Zinfandel Belloni.

Chocolate Chip Coffee Cake

2½ cups all purpose flour
1 teaspoon baking powder
1 teaspoon baking soda
¼ teaspoon salt
1 cup sugar
1 stick butter
2 eggs
1 teaspoon vanilla
¼ cup milk
¾ cup sour cream
1 (12 oz) bag semisweet chocolate chips
2 teaspoons cinnamon
½ cup brown sugar

Preheat oven to 350°F. Lightly grease a 9" springform pan.

In a large bowl whisk together the 2 cups flour, baking powder, baking soda, and salt.

In a large bowl or electric mixer bowl, beat together ¾ stick of butter and sugar until creamy. One at a time, add in the eggs, beating continuously. Add in vanilla, milk, and sour cream. Slowly add in the dry ingredients, ⅓ at a time, and mix just until combined. Fold in ¾ of the bag of chocolate chips and then pour the batter into the greased pan.

In a medium sized bowl, combine cinnamon, ½ cup flour, and brown sugar. Cut ¼ stick butter in using forks or pastry cutter.

Sprinkle cake batter with the topping mixture and remaining chocolate chips. Bake 35–40 minutes or just until a toothpick inserted in the center of the cake comes out clean.

Shortcuts!
You can substitute a box of yellow cake mix for the flour mixture and use just 1 egg and ½ stick of butter. Then bake

according to the directions on the mix box. Don't have a springform pan? This recipe works in a 9x9" baking dish as well.

Wine Pairings
Best served with dessert wines that complement the sweet notes, like a Moscato or Madeira. Some of Emmy's suggestions: Broadbent Madeira, Rosatello Moscato, Zind-Humbrecht Muscat.

Or when serving for brunch, try pairing with:

Chocolate-Hazelnut Coffee

1 cup of brewed coffee
½ ounce chocolate liqueur
½ ounce hazelnut liqueur

Stir together hot coffee and the two liqueurs.

Optionally, top with whipped cream and a dusting of cinnamon to complement the spices in the coffee cake.

Shrimp Scampi over Angel Hair Pasta

¾ pound of angel hair pasta
1 teaspoon salt, or to taste
3 tablespoons extra-virgin olive oil
4 tablespoons butter
4 garlic cloves, minced
½ cup dry white wine
¼ teaspoon crushed red pepper flakes, or to taste
Freshly ground black pepper to taste
1½ pound large or extra-large shrimp, shelled and deveined
⅓ cup chopped parsley
Juice of 1 lemon

In a large pot, boil water for the pasta. Add in ½ teaspoon of salt and a tablespoon of olive oil. (The olive oil helps keep the pasta from sticking!) Add pasta to the boiling water and cook according to the directions on the package—just until al dente.

While pasta is cooking, in a large skillet over medium heat, add 2 tablespoons olive oil and butter until melted. Add garlic and sauté about a minute. Don't let it burn! Add wine, remaining salt, red pepper flakes, and black pepper. Bring the mixture to a simmer and allow the wine to reduce for about 2 minutes. Add shrimp and sauté just until cooked, about 2–3 minutes. Add in parsley and lemon juice.

In a large bowl, pour shrimp mixture over the cooked pasta and mix gently. Enjoy!

Serves 4–5 people.

Shortcuts!
You can buy pre-shelled, cleaned, and deveined shrimp, which can save a lot of time. Just be sure they are not precooked.

Wine Pairings
Best served with a light, dry white wine, like Sauvignon Blanc or Pinot Grigio. Note: avoid Chardonnay, as the sweeter notes will

compete with the garlic in the scampi. Some of Emmy's suggestions: Rodney Strong Sauvignon Blanc, Duckhorn Vineyards Sauvignon Blanc, Santa Margherita Pinot Grigio

Lemon Artichoke Chicken

2 tablespoons olive oil
4 boneless, skinless chicken breasts
sea salt to taste
pepper to taste
Juice of 2 lemons
2 cups artichokes hearts (canned or frozen/thawed)
1 small red onion, thinly sliced
1 teaspoon dried oregano
1 teaspoon dried thyme
2 tablespoons butter
½ cup green olives
1 tablespoon fresh parsley
1 garlic clove

Preheat oven to 375°F.

In a large, oven safe skillet, heat olive oil. Rinse and pat dry the chicken breasts, then season chicken breasts with a generous helping of salt and pepper. Brown chicken breasts in the olive oil, about 5 minutes on each side. Add onion and cook just until tender. Add lemon juice, artichoke hearts, oregano, and thyme. Add one pat of butter to the top of each chicken breast, then place the skillet in the oven and cook for 25–30 minutes, or until chicken reaches an internal temperature of 165°F.

While chicken is cooking, finely chop olives, parsley, and garlic. Serve as a gremolata on top of the chicken.

Shortcuts!
If you're short on cooking time, marinate your chicken ahead of time in a large plastic bag with the olive oil, lemon juice, and spices. Let marinate for up to 8 hours, then cook in the skillet alongside the onions and artichokes for about 7–10 minutes on each side.

Wine Pairings
Best served with citrusy, crisp white wines, like Sauvignon
Blanc or Chardonnay. Some of Emmy's suggestions: Chateau St.
Jean Crisp Chardonnay, Keenan Chardonnay, Spy Valley
Sauvignon Blanc.

Wine Tasting Charcuterie Board

A Charcuterie board generally consists of cured or processed meats, cheeses, olives, and other dried or cured fruits and vegetables. They're great for parties and snacking, and as Emmy and Conchita found, they're easy to quickly throw together for impromptu guests if you have the ingredients on hand. They all start with a large board or platter, preferably one with a lip around it to keep food from falling off, but many different materials will work.

Below is a Charcuterie board specifically with wine pairings in mind.

Meats: Be sure you slice these cold and keep refrigerated until party time, as cured meats oxidize quickly, giving them a less appealing color.

Hard salami and Prosciutto paired with Riesling or Zinfandel
If you love red wines, note that saltier meats like salami and prosciutto do not pair well with full-bodied red wines, so either make sure your meats are lower in salt and spice (e.g., not peppered salami), or go with a fruitier red, like a Zinfandel. Fruitier whites also complement the higher salt content.

Chorizo or spicy meats with Tempranillo or Rosé
Reds that are too heavily oaked—like a Cabernet—will accentuate the heat in spicy meats, so go with little, crisp wines.

Pork Pâté with Pinot Noir or Sauvignon Blanc
The heavier textures of the pâté call for a wine that has enough acidity to cut through the fat, and both the Pinot Noir and Sauvignon Blanc have a creaminess to them that complements the pâté textures.

Cheeses:
Brie or Camembert with Chardonnay

Soft creamier cheeses pair well with the creamy, oaky notes in a Chardonnay. They're also fatty, so you'll want something with a little acidity to cut through that.

Gouda or Cheddar with Cabernet Sauvignon
Hard aged cheeses have a mild nutty flavor that pairs well with wines that have oaky notes or berry flavors.

Fresh Mozzarella or goat cheese with Sauvignon Blanc or Pinot Gris
Something light, crisp, and fresh pairs best with the creaminess of fresh mozzarella or goat cheese, without competing with the strong flavors.

Other additions:
Emmy tried to vary the additions on her tray to include sweet, salty, vinegary, and fresh. Her must-haves include sliced baguettes or crackers; spiced olive oil for dipping; grainy mustard; cornichons or pickles or other pickled vegetables, such as asparagus; olives; honey or sweet jams; dried fruit, such as apricots; fresh fruits and vegetables, such as grapes, cherry tomatoes, or sliced cucumbers.

Shortcuts!
Want a wine that will pair with all of the above? Go with a low alcohol content Pinot Noir, Zinfandel, or a crisp light Sauvignon Blanc. These are very versatile wines that will complement most flavors.

ABOUT THE AUTHOR

Gemma Halliday is the #1 Amazon, *New York Times* & *USA Today* bestselling author of several mystery series. Gemma's books have received numerous awards, including a Golden Heart, two National Reader's Choice awards, three RITA nominations, a RONE award for best mystery, and two Killer Nashville Silver Flachion Awards for best cozy mystery and readers' choice. She currently lives in the San Francisco Bay Area with her large, loud, and loving family.

To learn more about Gemma, visit her online at
www.GemmaHalliday.com

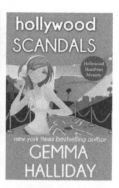

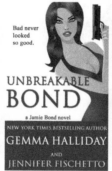
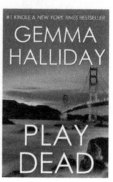